LYING with the DEAD

# LYING with the DEAD

*A Novel*

## MICHAEL MEWSHAW

**Other Press**
*New York*

Copyright © 2009 Michael Mewshaw

Production Editor: Yvonne E. Cárdenas

Book design: Simon M. Sullivan

This book was set in 11.5 pt Fournier MT
by Alpha Design & Composition of Pittsfield, NH.

10 9 8 7 6 5 4 3 2 1

LIBRARY OF CONGRESS CATALOGING-IN-PUBLICATION DATA

Mewshaw, Michael, 1943-
Lying with the dead / by Michael Mewshaw.
p. cm.
ISBN 978-1-59051-318-7 (pbk.)—ISBN 978-1-59051-355-2 (e-book)
1. Adult children of dysfunctional families—Fiction. 2. Domestic fiction.
3. Psychological fiction. I. Title.
PS3563.E87L95 2009
813'.54—dc22      2009008675

TO ARDEN PENELOPE MEWSHAW, MY FIRST GRANDCHILD

*Everything in nature has a lyrical essence,*
*a tragic destiny and a comic existence.*

GEORGE SANTAYANA

LYING with the DEAD

BOOK ONE

# Maury

I know the stars by heart. Not their names. Not what you'd find out through a telescope. But I know when they rise and when they fade, the ones that bring winter snow in the mountains and spring rain in the dry wash. Whatever the season I wake up in the dark and step outside and watch for the light. It's a long watch, and even when the weather's freezing I want to lie down in the sand and fall back to sleep. To stay awake I make a sound in my mouth that's like the wind scraping across the desert, and pretty soon my head starts in on memories of all those years ago at home.

That was back east in Maryland. Now I live out west in the Slab City. It's not a real city, just a crossroads near the California-Arizona line where people from around the country park their trailers. Old and young, retired or out of work, they spend the winter here. Then when the summer heats up they pack and leave, and I stay put and fix the slabs. The trailers leak water and oil and whatnot on the concrete. I wash that off and check for cracks and places that have chipped. There's times I have to rebuild a whole foundation before folks roll in for fall.

Nicky, she's the woman I work for and live with, she has me fix the fence around her property. It's barbed wire, but not near as high as at a prison. Bushes and baby trees grow through it, and if you let them get big, the branches eat the barbed wire strand by strand. They can tug the fence straight down. So Nicky has me chop off the limbs. Afterward there's chunks of wood stuck on the wire like strips of meat hung out to dry. I don't care to look at them.

My favorite job is carrying cinder blocks on a hod. A hod is a contraption, a kind of tilted box on a stick. The Mexican that trucks in the blocks unloads them into the box on my shoulder and I lug them out to the slabs. Each trip the blocks on the hod make a different design, a checkerboard of hollows and solids and black-and-gray squares. But just half-thinking about it, I can keep them straight in my mind, like I keep track of my memories in the box in my head.

This box in my head is big, with dozens of drawers. It reminds me of the wooden chest in the prison library where inmates used to work on their appeals. Day after day they crowded around it, dragging out these long drawers, flipping through the cards, then banging them back into the slots. I imitated the sound, a sort of pistol-shot noise, but quiet so only I heard it.

In the morning when I'm waiting and humming and watching the mountains for the first sign of daylight, I'll go to the box in my head and crack open a drawer. I'll sniff it and taste it, and if it doesn't smell too bad or taste too bitter I'll dip into it for a spell. Most times it's Cole I hunt for and crawl in with. Otherwise I'll pass from drawer to drawer, visiting Mom and Candy and Quinn. Whenever they telephone, once or twice a year, there's buzzing in my ears and water in my eyes, and it's hard to find words. But in my head, in their separate drawers, things are clear, and I have no trouble talking.

Sometimes I visit myself as a kid. The memory drawers go back to when I was little enough for Dad to give me a bath in the kitchen sink. He set my bare ass on the cold drainboard and shoved my head under the spigot and scrubbed my hair with a bar of soap. The suds burned my eyes. But he didn't stop. He plopped me on my feet and dried me with a starchy towel. His hands rubbed hard, like he was roughing me up, punishing me for something. Electricity went everywhere on my skin. That's when I did the thing I'll never forget. I balled up my fist and punched Dad in the face. He dropped his hands and the towel fell in the sink, and I busted out crying, knowing he'd hit me back.

That's one drawer I stay away from. There's others I break into, I'm so eager to climb inside. Only two drawers I've never been able to open. The first I figure has to be the day Dad died. The second I don't have any idea what it holds and I'm afraid to find out.

The morning sky fades from black to blue, the stars blink out, and the world turns bright without them. I see the empty slabs all around me, and barbed wire with hanging wood chunks around the slabs. Nicky's house is off in a corner. It's an adobe as brown and smooth as a mud dauber's nest.

The thing I like about living in the desert, there's not so many changes. Just hot and hotter, then a winter that goes by so quick you don't know where it went. No trees changing colors, no leaves falling, then burning with that sweet smoke that smothered me in Maryland, and none of the flowers that choked my nose in spring. Those in-between times were the worst, and I'm glad to live without them.

5

The same hour each day a plane from the West Coast swooshes past, up so high it barely leaves a nail scratch on the sky. In my mouth the wind sound becomes a motor. I'd love to fly. I know what it is to float. I feel that in my head a lot. But just once I'd love to be up there, looking down at the states between here and home.

The plane crosses the mountains from peak to peak. They're shaped in steps, like a moving staircase in a department store. But the mountains stay still, and it's the sun that jumps over the snow on the high places in a sort of signal that might mean good news or bad.

# Quinn

When I assure people that I'm happy and I love where I live, they presume that I mean London itself—the theater, the world-class museums, the Regency mansions and growing numbers of restaurants run by celebrity chefs. The whole vast thrumming multicultural megalopolis. But I feel little connection to that guidebook cliché. What I love is the leafy enclave of Hampstead, tucked away in the northwest corner of the city. For me it serves as a refuge, which despite its well-burnished history, carries no echo of my own fractious past.

I'm an actor, one whose career has reversed the arc traveled by an illustrious line of British entertainers. Unlike, let's say, Charlie Chaplin, Cary Grant, and Bob Hope, who crawled out of the English gutter, emigrated to the States, and reinvented themselves as Hollywood stars, I fled a scruffy precinct of the New World for the gentility of the Old. I traded the giant golden jackpot of America for a life of human and very handsome dimensions.

Plenty of Londoners don't share my enthusiasm for Hampstead, and I've taken considerable ribbing because of the neighborhood's reputation for designer-label living. Friends from edgier areas dismiss mine as trendy, snobbish, twee, a zone of house-proud toffs and politically correct kooks—the kind of constituency represented in Parliament by Glenda Jackson, for God's sake.

I don't bother to argue back. Nor do I waste my breath explaining that the village has historically attracted residents fleeing natural disasters and man-made catastrophes. The English raced to Hampstead's high ground to escape the Plague, the Great Fire, the flooding Thames and its miasmal vapors. The street names alone—Well Walk, the Vale of Health—promised miraculous restoration to a roll call of famous consumptives and neurasthenics who flocked here. So who can fault me for settling in happily after the tumult of my childhood in Maryland?

Every day on my afternoon walk up Frognal Lane as I reflect on the life I've made for myself, it occurs to me that it resembles the red brick path I follow. Lovingly arranged, meticulously tended, each brick has been laid in place like a piece of a beautiful mosaic. The overall pattern remains pleasantly comforting even if a deep-buried tree root does occasionally rumple the surface.

My house is a sanctuary within the surrounding Eden. A renovated abattoir with beamed ceilings, it has a fireplace in the living room, exposed stone walls in the kitchen, and a conservatory that looks out over the garden. Mal, my agent, jokes that a conservatory is an oil-and-cash-guzzling space dedicated to the proposition that anyone with sufficient income can deny the reality of the English winter. While I'll grant that it costs a bundle to cover the mortgage and keep the place ticking, I love sitting snug in the conservatory, ignoring the pissing rain or pelting sleet on the glass panels.

My garden is actually a ragged clump of shrubs and locust trees. Nobody's done any pruning in ages, and I rarely have the grass cut for fear of uprooting the wildflowers that bloom in spring and chasing away the critters that burrow in the weeds.

My neighbors, no kidding, buy tiger shit from the London Zoo and spread it over their flowerbeds. They believe its wild scent scares off animals. But I allow creatures large and small free rein of my property. Squirrels, hedgehogs, voles, and field mice (they mutate into rats and become fair game for traps if they sneak into the house) frolic for my amusement. On clear winter mornings, like this one, a tawny fox, regal as a lion on the Serengeti, sometimes stretches out in the deep grass, soaking up the feeble warmth of the sun.

Today, however, I have no time to admire the view or search for the fox. I'm booked for lunch with my agent and a BBC producer. Already late, I nevertheless stroll to the restaurant by a circuitous route, reveling in cold air that rings like crystal. On certain streets, the walls of cottages huddle close, none more than a hand span apart. Each door is a different color—lipstick red, royal green, Della Robbia blue. At Admiral's Walk, in front of the white wooden mansion where *Mary Poppins* was filmed, a brigade of tourists gape as if expecting to spot Julie Andrews sailing overhead, pulled along by her umbrella.

At Whitestone Pond, the highest point in London, the water is usually like a detergent-filled bucket stirred by a grimy mop. Today it glitters with jeweled ice. Convinced I've kept Mal and the man from the Beeb waiting long enough, I turn down Heath Street. The ethnicity of the restaurants along the road switches every month. Indian, Hungarian, Moroccan, Thai, Argentinean—maybe these joints just trade signs and go on serving the same grub. Only La Gaffe never changes. Despite the French name, it has an Italian menu, and attracts a clientele divided evenly between those who look like Peter O'Toole and those who crane their necks looking for him.

Until I insisted that I was too busy to travel into town, the gent from BBC proposed that we meet at his club, the Atheneum. This led me to expect a blimpish Oxonian nearing retirement age, someone who, instead of a gold watch, had been offered the opportunity to produce a last miniseries. But when I get to La Gaffe Ian turns out to be a short, trim fellow no older than Mal and with the same leathery tanned complexion. The two of them have the faces of hard riders to the hounds and hard drinkers after the hunt. They're dead ringers for a couple of flamboyant hustlers at the Beverly Hills Hotel. Next to them I appear threadbare and pallid in my beat-up old Barbour coat.

Well into a bottle of Brunello di Montalcino, Mal and Ian are boisterously discussing foreign real estate. They break off for a moment while we exchange names and handshakes. Then Mal returns to the previous conversation and flabbergasts me by revealing that he owns what he refers to as "a bolt-hole in Brazil." He must be doing much better for his other clients than he is for me.

As I pour myself some wine, Mal begins talking about a woman in Brazil who promised to introduce him to her "paralyzingly posh friends who have their own bolt-hole up the coast. There's no road," Ian says. "You reach the place by boat, a kind of local water taxi. It reminded me of a punt with an outboard motor and a fringed awning."

"Brilliant," Ian encourages him.

"As we put into this cove," Mal continues, "Anthea started stripping off her kit. 'Mal, be a darling,' she said. 'My friends are frightfully eccentric. They're not nudists per se, but when they're in Bahia they never wear clothes and neither do their guests. So be a love and do away with your swimsuit.'"

Ian leans forward, grinning, eager to laugh. None of this instills confidence in me that I'll come away from lunch with anything except a heavy stomach and a headache. Still, Mal is no fool and I figure he must have something in mind. So I resign myself to doing what actors do between roles—attempting to seem interested, but not anxious, patient, but not a pushover.

"We waded ashore naked," Mal says. "Don't get me wrong. In different circumstances, I'd have been delighted to be on a tropical beach with Anthea in the raw. But with strangers watching me it was like that nightmare when you realize you're at the office or in church."

"Or on television," Ian adds, "with no clothes."

"Precisely. But this was hugely more embarrassing because, you see, as we crossed the sand toward this thatched hut I noticed a dozen people, proper British people, at a table and"—Mal slows down for effect—"and every one of them was dressed as if for a dinner party at Le Caprice. Only we were starkers."

Ian guffaws, and a gout of wine, red as blood, spurts from his nostrils. Shielded by the menu, I don't catch a drop of it. But pink polka dots well up on Mal's Dunhill shirt. Through tears of laughter, Ian struggles to apologize. A waiter rushes over with salt and a seltzer bottle. At other tables people stop searching for Peter O'Toole and glare at us.

"Sorry, old man," Ian says.

"Don't be," Mal says. "Getting a good laugh out of you makes up for any number of wine stains."

"Do send me the laundry bill."

"Don't be silly. With all the pounds that Quinn and I plan to wring out of BBC what's a few quid for the cleaners?"

Ian guffaws again, refills his glass, and tops up mine. Then as abruptly as that, the prologue ends, and although the tone stays chummy, the pitch commences. It's not what you'd hear in Hollywood. No, this is London. It's more like an oral exam in an Oxbridge tutorial. Still, a pitch is a pitch.

"I suppose you're familiar with Aeschylus?" Ian asks. "The *Oresteia?*"

"Of course he is," Mal breaks in to save me from potential embarrassment.

"I haven't read it since college," I confess.

"But you remember the trilogy?"

"Who could forget it?" says Mal.

"We hope nobody has. Or nobody will once they've seen it as BBC means to present it. We're convinced the Greek classics can be relevant to a wide audience if they're properly formatted."

A hovering waiter leans in as if listening to Ian's project. But no, he's waiting to take our orders. We all ask for salads and pasta, and Ian resumes.

"BBC is prepared to commit to a play a night for three nights on the trot."

"Live?" I ask.

"No, tape. But we don't believe that'll compromise the intensity or immediacy. Our idea is to set the *Oresteia* in contemporary London, the House of Atreus in council housing. We want the characters to have the dramatic grandeur of archetypes, and yet at the same time human identities. They need to be people, real people, trapped in tragic dilemmas."

"Some of these council estates outdo the Greeks," Mal says. "You've read the headlines, haven't you, Quinn? Female circumcision. Forced marriages. Islamist terror cells."

"Don't get me wrong," Ian slows Mal down. "We're not planning to turn Aeschylus into tabloid journalism. But as we conceive it, the principal characters are Muslim immigrants. Very religious. From Pakistan, Afghanistan, someplace like that. Not political, just strict adherents to ancient traditions."

"You have a script?" Mal asks, no doubt wondering, as I do, where I fit in.

"Yes. It's Aeschylus, almost word for word. Only the context and motivation and a few scenes and lines have changed. Agamemnon is a fundamentalist patriarch who murders his daughter Iphigenia because she falls in love with a Christian boy. It's an honor killing. His wife, Clytemnestra, goes mad with grief and avenges her daughter's death by shooting her husband. Now her son Orestes is in agony, knowing he has to settle the score and kill his mother. The cycle of violence doesn't stop until the boy's trial, where the state replaces personal vengeance with institutional justice."

"Christ, that's quite a story," Mal says and he sounds sincere.

"We think so. Out of savagery," Ian recites as if from a cue card, "comes harmony. Through suffering the characters achieve grandeur and ritual significance."

"Hubris leads to nemesis leads to catharsis," I recall from my undergraduate course in Greek tragedy.

"Exactly. So you're interested?" Ian presses me.

"That depends," Mal chimes in.

"I'll let you two argue about money," I say. "My concern is the part you have in mind for me."

"We believe you could play both Agamemnon and Orestes."

"How's he going to do that?" Mal asks.

"Orestes doesn't appear in *Agamemnon*," Ian says. "He comes on in *The Libation Bearers*, years after his father's death. Then there's his trial in *The Eumenides*. We think you're the right age. What are you now, Quinn, early thirties?"

"Closer to forty."

"Okay, we'll age you for Agamemnon, but with a few touches of makeup you can still play Orestes. You're center stage all three nights. For a serious actor, it's the role of a lifetime."

"I'm interested." I keep it understated not just because I am with Brits. I have to hide my excitement from myself to guard against disappointment if I don't get the part. "Before I decide, I'll need to reread the plays."

"Plenty of time," Mal says. "Ian and I'll hammer out a contract."

"When do we shoot?" I ask.

"Ideally, this summer."

I nod, and as if on signal the waiter arrives with the first course. Ian moves seamlessly from pitch-master to talk show host and tries to round things off by razzing Mal about his bare-assed humiliation in Brazil. But Mal puts him on the spot, saying, "It's your turn. Tell us your worst embarrassment."

I assume this must be a fixture at meals for old boys from English public schools. Ian joins the game with no reluctance. In fact he relishes the chance to describe a recent prostate examination.

"You're probably too young to be familiar with the procedure," he tells me. "What you do is drop your trousers and bend over the examining table. In goes the glove, and the moving finger having rooted around should promptly move on. But my doctor has offices at a teaching hospital, and in his plummiest bedside manner he said, 'Hope you don't mind, but our urology students are making the rounds today. They'd like to observe.' What he meant was they'd like to do more than observe. He pulled his finger from my bum, and in wriggles one student's, then another and another."

This time, Mal guffaws. Fortunately there's no wine in his mouth. I suspect that they're both brewing to ask about my greatest embarrassment. On this score I have a rabid aversion to sharing. It's nobody's business, my hoard of childhood humiliations. My father's death, my jailbird brother, my crippled sister, my brutal mother who bitch-slapped me into manhood, I hold them as close to the vest as a bluffing cardsharp holds his hand.

I sip the wine, followed by a glass of water. I finish my salad, then my pasta, and mop the plate clean with bread. By the ceremonial gravity of my gestures I cast myself in a classical mode, a man who doesn't welcome personal disclosures. Refusing coffee, not tarrying to watch which one of them picks up the check, I step outside La Gaffe and into blinding sunlight. Down on Flask Walk in the tobacco-scented warmth of Keith Fawkes's bookshop, I buy a used copy of the *Oresteia*.

Before I had Hampstead or my house and its conservatory and garden, books were my refuge, words my first love and last line of defense. Mom claims this came from her side of the family—a clutch of long-winded, loudmouthed, poetry-spouting Irish. I wouldn't know. My encounters with my relatives tended to be brief and bruising, and I regarded reading as a way of avoiding them and everything else that pained me. But I don't see myself sinking blissfully into this Penguin paperback. It's not simply because it's freighted with scholarly footnotes, a glossary of Greek vocabulary, and a ninety-page introduction. From college I re-member my deep unease at Aeschylus, my shock of recognition at the House of Atreus. Too close to home, too close to home, I had thought, and tried to shut the tragedy from my mind even as I mechanically kept turning the pages.

Yet now what choice do I have? No matter the terms of the contract Mal manages to negotiate, I can't imagine turning down the part. As Ian put it, it's the role of a lifetime, the one I was born to play.

## *Candy*

Days when I take Mom Communion—that would be every Sunday and holy day of obligation—I attend Mass carrying what's called a pyx. It's round and gold-plated, about the size of a pillbox, and has room in it for half a dozen Hosts. In our parish you have to sit in a front pew and really push forward if you hope to receive the sacrament from a priest. Lots of times I wind up with a layperson, a Eucharistic minister, no different from me, and I whisper, "Two please," like I'm at Dunkin' Donuts.

I hold out the pyx in the palm of my left hand, its lid open so there's no mistaking where I mean for one wafer to go. The second goes in my mouth. These Eucharistic ministers, they're trained to deal with communicants carrying pyxes. Still, some of them get flustered and they'll forget to say, "The Body of Christ." Or else they'll mumble, "The Body of Christ," when they put a Host in the pyx, but not when they put one on my tongue. I don't suppose it makes much difference.

I tuck the pyx into a zippered compartment in my purse, completely separate from the mess of my keys, credit cards, and loose change. For the rest of the Mass, I'm hyper-alert to it on my lap. When the pastor taught me the prayers for the Communion of the

Sick, he emphasized—as if he needed to!—the solemnity of what I was doing. He discouraged me from chatting with friends after church or stopping along the highway to shop or fill the car with gas. "Be mindful," he said, "that you're more than a mere delivery boy." Blushing, he changed that to "delivery girl" and added, "Candy, you're as close to having priestly powers as a woman is ever privileged to come."

True enough. With a consecrated Host in the womblike safety of my purse, I feel, I don't know, somehow nearer to God than I do when I have Him in my mouth slowly melting. Strange.

Another oddity, this one even stranger, is that as I leave church, driving through the traffic jam on the parking lot, petrified I'll have a crash and drop the Host, I often find myself thinking about Dad, dead now all these decades. Maybe because his life was a car wreck, or maybe because I'm tense at bringing Mom Communion, I remember what I used to bring him and the tension I felt then.

"Candy, do your daughterly duty," he'd holler from the armchair where he sprawled in front of the TV.

This was my signal to sprint to the kitchen, snatch a bottle of beer from the fridge, pry off the cap, grab a glass and race back to the living room. Dad studied the second hand on his wristwatch and timed me like he did horses at the track. While I tipped the glass as he had taught me to do so the head didn't foam up too high or, God forbid, spill over, he tapped his foot. When I did it the way he wanted, it made me feel like I was his favorite.

If I finished the job in less than thirty seconds, he let me have the first cold, bitter sip. I never cared for the taste of beer. But I liked pleasing him, and when he was in a good mood and had had a run of luck that day with the horses or cards or numbers, he lifted me onto his lap, lit a cigarette, and blew smoke rings in my face. The feel of the smoke pouring back over my forehead and through my hair was like what I imagined a lover's caress would be. Remembering that gives me shivers. Part pleasure, part something else.

With Dad there was always that "something else," that downside that Mom complained made him hell to live with, then worse hell to live without. I don't think she ever minded covering for him, even lying for him, telling the neighbors he worked the night shift at the Census Bureau, and that's why he came and went at odd hours. But she never tried to fool me that he was anything except a full-time gambler. She had a soft spot for bad boys, and he was the worst.

She never asked me to pray for him to reform. That was just my instinct. Where another person might find strength in a bottle, I naturally depended on God. I still do. Of course, He doesn't always answer our petitions like we expect. Once Dad was dead, I was stricken with worry and wondered whether I had sent the wrong signal with my offered-up Masses and Communions. I prayed that he'd become a better man, not that he'd fold his cards for good.

This particular Sunday morning in January, when I leave church and head for Mom's, a hard freeze has glazed the windshield of my Honda with what look like big white ferns. While I hunch at the steering wheel waiting for the defroster to work, sunlight stings my eyes. The air is almost too cold to breathe. At least it's not sleeting or snowing. In the western corner of the state, out in Garrett County, Marylanders may know how to drive in foul weather, but here, close to the Chesapeake Bay, not a man, woman, or child doesn't lose all common sense when the roads turn slick.

Because of my bad leg I'm leery of walking on ice, and in the car I drive defensively. Still, ever since I caught polio as a kid, winter has been my favorite season because I get to wear boots and never draw a second glance. Back when girls were forbidden to show up for school or church in slacks, I was shy about my limp and hated wearing dresses and having people stare at my stringy calf. Nowadays I have a dozen pairs of boots that I value mostly for their camouflage. Seeing me hobble, people probably guess I twisted an ankle. Nobody pegs me as a poster girl for the March of Dimes.

In Mom's neighborhood, the frost has melted everywhere except in the shady places. Where the sun shines, the brown grass and leafless shrubs look dead. Back in the shadows every blade and branch looks starchy with life.

The scene's jumbled, and so are my emotions. Whenever I go home, I feel mixed up and can't tell whether I'm sick to my stomach because I'm stressed out or because I'm straining so hard to believe that my childhood wasn't all bad. I don't want to look at my life in stark black or white. I'd like to see Mom in shades of gray, too, but that's not easy. She doesn't really give you a choice.

Her thirty-year-old Chevy Nova sits in the driveway, like a hillbilly lawn ornament. The whole neighborhood used to be like that—a haven for white trash, a subdivision of folks who hated blacks and fled Washington, D.C. All during my childhood every house on the block seemed to have car or motorcycle parts spread over the front yard. But when blacks started moving to the suburbs, the area actually improved and now Mom's Nova is a last reminder of the way it used to be.

She quit driving after she had an accident on Ritchie Highway. Witnesses said she sailed through a red light and T-boned a VW van. Mom denied this and accepted no blame. She simply couldn't account for the damage to her car or how the van wound up turned turtle in a ditch.

"All I know," she swore to me, "is I woke up with a bump on my forehead and watched these little yellow people crawl out of the VW, like ETs from a spaceship that crash-landed. I thought I was dead or having a dream. I couldn't understand how these aliens got to be so shriveled and yellow. Then the ambulance came, and they gave me smelling salts and told me I hit a van full of Vietnamese. There must have been a dozen of them, all crying and caterwauling and pointing at me. It was awful."

For Mom the worst part was that the *Washington Post* published her age, then seventy-seven, for everybody in the Metro area to gloat over. She parked the Nova for good and depended on me to deliver her groceries and prescriptions. Except for doctors' appointments every few months, she never leaves the house now.

Eventually the car battery died, the tires went flat, and the door locks rusted shut. Still, Mom won't have it towed away. She considers the broken-down Chevy a kind of scarecrow against burglary. She's convinced that thieves, seeing it in the driveway, will steer clear.

Ever since integration, she's regarded herself as under siege. But she would never sell out and move. She swears she won't give "them" the satisfaction. When Asians and Hispanics arrived hard on the heels of the blacks, she wouldn't give them the time of day either. She locked her doors, drew her curtains, and never acknowledged that her new neighbors were better than the riff-raff they replaced. Instead of installing an alarm, she pinned holy cards over every window in the house—as if the Lord conspires in her racism.

Lawrence Leonard, my boss and best friend for the past twenty years, and my lover since his wife died, finds this and most of Mom's foibles knee-slappingly funny. He can't accept that she's not a comedian and that I have no stomach for playing her straight man. Dentists aren't famous for a sense of humor, but Lawrence has a big heart and a kindly knack of looking on the bright side and laughing—whereas I stew and steam, then break down and cry.

Of course, Lawrence doesn't have to deal with her day to day. After one ugly run-in, he backed off big time. He's learned that contact with Mom can be like tangling with a loose live wire.

A couple of years back, Lawrence ran a program on his computer and cranked out a plan to save Mom a chunk of money by refinancing her house. But when we sat down with her to go over the numbers, she behaved like we were aluminum siding salesmen out to cheat her. She hunched like a cat that's been backed into a corner. My brother Quinn describes her in this state as having her ass up on her shoulder blades.

"Why don't you two mind your own damned business," she snarled.

"Just trying to help." Lawrence spoke in a calm, reassuring voice like he does to root canal patients.

"I ever need your help," she said, "I'll ask for it. Don't hold your breath."

Lawrence and I left, and I couldn't speak until we were on the road to his house. Then I let go, gushing tears and apologizing and explaining that it had been this way all my life. Even now with Mom whittled down by age and listing to one side, she strikes terror in my heart. "She's lost the strength to haul off and slap me," I told Lawrence. "But she's got a mouth on her that's as bad as a fist."

"She hit you?" he asked. Stopping on the side of the road, he gathered me in his arms. "In the face?"

"She used to."

"That's awful. Jesus, baby, you should have told me."

"Well, over the years as it went from child abuse to adult abuse, it humiliated me more than it hurt."

"Why did you put up with it?"

That's a question I couldn't answer. Not on the side of the road with trucks rocketing past. Not unless I let Lawrence in on a whole raft of family secrets that I was afraid would chase him away.

Luckily, he filled the silence with sympathy, then with suggestions about how to cope with Mom and at the same time protect myself. On second thought, he said, it didn't make sense to refinance her house. She should sell it and plow the equity into a unit in an assisted living community. Then as if solving the last practical problem, he said that as soon as Mom was settled in a comfortable situation, the two of us should retire and marry and move to North Carolina, where he owned a condo on a golf course.

My reaction . . . my reaction was to burst out sobbing again. This was what I wanted, what I had been praying for since Lawrence's wife died. No, much longer than that—ever since I was a girl and yearned for someone to love me. But I went on blubbering because I knew it was impossible. Mom would never go to assisted living. And as for Lawrence's idea that we have her declared incompetent and commit her against her will, that would cause the kind of vicious, soul-scarring fight that's my family's signature, the brand burned into our flesh.

With my shoulder I wing open the door of the Honda, lift out my bad leg, and balance on my good one. After reaching back for my purse with the precious pyx inside it, I teeter there, collecting myself. Christ is tucked next to my heart. I need to focus on that. I'm here to bring Mom Communion, not wallow in self-pity.

I used to worry I'd show up one Sunday morning and find her dead in her bed or crumpled on the floor at the bottom of the stairs. But that fear's been replaced by one that she'll never die.

I'm sure I'll be punished for thinking this. I'll spend centuries in purgatory paying for my sins. But I'm fifty-five years old and stuck with a mother who never loved me, who hates Lawrence, and won't set us free. It's time for Mom to die. I just don't want to be the one to kill her. I'm convinced she's been hinting at it for months. But I'll be damned if I'll do it.

I slam the car door, press the chirping gizmo on the key lock, and clomp in my boots up the sidewalk to the house. A gray-shingled Cape Cod like the others on the block, it looks much too small. How did the four of us ever fit in here? How could these warped wooden walls contain all that chaos? I almost expect there to be a plaque out front with a skull and crossbones. Instead, there are rosebushes and azaleas, dead in this season. And in back, where there was once a forest, there's a fringe of trees. The bare upper branches thrash like witches' brooms at the sky.

Crowded as it was for Dad, Mom, Maury, and me, and later when it was just Mom, Quinn, and me, the house is now more than

Mom needs and more than she can take care of. To save her the hard climb upstairs to her bedroom, Quinn has offered to pay to make over the ground floor. But whenever I mention that she'd be better off sleeping in the dining room and having a closet rebuilt as a bathroom, Mom refuses.

That'll be the motto on her tombstone: I refuse. She refuses to quit smoking. "Let 'em kill me if they will," she says. She refuses to use a walker. "I'm old, not crippled." She won't wear Depends. Won't wear her hearing aid. "It's like plugging a Mexican band into my head." Won't have a cleaning girl. Won't eat Meals on Wheels. Won't cook for herself and won't take any nourishment except Ensure, candy, and ice cream. Won't do a damn thing any doctor, lawyer, priest, social worker, therapist, or her own children recommend. She means to die as she has lived—strictly on her own terms. To hell with everybody else.

And here I am bringing her Communion. I don't know why I bother. I don't know why she bothers! She hasn't set foot in church in years. She begs off with the excuse that she can't make it through Mass without having to pee two or three times. She claims she hates disturbing the congregation, crawling in and out of the pew. But I know better. I know she can't abide the new liturgy, now over fifty years old—the Mass in English, the singing and guitar strumming and tambourines, the handshaking and wishing your neighbor peace, the sweet upbeat homilies that she calls omelets. She misses fire-and-brimstone sermons. She'd phone in her confession if they'd let her. Grudgingly she accepts a monthly visit from a Filipino priest she accuses of being a homo, and just as grudgingly she depends on me to deliver Communion.

I knock at the door in the secret code she insists on. Three rapid knocks, a pause, and another rap. I start off lightly tapping my knuckles, but since Mom's hard of hearing, I end up pounding the wood with the heel of my hand.

At last she answers, but doesn't open the door. "I feel awful," she whispers in a ghostly voice. "It's one of my spells"—which is how she refers to what have been diagnosed as panic attacks. "I'm going to take a pill and go back to bed."

"You don't want a Xanax, Mom. Not at ten in the morning. You'll feel better after Communion."

"I'm not up to it, Candy. Leave it out there and I'll get it later."

"Leave it where? In the mailbox? On the doorstep?" My voice rises in outrage. "I'll do no such thing with the Body and Blood of Christ."

The security chain jangles, the dead bolt unclicks, and the door creaks open an inch, like she intends to stick her tongue through the crack. Instead, her hand drops from the knob and the door swings wide and she stands there small as a rag doll, her face red from crying. Or is it from a steely refusal to cry? Her eyes are mismatched, and not just because her glasses have lenses of drastically different strengths. She has a condition called heterochronica iridium—one blue eye, the other brown.

As a young woman she reminded me of a ferocious lioness protecting her brood—whenever she wasn't mauling us. Now she's a bedraggled old house cat. In spite of myself, I hug her.

I press her head to my breast. She's frail, her skin's cold, her hair's synthetic-smelling. Her arms dangle at her sides, and her shoulders draw up so that I suspect I'm hurting her. I let go.

Once the door's closed, the living room is scarcely warmer than the air outside. Mom wears slippers, flannel pajamas, a woolen robe, and over it a sweater that she clutches shut beneath her chin.

The house is as rank as a jungle, smelling of mold and cigarette smoke and food that has fallen to the floor and been stepped on and ground into the carpet. Mom appears oblivious to it, but the stink bothers me. The least a daughter owes her parent is to keep her and her house clean. But whenever I volunteer to break out the vacuum and spruce things up, Mom won't hear of it. If I argue, she unleashes her venomous tongue, accusing me of hinting that she's dirty. Which she is.

"I didn't sleep a wink last night," she says. "No sense laying there in the dark, I figured. So I got up, said my prayers, and started looking at my pictures."

Mom sags onto the couch. Beside her is a big cardboard box that she brought home from Safeway when she worked there as a cashier. It holds hundreds of family photographs that have never been cataloged by year, subject matter, or any other way. I've urged her to paste them in albums, or let me do it. But apart from a few framed snapshots on an end table, she keeps them in the box, all tossed together like kittens in a basket.

She lights up a Kent, and I sit in the rocking chair opposite the couch, aware of the Host in the purse on my lap. I'm also super-aware of the box of photographs and what it might signal. She's not normally the nostalgic type. When a sentimental mood does take hold of her, it's sometimes a short step to bad memories, then an explosion.

I decide to wait until she's between cigarettes before I bring out the pyx. I watch the Kent burn down toward her nicotine-stained knuckles and silently review the liturgy for the Communion of the Sick where Christ declares, "I myself am the living bread, come down from Heaven. If anyone eats this bread he shall live forever."

Like she's reading my mind and is duty bound to contradict me, Mom says, "No one should live this long. They ought to put me to sleep like a stray dog."

"A lot of people your age still enjoy life."

"Name two."

"Lawrence and I see them out on the golf course."

"Great! Buy me a bag of clubs."

She dragon-snorts smoke from her nostrils. I don't suppose there's anything worse about an old woman smoking than a young person poisoning her system, not to mention my system, with cigarettes, but she's about to receive Communion. Do I dare ask her to brush her teeth?

Instead, I say, "I'm sorry you had a bad night."

"Wish I could describe what they're like, these spells of mine. It starts with music," she says. "Eerie music and a hot flash in my chest that turns to goose pimples on my spine. All of a sudden I'm trembling and seeing colors. Streaks of brown and green. Excuse me, Candy, I know you're a prude about language, but it's like I have shit in my eyes. There's an awful smell and something I'm dying to see but scared to see at the same time. I don't know. I can never dial it in clear. I just wish there was a pill to cure it."

Since Mom downs a dozen medications a day—thyroid pills, antidepressants, beta-blockers for an arrhythmic heartbeat, anti-anxiety tablets, blood pressure pills, sleeping pills, pick-me-up pills—I timidly allow as how her panic attacks might be a side effect.

"No, it's a punishment," she insists. "It's God or the Devil getting revenge."

"For what?"

"For my sins."

"Don't be silly. You're in a state of grace."

"Don't be so sure of that." She lights a fresh Kent off the butt of the first. "I'm paying for the past."

"You shouldn't dwell on the past," I tell her. Yet it surprises me that she's examining her conscience. Is that another tip-off, like the pictures? Sign of a mood swing? Last week she shocked me by asking whether she had ever hit me. I feared a trap and didn't answer at first. The fact is, she's belted me so often, it's just the big occasions that stick in my mind—the black eye on my thirteenth birthday, the bloody lip for high school graduation, the boxed ears the day Quinn flew off to Europe. Finally, without dwelling on dates and details, I told her yes, she hit me.

"And Maury?" she asked.

"Well, hitting I'm not sure, but there was the time you pushed his face into a bowl of hot pea soup."

"I did?" she said, amazed. "What about Quinn?"

"You'll have to ask him." It's like her brain is a sieve that no longer retains anything so minor as a memory of walloping us.

From the box she lifts a snapshot of Maury as a boy. Knees bunched under his chin, he's crammed into a fruit crate that Dad nailed in the branches of an oak out back. Maury called it his tree house. He loved to hide there, alone and out of reach.

He was always climbing things. Agile as a monkey, he shimmied down from his high chair even before he could walk. To keep him in his crib, Mom and Dad had to flip it upside down and lower it over him like a cage. I remember him staring through the wooden slats, a little prisoner.

But when Mom asks what I recall about Maury, I don't mention cages. I don't mention her or Dad shouting at him. I say what a beautiful baby he was.

"He's still a handsome man," she insists.

I agree, although neither of us has laid eyes on him for years.

"When did you first notice something was wrong with him?"

There's no predicting what Mom wants to hear, except, of course, that she didn't cause his problems. Maybe she believes there's nothing wrong with him at all; he's just unlucky. When Lawrence showed me a newspaper article about Asperger's syndrome, and I passed it along to Mom, thinking it matched Maury's symptoms, she rejected any notion that her older son might be "an Ass Burger."

"I love Maury so much," I tell her now, "I never noticed anything wrong with him."

"That's crap, Candy."

"Well, only that business with the fan, the way he watched it and made a whirring sound."

"Yeah, then when we got air-conditioning," she says, "you couldn't drag him away from the window unit. He'd squat there staring through the vent. I hoped he'd grow up to be a repairman. But no such luck. Remember how he played wrong with his toys? Give him a truck and he'd flip it over and spin the tires until he was hypnotized. Then he got that Hopalong Cassidy gun set for Christmas," Mom goes on, "and treated the pistols like cars and crashed them into each other. By the same token, you'd expect he'd pick up a toy truck and shoot it. But there was never any logic." Mom shakes her head. "Still, it wasn't until Maury started school and other kids teased him that I knew something was wrong."

How could she not have caught on before then? I'm fifteen months older than Maury. It's not like Mom never saw a normal child. Didn't she wonder when he fell to pieces every time she switched on the vacuum cleaner? He was scared of being sucked into the bag, just like he was of getting washed down the drain when Mom pulled the bathtub plug.

When it was empty, though, he loved the bathtub. He'd climb in with his clothes on and snuggle up. He liked the feel of the porcelain. I never figured out how to square this with the fact that he couldn't bear to be touched. He loved me the most. He told me that all the time. But whenever I tried to cuddle him, he squirmed away.

Mom passes me another picture. I must be about four, Maury just shy of three. Both of us have curly blond ringlets and we're wearing matching white shoes and flouncy pinafores. Mom claims it wasn't unusual in those days to dress little boys in girl's clothes. But cute as he and I look together—honestly, Maury was prettier than me—I don't think it was smart to twin us.

"Isn't this sweet?" Mom holds up a shot of me pushing Maury in his stroller. Then in what I don't fancy is an aimless fall of her hand on a similar picture, she flashes one of Maury later on pushing me in my wheelchair. Like it might have slipped my mind, she asks, "Remember when you had polio?"

The snapshot shows me smiling. Or fake-smiling. Sure, I was happy to be out of the hospital. On the other hand, I recognized even then that I was playing a role. Nobody loves a complaining drama queen. The script called for cheerfulness. That was the only part available to a kid who pulled through polio.

Lately total strangers have started asking me about it. They're not shy, and I don't fault them for it. Who can blame anybody for being curious about a disease that doesn't exist nowadays? A woman writing a book on polio even sent me a questionnaire. Everyone wants to know what it was like.

How I caught it is a complete mystery to me. Mom kept Maury and me indoors during the hottest hours of the summer epidemic, and neither of us swam in a pool, public or otherwise. Yet polio singled me out and hunted me down like a dog after a rabbit.

I had it a month before anybody realized I was sick. The chills and fever, the pins and needles in my leg, the fatigue and limping, they got lost in the family's bigger problems. Things had gone belly up for Dad and he couldn't pay his gambling debts. Scared of having his legs broken, he left town and laid low until he could make restitution. Meanwhile Mom found a job checking out groceries at Safeway. Surprisingly, she didn't seem to have any problem dealing with the public. She kept the cutting remarks to herself until she got home. But she did claim that being around food all day sickened her so bad she couldn't cook dinner. She gave Maury and me cold cuts.

Sometimes she took Maury to Safeway with her and he spent hours jumping on and off the mat that opened the automatic doors. He wouldn't or couldn't stop until Mom gave him a good smack.

She tried to cure me of polio in the same fashion, with a stinging slap to the face. "Straighten up and walk right," she demanded. But when that didn't scare me into good health, she drove me to a doctor who took one look and declared, "Your daughter has P-O-L-I-O." He spelled it out like the disease had gone to my brain and I couldn't understand the word.

Mom wobbled and sobbed, then promised me, "You're not going to die."

The doctor hadn't mentioned dying. I had never thought I'd die. Now I couldn't think of anything else. It didn't help my spirits that Mom removed the Miraculous Medal from her neck and looped the chain around mine. "Pray to the Blessed Mother for a miracle," she shouted, as an orderly with a mask over his nose and mouth wheeled me into the hospital.

The children's polio ward was strictly black and white. Nurses in white bustled around, their starched uniforms crackling. Nuns wore crow-black habits with rosary beads rattling from their belts. The white doctors and priests dressed in dark suits, and the black orderlies in white smocks. The patients—boys, girls, and babies—were white. Black kids with polio got sent to a different hospital.

The ward was the first air-conditioned room I ever slept in. A summer blessing, believe me, for Washington, D.C. But the stink of disinfectant and medicine made me gag. Every breath of air tasted like another swallow of sickness. I wanted to hold my breath and squeeze my eyes shut so nothing of that place entered me. But you couldn't block it out. It was too strong, and I was weak and I couldn't quit looking.

At night, I sneaked out of bed and spied on the other kids. The refrigerated air cooled my backside through the slit hospital gown. But I shivered less from that than from what I saw. Kids with heads lolling on pipe-stem necks. Babies as twisted and bent as one of Mom's discarded bobby pins. My roommate was a bundle of sticks in an iron lung. She breathed through a machine that wheezed and groaned while she gazed up at a mirror that showed her hollow-cheeked face. That's how we talked, the two of us speaking into the mirror, her face paralyzed in a smile, mine frozen in disbelief. The worst thing was—I mean the weirdest—she had toys with her in the iron lung, but couldn't move her hands to play with them.

The black orderlies didn't mind that I roamed the ward. I guess they agreed that I wasn't sick compared to other patients. But the nuns and nurses warned me never to get out of bed by myself even to go to the bathroom. They made me use a bedpan, which I wouldn't do until they threatened me with an enema.

Polio had no cure in those days. It had to run its course. Some died. More wound up crippled. While you waited to see how things worked out for you, all you could do was stay limber. Each morning an orderly lifted me under the arms, lowered me into a tub of hot swirling water and told me to kick my feet. Kids who had no control of their muscles got dunked up and down. Their scrawny legs quivered like spaghetti strands in a boiling saucepan.

After the whirlpool, a physiotherapist told me to reach for my feet. That, she said, was how they'd know when I was healed—when my fingertips touched my toes. In the beginning I could barely grab my knees. But I kept at it—the physio kept me at it—and my hands eventually moved down to my calves, one plump, the other stick thin. When I made it to my ankles, I was just six inches from home.

In the evening, orderlies dragged metal cauldrons onto the ward, and the kids right away started crying. It was like a siren on a timer. One minute total silence, the next nothing but bawling. The orderlies jabbed tongs into the cauldrons and yanked out hot compresses, then went from aisle to aisle, wrapping our arms and legs. They burned like fire, those compresses, and my pink skin didn't stop stinging till bedtime.

But I wasn't in so much pain that I didn't notice something strange. Kids on the ward started wailing even before the orderlies wheeled in the cauldrons. They knew, their skin knew, what was coming.

When I told this to Lawrence, he explained about Pavlov's dogs. Right off the bat I realized that that described polio. It was a disease that reduced you to a howling mongrel.

After three months, they discharged me to what I dreamed would be happiness at home. But I had to stay in the house and rest most of the day in bed. With Mom at Safeway and Dad still hiding, Maury was all the company I had.

Out the window, I watched people on the sidewalk across the street, staring at our house and whispering, just as they did years later after Maury was arrested. Neighbors and rubbernecking strangers from around town had read in the newspapers about me, the umpteenth polio victim of the season, and they were anxious to have a look. They kept their distance, though. Like with AIDS today, people didn't know whether to feel sorry or disgusted.

Parents wouldn't even let their kids play on my side of the street. One daring little friend did dart over, and for a minute we hollered back and forth, me at the open window, she down on the lawn. But then her mother swooped in and toted her off to safety.

I suppose that's when it started, this sense I have that I'm excluded, that my feelings don't matter and I might as well not have them. That's been the hardest part for Lawrence to handle—the way I act like if I ever drop my guard the past will eat into every corner of my life.

"Candy, you're daydreaming," Mom breaks in. "Shut your mouth before you catch flies."

"I'm listening."

"Not to me, you're not."

"I'm here as a Eucharistic minister," I remind her. "I'm concentrating on the prayers. Are you ready?"

"I told you, I prayed all night. I have so many special intentions," she says between cigarette puffs, "there aren't enough hours in the day. 'Hear me, Lord,' I beg. 'Your will, not mine, be done.'"

I know she prays for me to land a good man, which I regard as an insult to Lawrence. She prays for Maury to find a good woman and for Quinn to win an Oscar. Then on top of the missionaries and the souls in purgatory, she prays for God to have mercy on an A-list of dead celebrities—Audrey Hepburn, Elvis, Natalie Wood, Rock Hudson . . .

"Oh Lord, life is hard," she groans. "The old griefs, the memories, so much pain."

"Why don't you just tell God that He knows what you need and leave it in His hands?"

"I'd rather itemize. It calms me down. At least it did. Now I'm so nervous you'll ship me off to assisted living, I pray I'll die soon."

"What do you have against living in a nice room with all your needs looked after?"

"Roaches," she says. "Those dumps are crawling with roaches."

"We'll find you a clean place."

"And they're expensive. A couple years of living like Lady Bountiful and there'd be nothing left for you and Maury."

"Don't worry about me. And you can count on Quinn to look after Maury."

Mom flicks an ash from her cigarette. It misses the ashtray and floats to the floor. "Promise me one thing. Don't commit me against my will."

I tell her the truth. I wouldn't dare to do anything against her will. If I did, she'd attack tooth and nail. They'd have to strap her into a straitjacket and stuff a gag in her mouth. Mom's like those guys Maury did time with, cons who can turn anything— a rolled magazine, a comb, a toothbrush—into a deadly weapon.

As she gropes in the box for more photographs, she resembles a dealer plucking cards out of that gadget called a shoe. She deals me a shot of Dad, his hair brilliantined, his sport shirt splotched with Hawaiian flowers. Gamblers, I've heard it said, stay in the game secretly hoping to lose. But judging by his cocky grin, Dad wasn't that kind. He always looked and dressed and acted like a guy with an ace up his sleeve and a joker to play. He had a wicked sense of humor.

I remember once he returned from a fishing trip on the Anacostia River lugging a snapping turtle by its tail. He chased Maury and me around the backyard until the turtle crooked its long neck over its shell and bit at Dad's hand. That did it. He slapped it down and chopped its head off with an ax. Blood splashed everyplace and the headless snapper stumbled blindly in the grass.

Maury, who loved animals, dropped to the ground next to it, and rocked and moaned. I felt sick and upchucked on my Mary Jane sandals.

"When I think about it—" Mom breaks my train of thought. "Maury, when he was born, seemed like any other baby. Slept a lot, didn't cry much. You need to nurse them, read their minds. The little devil's got no words. But I quit breast-feeding him because he was a biter."

This is my cue to say, "Don't blame yourself, Mom."

"Soon as he could walk," she continues, "he did nothing but fall on his noggin. Not a week passed that we didn't have to rush him to the emergency room for stitches. That's the difference between Maury and Quinn. Quinn could fall in shit and hop out smelling like a rose. But poor Maury, his life is one long stumble of fits and starts and stutters and farts. The last straw, the final blow, was you coming down with polio."

"How did my polio hurt Maury?"

"He loved you!" Mom exclaims, shedding a long ash from her Kent. "You were his favorite. Those months you were in the hospital, he never stopped moaning."

Having polio was a pretty poor time in my life too, but I've grown accustomed to being a bit-part player in the family melodrama. The main plot has always been about Mom or Maury or finally and forever about Quinn.

Shoving up off the sofa, Mom announces, "I have to pee," and walks briskly across the living room. Perhaps this spryness is meant to prove she doesn't need to be in an old folks' home. But at the bottom of the staircase she hesitates and like a tightrope walker slides a foot forward, then teeters and grabs the banister. She climbs a step at a time, planting her left foot and pulling the right one up after it, planting the left foot, pulling up the right.

There's a sympathetic twinge in my leg, and I want to run and help her. And at the same time, I want to run away.

# Maury

My room in Nicky's house is at the top of the stairs, under the slanted roof. First time she showed it to me, she said, "Painted green, it's like you're in a tent." It reminded me of Mom's attic back in Maryland. After my parole from Patuxent, I spent months up there building my boat. Not a model. A big one, fourteen feet long. I stretched out in the bottom of it and stared at the nails in the rafters like I do at the stars over Slab City. Once I finished the boat, I planned to float across the Chesapeake Bay and into the ocean. Instead, I caught a bus to California.

In the desert summer, eight months long, the window unit in my room shakes and jangles and shoots lukewarm air across the bed. It's strong enough to blow the hairs on my bare arms and legs, but never cold enough to stop me from sweating. This time of year, I like it with the AC off so I can hear the wind against the roof. It sounds like snow, but it's sand. Hissing through my teeth, I can make the same sound.

We don't get snow in the desert. Only up in the mountains. Some days, in the bright sun, the dunes look like snowdrifts, but when you press your hand to the ground, it's hot even in winter.

Long as it's been since I touched snow, I still dream about it. Nicky claims it's natural to dream about blizzards in a place that's hot. "Just like up north where it's freezing, you dream about a warm beach," she says.

I don't really dream about any kind of weather except snow, and it's more I'm remembering being a little boy and praying and watching for the first flakes to fall. If they stuck to the streets and turned slippery, that meant no school tomorrow. And if it got deep, then Dad couldn't drive home from wherever he was playing cards and we'd all have a free day. I prayed for snow that would never melt.

At Patuxent, I used to watch it from my cell window. The glass had a spiderweb of wire in it so you couldn't break it and cut your wrists. As the snow came down and covered the yard, I got more and more excited, hoping when it was knee deep they'd let us go outside and have a snowball fight. Of course they never did.

After dinner I'm in bed hissing the snow sound on the roof when Nicky shouts that I've got a phone call. That has to mean Mom or Candy, and because I've been remembering winter in Maryland, it's like the call's an answer to a brain message from me. But then I'm always remembering them and they almost never call.

From the top stair I watch Nicky at the bottom. She's a big woman and blocks my way to the phone. I wait for her to move. She grins and makes me squeeze past, knowing I hate to be touched.

One night right after I moved to Slab City, she rubbed up against me in the hallway and I felt static, like I do walking over a rug on a cold day in the wrong shoes.

"Anything the matter?" she asked, seeing me jerk back.

"You surprised me, is all."

She crowded in close again. She always wears baggy cotton dresses, the kind they sell across the border, with bright flowers sewn on the front. There's no guessing what's underneath. She has a good smile and her face is dark brown so her teeth shine. She tells people all the time that she has Indian blood. I believe her. When she stepped near me, I dropped back more.

"What's wrong?" she asked. "You a homo?"

I told her I wasn't. "I just don't need problems in my life."

"What kind of problem can it be working all day and hiding in your room at night?"

"I'm not hiding."

"Don't you ever get lonely?"

"I have all the company I need." I didn't mention the drawers in the box in my head and how I can be with Candy or Quinn or Cole whenever I want.

"Me, I'm lonely," she said. Her husband, who left her this place, died years ago.

"I'll be your friend," I said. "But not that kind."

I thought she understood. Still, there's times she stands so near I feel a shock, and she thinks it's funny. Now she steps aside, and I walk down the hall to the table with the telephone. The table's another thing she bought across the border—a big round tray with jagged edges and hammer marks on the copper. I sit on the leather stool beside it, and Nicky stays close enough that she hears what Mom has to say.

Mom does most of the talking, and she talks loud. She asks me to come home one last time. I say I haven't ever been home since I left, so this would be the first time. She isn't listening. She says she has something to give me and something to tell me in person. With her talking and Nicky listening, I start to feel dizzy. But I don't dare lie down on the floor and rock. Not with Nicky's broad brown feet in their sandals taking up so much space. Her toenails are blood red.

When Mom hangs up, Nicky says, "She's got something to give you."

I need to go to my room and think. But Nicky blocks the stairs and says, "I bet it's money."

"She's not rich."

"I hope it's money."

Nicky has money on the brain. In her job I guess she's got to. You can't always trust people in trailers. Some of them leave Slab City in the middle of the night, skipping out on months of rent. I pay for my room and meals with chores, not cash. Nicky has to have a machine to keep it all straight in her head—the money she's owed, what's dribbling in, and what's leaking out. There's a computer on a desk in the dining room, and she shoos me in there to show me the problem.

The screen has white numbers running across it. Maybe they add up to her. To me they just stream on and on, down one blue page and onto the next. Nicky moves them with her finger, saying, "See, see." But what I'm watching is her fingernail tapping at what she calls "the mouse." I don't know why that name. It looks like a clamshell.

"I'm almost broke," she says, "I might have to sell the property and move away. What'll you do?"

"Go with you."

"Not without money or a job you won't. I'll barely have enough to live on myself."

I fix my eyes on her finger. Then the screen. So many numbers, so much debt. I doubt whoever buys the place from Nicky'll let me stay on.

"Is there room for you at your mother's house?" she asks.

"I don't think so." Mom's the one that sent me packing in the first place.

"Then you better damn well hope it's money she has to give you. Who's going to pay your way back east?"

"My brother, Quinn."

"Can you stay with him?"

"No, he lives on the other side of the ocean. What would I do there?"

She switches something that makes the numbers disappear from the screen. "You're not all that much company," she says, "but I'd hate to lose you."

I don't say it, but I'd hate to lose her too.


Back upstairs in bed, I think about money and how to get it. I shut my eyes and wonder what Mom has to tell me. Will she say it's all been a big mistake? Not that things didn't really happen, but that I looked at them wrong and didn't understand. Her asking me to leave Maryland, it wasn't that she didn't love me. It was just the cops kept picking on me.

With the sand blowing against the roof and me wishing it was snow, I might as well be outside on a slab and wishing I was on an airplane. It's stupid to worry about money or what Mom has to tell me when the biggest worry is she's old and she's dying. She didn't say it on the phone. She didn't have to. I know when you're old, you die. Unless you're already dead when you're young, like

Dad. Then they lock you in a box and bury you in the ground. Unless they burn you. I'd rather a box. I know boxes. I lived in one for twelve years and there's the box in my head where I have everything stored. Burning is something I can't bear to think about. But Mom always has her own ideas.

# Quinn

On my daily hike through Hampstead I carry the *Oresteia*, reminded of years at the University of Maryland when I crossed
the campus feeling simultaneously self-conscious and self-
congratulatory about the paperback in my hand. I never went
anywhere, not even a football game, without something to read.
There wasn't a moment to spare in my forced march of education and improvement.

But whereas those books buoyed me up with promises of a
vivid future, the *Oresteia* has been dragging me down and into
the past. Say what you will about Aeschylus, he isn't reluctant to
depress his audience. A close reading of the trilogy, much of it
out loud to savor the cadence of the verse, has left me, as I guess
Greek tragedy is meant to, more than a little heartsick. It's been
like plunging into a submarine cave wearing a defective air tank
and a mask that wildly magnifies every detail. I can see where I'm
going, but have no confidence I'll get out alive.

Curses that run on for generations, dead fathers, frenzied mothers, sacrificed children, and pursuing Furies. At times I have the
impression that I'm not reading so much as reliving my family history. Seven pages into *Agamemnon*, I trip on a line that tempts me

to abandon the whole project. "We cannot sleep, and drop by drop at the heart / the pain of pain remembered comes again."

I don't want to remember the pain. I thought I had put it behind me when I settled in England. But now after nights of violent dreams, I stand in the bathroom each morning under the pulsing nozzle of the power shower and try to wash Aeschylus off me. It doesn't work.

Is there any bigger bore than one who inflicts his nightmares on a captive audience? In plays and movies, dream sequences strike me as pretentious at best, lazy exposition at worst. I detest the trite symbolism, the dark foreboding, and Freudian mumbo-jumbo. And yet the pressure to keep my dreams private seethes in my skull. Memories rush over me like those yobs on the tube who elbow passengers, itching for a fight.

Some days I wake convinced that I've committed a great crime and I'm haunted with guilt. It's then that I recall Mom's promise to me as a kid. She swore she'd always love me. She swore she'd love me even if I killed somebody. I didn't doubt her for a second. After all, she loved Maury. But she repeated her vow so often, I started to suspect that she had a person in mind for me to murder.

Ratcheting up my nerves and irascibility these days, negotiations with BBC have turned, as Mal pungently expresses it, tits up. They say they still want me. And despite my disquiet over the *Oresteia*, I still want them. I desperately want the part, both out of pride and frankly because of the payday. But they've oh so politely declined to meet my quote.

Like every actor of my stature, I have "my quote"—the price I feel I should command. BBC has offered a "no-quote" deal, a low-ball figure that they promise will never be made public.

We're in an industry, however, where there are no secrets and everyone can calculate your value down to the last decimal point. As soon as you accept a no-quote contract, you can kiss your quote good-bye and gird yourself for a career of cut-rate paychecks.

As the dickering drags on and Aeschylus eats deeper into my dreams, I find that the random abrasions of daily life—a shoulder bump on the High Street, an inept bank clerk, an impertinent question from an interviewer—fill me with unreasonable anger. The English winter seems gloomier, the view from my conservatory dull, lifeless. Suddenly I start to stumble on the brick pavement and curse out loud.

Then things turn worse. I get into a scuffle at a cab stand when a drunken couple breaks into line ahead of me. In the States the incident would pass unnoticed. But in the UK, the bottom-feeding tabloids are omnivorous and they play it as a man-bites-dog story. "Furious Yank Actor Defends British Queue," reads the headline. Friends notice I have a black eye and rib me that I'd better mind the booze or else take boxing lessons.

The good-natured joshing stops when I explode at a press conference. Fed up with an outrageous line of rottweiler questioning, I clamp a hand over a reporter's mouth and shout that I won't speak again until the harassment ceases. That the reporter is a woman doesn't help matters. The upshot—an out-of-court settlement and a caution from my accountant that further impersonations of Russell Crowe should be shelved until my assets match the Australian's.

I downplay these dustups, urbanely citing the show biz mantra that there's no such thing as bad publicity. It'd worry me far more, I maintain, if my outbursts didn't make the papers. But inside I'm spoiling for trouble.

One drizzly afternoon as I cross Golder's Green en route to my weekly doubles match, two teenagers shout, "Look at the fucking tennis tosser." I call them a couple of assholes. Insult follows insult, menace leads to menace, everything expressed in alternating British and American obscenity. It might have been amusing, laughable, if one boy didn't pull a shiny object from the pocket of his hoodie. Sure it's a knife, I unsheathe my racket, a male menopausal model brand-named the Thunderstick, and let both of them have a taste of it. One lout comes away with a fractured wrist, the other with a string pattern on his mug. I come away with an unflattering picture in the evening papers and charges of serious affray. What I imagined was a knife proves to be a cell phone. The boy claims he was terrified by my behavior and intended to dial 999.

In America, this series of farces might lead to a plea for the court's mercy and an agreement to enroll in anger management. But to avoid the full weight of British justice, I have to submit to a battery of assessments and a course of treatment by a bona fide, pipe-sucking psychoanalyst. His offices are not far from me, at the bottom of Fitzjohn's Avenue, down near the Tavistock Center, where a bronze statue of Sigmund Freud broods over the stalled uphill traffic.

Dr. Rokoko, a burly New Zealander of distant Maori antecedents, looks as if he belongs on a rugby pitch. When he rolls up his shirtsleeves, it's a shock that he doesn't have tribal tattoos on his massive forearms. Far from the caring-sharing type, he has a scrum half's blunt, no bullshit manner. Or perhaps this is just the position he takes with antisocial offenders assigned to him by the court. Our sessions commence not with an invitation to confide my problems, but a pugnacious interrogation delivered in a clipped antipodean accent.

"Inny histry of childhood vilence?"

"Are you asking what I experienced or what I observed?" Eager to get this over with and to reveal no more than absolutely required, I start off with the intention of speaking as little as possible about Mom, Dad, and Maury. I figure any mention of Dad's murder is likely to keep me in mandatory observation for the rest of my life.

"I'm asking did you git in many fights growing up?"

"Very few. Actually none."

I don't mention that this was the one advantage of having a convicted killer for a brother. Nobody messed with me for fear that I might prove to be as unhinged as Maury. By the time I reached high school there were a few hard-ass delinquents who might have relished taking their chances, but by then Maury was home on parole to protect me.

"So you claim," Dr. Rokoko says, "that you never hit anybody until recently?"

"Correct."

"And no one hit you?"

"Never." I deliver the lie with complete aplomb.

"Inny histry of ibuse?"

"Physical? Verbal? Sexual?" I ask.

"Sexual. Let's start with that," he says, tamping tobacco into his pipe.

It's difficult to suppress my normally expansive nature; my impulse is to be a raconteur, an entertainer.

I've long dined out on comic tales of Mom's bare-knuckled discipline. In addition to leaching the sting from old wounds, people's laughter allows me to savor the humor myself. A tiny woman terrorizing her family and everybody else who crosses her path—the very idea has intrinsic hilarity. But Dr. Rokoko's question about sex abuse taps into unrehearsed territory, and I have no better explanation of what surges from me than I do of the berserk episodes that sentenced me to a shrink in the first place.

Behind our house, I tell him, there was a copse of woods. As a boy, Maury had a tree shack back there. By the time I was in school, nothing remained of it except rusty nails in an oak tree and a clear patch around its trunk. On warm afternoons, this lonely latchkey kid sat in the shade doing his homework or daydreaming until Mom and Candy got off work and fixed dinner.

One day, to my amazement, a man had pitched camp under the tree and was roasting hotdogs over a bonfire. He must have been in his early twenties, a dozen years older than me. My automatic instinct was to run. Yet I stayed. Worse, I stepped into the clearing.

Mom had warned me about strange men—never talk to them, never accept a car ride or candy. If a man touched me, I was supposed to scream bloody murder. Her cautions didn't extend to what I should do in the case of strange women.

What kept me rooted to the spot was what should have raised the shrillest alarm. The guy had a gun—a .22 rifle—and cartridges slung bandolier-style across his chest. From the webbed belt around his waist dangled a Bowie knife and a pair of handcuffs.

"How about a hotdog and a beer?" he asked me.

"I'm only eleven."

He laughed. "That's old enough."

"Not to drink."

"Good. That means more for me." He popped a can of Gunther with a church key from his knapsack.

Every bit of his equipment excited and unsettled me in equal measure. I longed to handle the weapons. The man had to have sensed that. "Like to see my rifle?" he asked. "Don't be afraid. It's not loaded."

He handed over the .22 and sidled around behind me. "Press it against your shoulder and pull the trigger." Encircling me in a loose embrace, he inserted my finger into the trigger housing. The click of the firing pin was no louder than a snapped twig. Although discomfited by his closeness, his laying on of hands, his breath on my neck, I still didn't run.

"Wanna see my knife?" He yanked it from the scabbard and flipped it at my feet. The blade sank in soft leaf mulch between my tennis shoes. "Go ahead. Pick it up."

I hefted the knife by its carved bone handle. Nothing had ever seemed more seductive and beautiful to me.

"Do me a favor and you're free to keep it," he said.

"My mother won't let me."

"Let you what?"

"Have a knife."

"Hide it from her. Don't you have secrets?"

I told him that I didn't.

"I don't believe that," he said. "Me, I got plenty. Even where I am and where I go's a secret. I'm traveling around the country meeting young fellas like you and looking to get laid. Can you help me?"

"I'm only eleven," I said again. "I don't know any girls your age."

He laughed soundlessly. "Me neither. But we have each other. If you wanna be friends and have some fun, you're welcome to the knife."

"I gotta go home. My mother's waiting dinner for me."

"Hold on a sec." He grabbed the waistband of my blue jeans and shoved a hand down into my underpants, all the way to the sack of my balls. "I won't hurt you."

I thrashed to get away, but he tightened his grip. His whiskery chin scraped my face. I screamed, and while it wasn't the kind of bloodcurdler Mom recommended, he let go.

"Hey, I didn't do anything wrong," he said. "Go ahead and keep the knife. And keep your trap shut. Nothing happened."

I told Dr. Rokoko that I grabbed the knife and raced home. I didn't mention that Mom wasn't there yet, allowing me time to think things through. I went up to my room and lay in bed with the knife on the covers beside me. The blade had a dull sheen and was cold to the touch. The bone handle was smooth and warm.

The man, I decided, had been right about one thing. Nothing had happened. Or not much. But if I confessed to Mom that I stayed in the woods with a stranger when I should have run, she'd beat me black and blue. Then she'd call the cops and I'd have to own up to them that the guy stuck his hand down my pants. They'd ask where he touched me and why didn't I fight back? Why didn't I use the knife? Did I want to do what he said? And what exactly was that? I had a hard time imagining sex with a girl. I couldn't picture what the man was suggesting.

After the cops caught him, there'd be a trial and I'd have to repeat the story in front of a flock of people. Then the guy would go to prison. All because I didn't do what Mom told me to. All because, as she frequently complained, "You're never happy unless you're making other people miserable." All because I had been spellbound by the knife, and because the man had sex on his brain, something I had more and more on mine. He wasn't to blame. I was.

So I never told her about him, just as I didn't admit to Dr. Rokoko that I hadn't emerged from the incident unscathed. But the scar wasn't emotional. When Mom found the knife hidden in my closet, and I refused to say where I got it, she whipped my bare ass with a wire coat hanger. She whipped me so hard I bled. "Don't you understand what knives have done to this family?" she screamed. "Don't you understand?"

In the face of my silence, Dr. Rokoko draws ruminatively on the tobacco-filled pipe that he hasn't lit. He puffs and appears to be mulling over the story, evaluating it and me. "What am I supposed to do now?" he finally asks. "Applaud? Offer you a curtain call and a standing ovation?"

"What am I supposed to do?" I shoot back. "Go ballistic so you'll know what I'm like when I lose my temper?"

"I'd rather that than listen to more glib BS. Save your anecdotes for talk shows. Were you breast-fed?"

"Oh Jesus, spare me the psychobabble."

"I bet your mother's milk dried up. You're a very hungry man. That's why you talk so much crap. You have a mania for force-feeding people because you weren't fed."

I sigh and say nothing. I don't care to add credence to his diagnosis by talking more. Still, I realize I can't stay silent forever if I hope to avoid being hauled back into court. So in subsequent sessions, I narrate a highly selective account of my childhood. I concede that Dad's dead, but don't add that he was murdered by my brother. I describe Mom as a Penelope-like figure, struggling with three kids instead of a houseful of suitors, but I don't acknowledge her seismic temper. I speak of Candy's polio, and in a politically correct manner, I admit that Maury's "an Aspie," an example of neuro-diversity. But I don't tell him how deeply this distressed me. I refer to our family as dysfunctional, but don't reveal just how truly fucked up we were.

Not long after I start in with Dr. Rokoko, I sign a contract to write my memoirs. Of course, this sounds very grand, the sort of preening star turn, the capstone for an actor that might come much later in his career. But the publisher has in mind a manuscript that's less about me and more about my famous enemies and friends. The escapades of Lord this and Dame that, greenroom spats, sexual peccadilloes, a peek behind the arias.

With the BBC negotiations still stalled, money is a major incentive for me. Still, my ambition is to produce an unimpeachably literary book, not a celebrity trash wallow. In the area of writing, I'm not an utter novice. I have the reputation of being a thoughtful actor, a serious interpreter of texts, and I'm often invited to judge publishing awards, appear on panels at the Edinburgh Festival and supply voice-overs for high-minded documentaries. BBC has presented several of my radio plays, and I have a file cabinet of scribblings for prospective film scripts.

As I do with Dr. Rokoko, I start off going easy on family revelations and discussions of my low-rent upbringing. I leave it that I grew from nontheatrical roots. With a quote cadged from Cary

Grant (né Archie Leach), I write, "I pretended to be somebody I wanted to be until finally I became that person. Or he became me." Then I cite Marlon Brando, who said, "When you are a child who is unwanted or unwelcome, and the essence of who you are seems to be unacceptable, you look for an identity that will be acceptable." And what better identity to assume, I ask, than one created by Shakespeare, Shaw, or Strindberg?

Aeschylus, whom I toil over every day, doesn't come in for a mention. And at first Mom doesn't come in for more than a cameo appearance. But gradually it feels like matricide to eliminate her from the memoir and she moves to center stage. After all, she *was* my original producer, my earliest director, and sternest ongoing critic. She groomed me for stardom not like a typical doting stage-door mother, but like one of those merciless Indian matriarchs who cripple their children to improve their begging prospects. She pulled my hair to stand me up straight. She pinched my legs so I'd stop fidgeting. She spit into a Kleenex and scrubbed my face clean. She smacked the crown of my head to smooth my cowlick. To hurry me up or slow me down, she cracked my arm like a whip.

Paradoxically, as harsh as she could sometimes be, she was also smotheringly protective. She wouldn't even allow me to join the altar boys—she was afraid to let me leave the house before daybreak to serve at six o'clock Mass—until Monsignor Dade declared that I might have "the call." Ecstatic at the prospect of a priest in the family, she summarily shoved me out the door into the darkness.

Little did she realize that her single loosening of the reins would free me for a different fate. Instead of sticking my neck into a clerical noose, I wriggled away from the future she and Monsignor

Dade envisioned, and became the man I am. This narrow escape reminds me of the French playwright Jean Genet, who passed almost his entire childhood in prison. When later asked how juvenile detention might be improved, he replied that to the contrary it should be made crueler and universal. If everybody were savagely punished in youth, Genet said, there'd be far more beauty and poetry in the world.

This theme of a beneficially stunted adolescence, set against the backstory of my stint with the altar boys, constitutes an early chapter in my memoir and is the first chunk that I feel comfortable sharing with the public. When invited to speak at the Burgh House about how I became an actor, I bring along a sheaf of typed pages. To prime the audience I joke that inside every Catholic boy there's a spoiled priest and inside every Irishman a spoiled Proust. Then I don't read my manuscript so much as perform it.

Every summer, as a reward for our devotion, Monsignor Dade chartered a bus and drove a dozen altar boys to Glen Echo amusement park. The carnival rides didn't start up until the afternoon, but the swimming pool opened early. While other kids spent the morning frisking in the cool water, I was stuck high and dry. Mom wouldn't permit me to dip so much as a toe into what she called "that awful pee pod." After polio had crippled Candy, she wasn't about to lose another child to disease. I argued that no microbes could survive in Glen Echo's astringently chlorinated pool. Still, Mom wouldn't relent.

So I clung to the fence, like those convicts I saw on Sunday at Maury's slammer waiting in the yard at the hurricane wire, hoping for visitors. As if I didn't feel excluded enough on my own, Monsignor Dade crowded in beside me in his black suit and starched collar.

"Why aren't you swimming?" he asked.

"My mother won't let me. She's afraid I'll catch something."

"And you obeyed her," he marveled. "Even though you could have sneaked into the pool."

What was the point of explaining that I didn't dare do anything behind her back? It was her punishment, not God's, that I feared.

"That's wonderful, Quinn," he said.

Seeing nothing wonderful in my plight, I wandered off through the deserted park. Footsteps followed me. Monsignor Dade's. Even after my run-in with the creep in the woods, I had no fear—the idea didn't exist in those days—that a priest might groom a boy and crave his body. It was bad enough that he craved my soul. To me a religious vocation threatened to intensify the prison I was already trapped in. Holy orders, as I saw it, would sentence me to an eternity on the wrong side of the fence.

As I ambled along, I heard workers tinkering on the innards of the Tunnel of Love, hosing down the Fun House and rattling utensils in closed food stalls. The smell of buttered popcorn made my stomach rumble. I debated whether to dig into the bag lunch Candy had packed for me. If I ate now, I'd starve later. But there was nothing else to do during this dead time.

At a picnic table, I unwrapped a peanut butter and jelly sandwich and wolfed it down under strands of unlit bulbs that swayed overhead like a galaxy of spent stars. Everything at Glen Echo—the coiled snake of the roller coaster, the stopped clock of the Ferris wheel, the scorpion stingers of the Dodge'em Cars curled against the roof—everything appeared to be suspended in anticipation, waiting like me for my life to begin. Sparrows and pigeons provided scant back action, flitting above the rubbish bins. When I clapped my hands to scare them away, I noted that this glen had no echo.

It dawned on me that this might be what Maury did every day in prison—kill time so that it wouldn't kill him. Pay strict attention to the fleeting minutes so that he'd have power over them rather than let their randomness rule him.

Then a shadow swept over me and Monsignor Dade lowered himself onto the bench. He tried to make small talk. That wasn't easy with a kid who had had it dinned into him that he should never discuss family business with outsiders. Dad's murder, Mom's mood swings, Maury's crime—there were so many things I was compelled to stay mum about.

A pink-cheeked, talcum-scented man of late middle age, the monsignor soon zeroed in on the subject that obsessed him—my vocation. "To receive the call of God," he said, "is the greatest honor that the Almighty God can bestow upon a man. No king or emperor on this earth has the power of the priest of God. No angel or archangel in heaven, no saint, not even the Blessed Virgin herself."

He concluded by promising to pay my tuition to Catholic high school and on through university if I'd give prayerful consideration to becoming a priest.

Heightening the drama of the moment, the air at Glen Echo started to throb. Throughout the amusement park, engines coughed and the PA system shrieked. The metal facades at the ring toss and the shooting gallery thudded up, and the roller coaster took a thunderous trial run without riders. Rolling my lunch bag, I slammed it between my cupped hands with a loud pop. Monsignor Dade flinched, perhaps believing I had rejected the deal. But ruthless little schemer that I was, I recognized my ticket out, and in a masterful impersonation of earnestness I agreed to do what he asked of me. Son of a single impoverished mother, I agreed that in return for an education I could never have afforded, for an opportunity available to no one else in my family, I would pray over my vocation. And as good as his word, the monsignor continued to cover my college tuition even after it turned out that my vocation was to be an actor.

My reading at Burgh House prompts a polite round of applause, loud and long enough to persuade me that I've done well by British standards. The inevitable few people linger to have a word. Only one person fully engages my attention, and as I speak to the others, I'm aware of playing to this ravishing brunette. Tall, lean, and as self-possessed as a fashion model, she's dressed like an impecunious grad student in unbecoming corduroys and a loose-fitting sweater. A jumper, she'd call it. When it's her turn to talk, I complacently expect compliments. Instead she says, "Don't you think you should footnote the quote you stole from Joyce?"

"Afraid I don't remember Joyce. Are you a friend? Her sister?"

"James Joyce. What the priest said is verbatim from *A Portrait of the Artist as a Young Man*."

"You're kidding. Are you accusing me of plagiarism?" I joke it off. "You need to speak to Monsignor Dade."

"Maybe I should," she says with a taunting smile.

"Afraid he died decades ago. Thank God I didn't fall for a sales pitch he cribbed from a novel. He might have tricked me into taking vows of chastity and obedience."

"Like you tricked him into paying for your schooling."

"And thank God I have you to keep me honest."

Having met "cute," as every romantic comedy demands, she and I go for a drink at Toast, a restaurant improbably located above the Hampstead tube station. Her name is Tamzin—"that's with a zed," she informs me. As I suspected, she's a graduate student in literature at University College London and works part-time at the British Library. With no false modesty, she swears that she can track down any quote I'd care to use in my memoirs. I promise to keep her services in mind.

"*Non serviam.* That's from Joyce, too, and it's what you should have told the priest. I will not serve," she says. "But I'll work for you if you need me."

"Oh, I do."

Stepping out of Toast, we stumble into a rainstorm that slashes down like drill bits. What a shame, I say, that Tamzin has to catch a bus to her bedsit in Kentish Town when my house is close by. "Wouldn't you like to spend the night?" I pose the question in a voice that hovers between that of a jolly uncle and a patently bogus gallant.

Tamzin bats her lashes in theatrical bafflement. "Why would I do that?"

Why, indeed? I might say, *So that I can wake in the morning to worship your green eyes.* But it's tiresome to keep talking in italics. "Quite right. Let's find you a cab."


In the following days, her question persists. Why would she do that? She's at least fifteen years younger. Not an embarrassing age difference, but one that gives me pause when combined with her corduroys and schoolgirl jumper. Still, I arrange for us to have coffee. Then the next night we split a bottle of wine. Then we have dinner at a ghastly gastro-pub and go back to my place and end the evening with a kiss and a call for a taxi to take her home.

I like her spirit, her sassiness, and while I assume she's more attracted to my persona than to my corporal presence, she's no pushover intellectually or in other respects. To impress her with my intellectual gravitas, I tell her about the *Oresteia* and BBC despite my superstition that it's wrong to mention a deal before I have a contract and a cashable check. Then I invite her to fly to Venice for the weekend. Since it's during the film festival, I camouflage the trip as business and urge her on by saying she can keep my quotes straight.

What she infers from all this I have difficulty reading. The young are from a different country with their own dialect. That I'm American, rich, and in her eyes famous exaggerates the differences. Or so I suspect.

Still, my hopes rise when she climbs into the taxi to the airport wearing a dress, a nice one that shows off her legs. On the *aliscafo* over to the Lido, Tamzin says she has a gift for me. Hair swirling in the wind, sturdy legs bracing her against the lagoon's rough chop, she gropes in her shoulder bag and brings out a copy of *Clifford Odets, American Playwright*.

At the hotel, I've booked us separate rooms. I go to mine and browse through the biography. Tamzin has underlined a passage from a journal where Odets noted about his mother, "She wanted to be consoled. So did I. She was lonely, distressed, aggrieved. So was I. As a child, I expected to be petted, brought in (not cast out), consoled and comforted; and she begrudgingly would do none of these things for me; she was after all a child herself."

Has Tamzin somehow been channeling my sessions with Dr. Rokoko? How does she know about Mom? I don't need this. I put down the biography and pick up the *Oresteia*. Then I put it down too and go to the bar and begin drinking.

By the time Tamzin joins me for dinner, I'm still drinking. I suggest we skip tonight's films and eat at the hotel, far from the festival's frenzy. In the all but empty dining room I continue drinking and to my surprise and shame commence babbling about my sad-assed childhood. Clifford Odets and the *Oresteia* have opened the floodgates and I feed for fear of not being fed. Not that I'm a depressing raconteur. Unreliable, yes, but never dreary. My monologue, I'm confident, sparkles with poignant reminiscences and self-deprecating wit.

But Tamzin seems subdued and picks at her food, pushing a seared fish around her plate. Then she shoves it aside and sits back, and I wish I'd shut up. I natter on as a cat sidles out of the darkness over to our table. After rubbing against her legs, it leaps onto Tamzin's lap, and she breaks off chunks of the fish and feeds them to it.

How long I talk, how long she lets the famished cat eat from her fingers, I can't estimate. I only know I've finished a bottle of Greco di Tufo and Tamzin has reduced the fish to its skeleton. Just as I'm about to suggest ordering a second bottle, the cat stands up. It's choking on a bone and convulsively gags into Tamzin's lap every bite that it's eaten. I rush around and fumble at her dress with a napkin. Suddenly we're caught in a skit from an off-color cartoon, an underground clip of Charlie Chaplin in his cups. My hands are all over her. And she doesn't object. In the elevator, I keep up this pantomime of pawing and cleaning, and murmur an apology.

"For what?" Tamzin asks.

"Your dress is ruined. The evening's a shambles."

"It'll wash off."

We're barely into her room, the door half-shut behind us, when she stoops at the waist, seizes the hem of the dress and strips it off as she straightens up. Easy as . . . easy as skinning a cat. She draws a bath and plops the dress, not herself, into the warm water. Then it's off with the rest of her clothes. Her skin is so pale and flawless, I'm afraid it'll smear to the touch.

"Thank God for that cat," Tamzin says, stepping into my arms. "I thought you'd never quit talking."

# Candy

While Mom's upstairs, I shuffle through the photographs. It's a melancholy business, this revisiting the dead and their out-of-date clothes and old cars and furniture that ended up in a Goodwill dumpster. I'm glad all that's over and done with, and I don't have to live through it again. It's fading in the rearview mirror, like a crash you zoom past on the interstate.

But a clutched-up feeling stays in my throat. When Mom comes back, I'm afraid she'll pick up where she left off and plow on toward the ending where we've been too many times before. She's like one of those old women with rosary beads reciting the same Sorrowful Mystery over and over. I've heard it so often, I could trade places with her and tell the story myself.

Maury killed Dad on my fifteenth birthday. I was out of the house, treating myself to a matinee. I'll never forget the movie, *Splendor in the Grass*, which was about whether Natalie Wood should have sex with Warren Beatty or go insane. Her dilemma hit me hard. Although I didn't have a boyfriend and had never been on a date, I was sick with worry that if things didn't work out for a beauty like Natalie, what hope did I have?

On the walk home, I was chewing over the film's sad ending— Warren married to a fat Italian, Natalie mulching the past into poetry—when I noticed that our house was decorated with yellow ribbons. My first foolish thought, I'm ashamed to admit, was that Mom had thrown me a surprise party. But then I saw neighbors milling around on the sidewalk, and there were squad cars and an ambulance with bubbling roof lights.

"Here's his daughter," someone shouted. "It's his sister," another one said. At the crime scene tape, I cried out, "What happened?" And people hollered, "She lives here. Let her through."

"I've got my orders," a cop said.

"Where's my mother?"

A detective in a brown suit and snap-brim hat told the cop he'd take charge. He lifted the tape and motioned for me to duck under it.

"What's wrong?" I asked, although I was afraid I knew. I figured Mom and Dad had been fighting again. Neighbors were always complaining about their shouting and shoving matches.

"Your father . . ." The detective hesitated, searching my eyes. ". . . he's in bad shape."

"Where is he? In the ambulance?"

"Still in the house."

"And my mother?"

"She's there, too, answering questions. Do you feel up to talking to us, hon?"

"I want to see my mother."

"In a minute. After we talk."

A few reporters rolled in. I didn't understand that. A flashbulb popped, the first blinding shot in what became a barrage. Questions splashed over me like water bursting from a hose. I ducked my head, but the flood of noise and the flashes didn't stop.

"Let's go inside." The detective hurried me along until he realized that I limped. Then he gentled me toward the front door.

The living room, dining alcove, and kitchen were churning with cops, the rescue squad, a priest, a doctor, a man with a measuring tape, and a guy dusting for prints. I begged them to be careful. If anybody broke Mom's knickknacks, there'd be hell to pay.

The detective led me over to the new sofa. Covered in clear plastic, it was off-limits to Maury and me. When we watched TV, Mom made us sit on the floor. The sofa was reserved for grown-ups. I didn't want to have to explain this to the detective. So I sat down and hoped Mom wouldn't find out. The detective settled in beside me, and the plastic gave an embarrassing squeak under his butt.

"Did they fight a lot?" he asked. "You can trust me, hon. Just tell the truth, and help us help your family."

Maury and I had been raised as close-mouthed as a Mafia clan. Whenever bookies or collection agents pounded at the door, we knew not to answer questions and never to blab about Dad's whereabouts. For years he'd been in and out of hiding. So it shocked me to hear the detective say, "Your mother's already told us plenty."

"Like what?"

"Like they fought a lot."

That described Mom and Dad to a T. But I argued, "They don't fight any more than other married couples."

"I'm not talking about your parents. It's your brother. He and your father didn't get along, did they?"

I didn't know what to say. With Dad and Maury, the fighting was all one way. Dad just didn't have any patience with Maury's quirks.

The detective removed his hat. His large-pored face became blurry as my eyes teared up. "Did your brother threaten your father?" he asked. "Did he say he meant to hurt him?"

"Maury never hurt anybody. He hated it when anyone hurt an animal, even a turtle. He doesn't like to be touched, himself, and he doesn't touch other people. Whenever Dad spanked him—"

"Maury'd get mad?"

"No, he'd fall into one of his fits."

"And do what?"

"He'd moan on the floor and rock back and forth."

"What your mother tells us, he did a lot worse today. He stabbed your father."

I shook my head no.

"He confessed."

I started screaming. Not saying words, just screeching. That brought Mom out of the bedroom. Blank-faced and slow, she led a procession of detectives down the stairs. There was blood on her hands, on her arms and the front of her blouse. She looked like the butcher at Safeway, gory in his apron behind the meat counter. When she came near, I cringed and kept screaming. She hugged me, and the blood was hot to touch.

Only her eyes had expression. Compared to her empty face, they had every possible emotion in them, all at the same time. I was put in mind of staring out a window. On top of what you see through it, there's your own image in the glass and a reflection from the wall behind you where a mirror shows the scene backward, and on and on. That's how full Mom's eyes were with panic and pain and sadness and anger.

"Is Dad dead?" I asked.

She nodded.

"Maury killed him?"

She cut her eyes to the detectives. She didn't want to talk in front of them. "I gotta go to the police station and be with your brother."

"Let me go with you."

"You have to stay and look after the house. Go up to your room and wait there."

"How can I look after the house up there?"

"Don't argue, Candy. Just do what I tell you."

"One of my men'll keep her company," a detective said.

"She'd rather be alone. Wouldn't you?" Mom prompted.

I had no choice but to trudge upstairs and change out of the clothes she had bloodied. I soaked my birthday dress in the bathroom sink, and bloodstains swam off the wool like stingers from a sea nettle. The sight of it made me sick to my stomach. But even sticking a finger down my throat, I couldn't bring anything up.

I sat beside the window in my bedroom, hidden by a curtain. The crowd on the sidewalk grew bigger, and reporters interviewed neighbors and snapped pictures of the house. Everybody pressed against the yellow crime scene tape and gawked. Nobody wanted to miss a thing.

I felt . . . After all these years I'd just be guessing what I felt at fifteen. I'm positive self-pity topped the list. My birthday was ruined and so was my dress. The idea that my family and my life were ruined followed next. Then shame pushed everything else aside.

It was like the summer I caught polio and came home from the hospital to find people staring and pointing and whispering. Now it seemed I had contracted another disease and if I didn't agree to quarantine myself, people would do it to me.

Later I sobbed to Mom that I felt scalded with shame. "Don't be such a sissy," she said. "You make it sound like you've been peed on."

Which was exactly how I felt.

After the rescue squad carried Dad's body out in a black bag and the crowd drifted away, it hit me how much I'd miss him. Because of my bad leg it had been years since I'd run and fetched him a beer. Now I'd never do it again, nor climb onto his lap while he blew smoke rings through my hair.

After a few hours, I disobeyed Mom and left the bedroom. Downstairs, the living room and dining alcove had a scattering of gum wrappers, cigarette butts, and scorched matchsticks. Because the police hadn't cleaned up after themselves, I did it, same as I did every time Mom and Dad stumbled off to bed leaving the house a mess.

I postponed going into the kitchen till last. I was afraid there'd be blood wall to wall. But when I pushed through the swinging door, things were spic and span, every plate, glass, and piece of silverware in its place. Only the butcher knife was missing.

I crossed the gummy linoleum floor in my bare feet. I got no spooky feeling that somebody had died here. That was the creepiest thing—the sense that nothing seemed to have happened, yet everything had changed.

I pulled at the refrigerator door, and the rubber seals yielded with a moist pop. This was forbidden territory. Maury and I weren't supposed to eat between meals. Snacks and soft drinks were against the rules except on Saturday night. Since I was sinning already, I grabbed a beer instead of a Coke. If there had been a pack of Dad's Camels handy, I'd have fired one up and blown smoke rings through my own hair.

With a second bottle of beer, then a third, a nice glow took hold. This, I decided, was how I'd survive. I'd sit tight and I'd stay tight. The beer pooled deep inside, freezing me at the center so that I felt less and less, then nothing.

By the time Mom came home, I had passed out with my cheek glued to the kitchen table. It was after midnight, and she must have known I was exhausted. But that didn't stop her from shaking me awake and yakking into the wee hours.

The fight with Dad had started over nothing, she said. "Who knows what riled him? Some nights you needed to throw a net over that man. Not that it was anything Maury hadn't heard before. Just the typical hollering and cussing. But it upset Maury and he grabbed the butcher knife and stuck it in Dad's belly."

I heard her through a haze of beer, and as she talked on, the room started sliding under me. Some of the words didn't stick. I didn't want to picture Maury stabbing Dad. I didn't want to know what he confessed to the police, or how he acted when they locked him in solitary confinement for his own safety.

Maury probably preferred that to a cell full of prisoners. He liked to be alone in little places. I imagined him stretched out on his cot, like in the bathtub, his hands rubbing the walls for reassurance. Then tomorrow morning some smart person—a policeman, a lawyer, a priest—would show up and declare that he couldn't be held accountable.

But Mom soon busted that pipe dream. "What we have to pray for," she said, "is they give him life, not the death penalty."

"He's just thirteen."

"They booked him as an adult. It's a capital crime. If they prove premeditation—"

"Maury never premeditated anything."

"That's the point. Anybody asks, you tell them he wasn't capable of planning ahead. That's our best hope."


But nobody asked me that or anything else. Nobody spoke to me at all except Dad's relatives, who carped out loud, never caring who was in earshot. Heavy drinkers and hell-raisers, railroad men from Pennsylvania and oil roustabouts from Louisiana, they made it a point to take me aside and tell me that Dad had married a hardhearted woman. It went unsaid that she had produced damaged kids, one sick in the head, the other crippled in body. But it was clear they believed he had had less luck in life than at cards. Now we simply had to hope that he had gone to a better place.

Mom never asked me anything either. Not how I felt nor whether there was something she could do for me. She expected me to do for her. I became her dogsbody—honestly, that's the term she used. I prayed Dad's death would bring peace at home. But the battle between husband and wife turned into a mother-daughter donnybrook, and it took her no time to beat me down.

The worst of it was I had to go through this without Maury, who loved me like no one else in the family. With him in jail and me on my own, a hunger took hold that was as raw and stinging as a skinned knee. Nothing eased that ache until Quinn was born, and I had an infant to fawn over. I dressed and undressed him, bathed him and pushed him in his stroller. He was a doll, my living doll, and all I had to love until Lawrence happened into my life.

Still, I can't complain that Mom had it easier than me. She wore herself to a nub working for Maury's release. And when the public defender convinced her that that wouldn't happen and that he should plead guilty to second-degree murder in exchange for a life sentence, she didn't despair. Roaming the halls of the County Service Building, she cornered lawyers and begged them to do his appeal for free. She wrote petitions to shrinks and social workers pleading for help. Driven by a love hard to separate from lunacy, she paid out of her Safeway salary for tests that were supposed to prove his diminished responsibility. Finally she managed to have him transferred to the Patuxent Institute for Defective Delinquents, where he got psychological treatment and a chance for parole once he was no longer a threat to society and himself.

After that, I expected Mom to move on with her life and move out of the house where the murder was committed. But she fixed her course and wouldn't swerve from it till her son was free. I don't know where she drew the strength.

People insisted I was strong too because I stuck by Mom. But I knew better. I knew I stayed with her out of weakness.

"Candy!" she calls from upstairs. "Candy, where the hell are you? I've been hollering for five minutes."

Afraid that she's fallen and hurt herself, I scramble from the rocking chair and risk my neck on the stairs, climbing them two at a time. Dust rollers nestle in every corner of the second floor. I'd lay money she hasn't vacuumed or changed her sheets since last summer. She's living in her own house like a bag lady in the streets.

The door to her bedroom is shut. She shouts again, summoning me to the bedroom that used to be mine. Nothing's left of me here, and Mom calls it "the library." It has a shelf full of paperbacks, some of them from when Quinn was in college. Eventually, Mom read them herself, dead set on keeping pace with her son. But I have to say that where they fed his mind, all those books seemed to feed her mouth. Even at her age, nobody can outtalk her. There's also a card table where she wrote letters to Maury in prison, then later to Quinn in London. Now that her dealings with the boys have dwindled to phone calls—about once a year from Maury and twice a month from Quinn—the room has become a catchall for every type of keepsake.

Like I feared, Mom's down on the floor, propped up by a bony elbow. "My God, what's wrong?" I exclaim.

"Not a damn thing except you fell asleep on me."

"Lemme help you up."

"I'm okay where I am." She gives a dismissive flick of the fingers that hold a lighted cigarette. "Sit down."

I'm in my church clothes and the carpet's filthy. Still, I do as I'm told. I know there'll be trouble standing up again. Mother and daughter, we'll be like a couple of turtles flipped on their shells, struggling to turn upright.

"I've saved some stuff in the cedar chest," she says, "in case Quinn wants it."

I doubt he wants anything, not from her, not from me. I doubt we cross his mind except as burdens. In my low moments, I suspect Quinn cracks jokes to his English friends about his threadbare Irish family. I know he's honed a pitch-perfect impression of Maury, something resembling Dustin Hoffman in *Rain Man*. I've laughed at it myself so I'm as guilty as he is. I just hope he never imitates my limp.

Mom scoots around on her scrawny shanks and leans against the cedar chest. There are photos in it, too, and she hands me a stack of them. Then she tilts her head like a sword swallower and drags on the Kent, letting the poison stab deep into her lungs. After a lifetime of cigarette smoke, they must be as black and wrinkled as leather handbags.

"How long is it," she asks, "since Quinn brought that woman to visit?"

"About ten years." I don't mention his more recent visits when Mom refused to open the door for him. She warned him by phone she didn't want to be seen in her sorry shape. Still, he assumed if he stopped by the house she wouldn't turn him away. He assumed wrong! Insulted, he threatened to stop sending her money. But he cooled off and never missed a monthly check.

"What a stuck-up twat she was," Mom says. "She eyeballed my furniture like her skinny ass was too precious to sit on it. Everything she ate, even soup, she worried she had food stuck between her teeth and trotted off to the bathroom—the loo!—to check in the mirror."

Mom laughs, then coughs, then fights to catch her breath. "And that nose of hers, I'd love to have it full of nickels."

"I thought she was very elegant and aristocratic."

"Aristocratic my ass. I bet she knew some tricks in bed. Otherwise Quinn wouldn't have been with her. You believe what the nuns taught you about love, and how it depends on holding hands and looking into each other's eyes. But you'll learn soon enough if you stay with Leonard that it comes down to what you do in bed. Your father claimed that's how he wanted to die—during sex. But what about the woman? That'd put a gal off love for good."

"Mom, please!"

"He'd stagger home drunk after winning at cards and want to rush me before I was ready. I liked it better when he lost. He was slower and grateful then."

"Save this for Quinn."

"Don't think for one minute I didn't teach him the score. I hope he was listening. Doesn't look like you or Maury'll give me grandkids. So it's up to Quinn to make sure the family doesn't die off."

"Does that really matter?"

"Damn right. What mother doesn't like the line to go on?"


I riffle snapshots of Quinn that show his career with the chronology scrambled. One moment he's onstage at the Old Vic with Laurence Olivier, the next he's dressed as one of the magi for a grade school Christmas pageant. In the oldest pictures Mom's always hovering nearby. Whenever she wasn't spanking him, she spoiled him rotten. Soon as he started talking—and that was early—she never punished him for pretending to be something he's not. From the word go, they were in it together. But unlike

Maury or me, he gave her as good as he got. He was her favorite opponent, and she loved tangling with him.

She believed it would always be the two of them costarring in a script she wrote. But early on he brushed her off. I'm not talking about when he flew to Europe and never came back. I mean as a kid, he was already aiming for a wider audience.

What did she expect? Even before he was born, Mom made him the center of attention. She paraded around pushing her belly forward, like a man proud of his chest, and invited total strangers to touch it. Soon as he was weaned, she brought him to Patuxent Institute with us on visiting days, and let him fill up the silence. He'd jabber away, entertaining everybody—guards, inmates, other families. On the way home, Mom claimed to be too tired to drive, and since I had my learner's permit, I'd take the wheel while she'd lie in the backseat crooning to Quinn. Damned if he didn't croon back to her, the two of them in harmony. I sometimes wondered whether this, not seeing Maury, was the point of the trip.

For a kid who was such a charmer, Quinn never had many friends, and as a teenager he didn't date girls. As Mom put it, he was too smart to knock up some local tramp and waste his life like so many neighborhood boys did. She thought he was saving himself for the right woman. But I believe he was waiting for better opportunities.

I once cut loose with both barrels and told him that if it wasn't bad enough having a brother with Asperger's syndrome, I had a second one that was an Iceberger. But I really don't blame Quinn for his calculating nature. If I had his brains and ability, his good looks and good luck, I'd have done the same thing he did—get away at the first chance.

. . .

"Kids," Mom mutters half aloud. "I used to figure nothing pays off like kids. Now I'm not sure. Every time Quinn calls, he sounds so bored."

"It's five hours later in London. Maybe he's tired and ready for bed."

"Nah. He's just tired of me."

I toss aside a publicity still of Quinn in a Shakespearean costume that's as flouncy as a 1940s cocktail dress, and she picks it up. "Kids'll drive you crazy. Life'll make you nuts. After a while it all wears you down. It started for me when your father was in the army. During the war I virtually lived in the bathroom."

I assume she means she was sick to her stomach for fear that her husband would die in battle. But she says, "There were blackouts every night. The whole city of Washington was scared the Japs or the Germans would bomb us. When the siren wailed, I'd take shelter in the bathroom until the all-clear signal. I tacked tar paper over the window so I could leave on the bulb over the sink and read a book. I spent so many hours on the john smoking and reading, it's a wonder I didn't die of hemorrhoids. Sometimes I feel like I'm still holed up in that one bitty room, shut off from the world."

What am I supposed to say? Get out more often? Join a club? Take up a hobby?

She stares at the picture of Quinn in the cocktail dress. "Who are you?" she asks. "Where did you come from?" Her voice grows shaky and she starts to sob. "God knows, I did my best. I loved Quinn like all my children. Now he hates me."

"He doesn't hate you." I slip an arm around her shoulders.

"He'd hate me if he knew the truth. So would you."

This is my hint to ask, *The truth about what?* But I do no such thing. In fact, I move my arm off her.

"What's the matter? Can't you take the truth?" she asks.

Again I don't answer.

"He was never supposed to be born. Quinn was an accident."

"A happy accident," I say. "A gift from God after Dad died."

She cries harder, hacking and straining to haul up something from deep inside her, like a buried anchor from mud. "I considered aborting him. Honest to God, I did. I beat my belly so hard it left bruises. I would have done worse. But I had a girlfriend who got pregnant by a sailor while her husband was off in the army. She took a coat hanger to herself and bled to death. I didn't dare chance that. Not with you and Maury to worry about. Damned if I'd let you be raised by your father's family."

"You must have been under terrible pressure." I can't think of anything else to say.

"That's what the priest said when I confessed to him. He didn't blame me for being tempted to get rid of my baby. The point was, I didn't do it. He told me to pray for my dead girlfriend. I've been doing that since 1944."

"I think it's time for you to let go and let Christ take over." I repeat the homily from this morning's Mass. "Life is like water-skiing. The Lord's job is to steer the boat, and ours is to hang onto the rope while He does the driving." This image of me up on water skis requires a leap of faith, but I manage it and enjoy the idea of zipping across Chesapeake Bay with God at the controls.

Mom, however, can't make the jump. "I haven't worn a bathing suit in forty years," she says.

"Then forget about waterskiing. Just have faith in God's forgiveness."

She shakes her head. "After all I've done, God won't forgive me. There's so much you don't know and I've never told you."

And there's so much I'd rather not hear, I want to holler. Instead, rocking her in my arms, I murmur, "Go to your happy place."

This is what Mom told Maury and me when we were sad or sick or scared. "Go to your happy place," she'd say, "and tomorrow'll be a better day."

"The only place I'm headed," she says, "is hell."

"That's not true."

"Yeah, it is."

Rocking her harder, I whisper, "Let go. Just let go and let the Lord do His job."

Mom heaves and shudders. The spasm is so powerful, I'm afraid it's a seizure. I pull back and examine her lopsided face, the blue eye and the brown eye behind mismatched lenses.

"Quinn's not your brother," she blurts. Then she corrects herself. "He's not your full brother. He's a half to Maury and you."

I don't bother to ask whether she's lying. When it's a question of bad news, Mom never lies.

"Does Quinn know?" I say.

"Of course not," she spits out indignantly, like how dumb can you be? "You're the first person I've ever told, the only one I'd trust."

"Lucky me!" In my shock I want to lash out at her. Lash out at something. But I bite my lip. "Don't you think he deserves to know?"

"That's what the priest claims, the Filipino. For my penance, he wants me to admit the truth. But after hiding it all these years, how can I do a thing like that to Quinn?"

"Same way you did it to me."

"I'd rather die," Mom declares. "I'd rather be put out of my misery."

I'm stunned, appalled. "Suicide is a mortal sin. You know that. It means damnation and no burial in consecrated ground."

"I'd never kill myself. But I'm afraid what Quinn'll do if he finds out."

"He certainly won't kill you."

"I wouldn't count on that. Promise you'll never tell him," she pleads—which is precisely what she's angling for me to do, call Quinn and let her off the hook.

"I couldn't do it if I wanted to. He'd have hundreds of questions, and I don't know a thing about it."

"I'll explain everything to you."

"I don't want to hear." I clap my palms over my ears. "This is between you two."

"You're not curious who his father is?"

"Not on your life. That's for Quinn to find out, if it matters to him." Then it dawns on me that there is one thing I would like to know. "Is this what you and Dad were fighting about the day he died?"

In a kind of palsy, she claws the glasses from her face, blinding herself and making me invisible. "That's a shitty thing to ask your dying mother."

"Not half as shitty as leaving me to wonder."

"Sounds to me like you've made up your mind."

"You haven't denied it."

"What I haven't done is dignify the question."

"This is a strange time to stand on dignity. Why start so late in the day?"

"I can't believe you're talking to me like this."

"Ditto," I say. Getting up on hands and knees, I climb to my feet.

"So that's it. You're abandoning me." She jabs her glasses back on. "You won't help."

"I'm late meeting Lawrence." I reach her a hand.

"That's not the help I need."

"It's all I have to give. I'm not telling Quinn he's a bastard."

"I've known you to call him worse. Won't you do me this one favor?" she says. "Phone and tell Quinn I'd like to see him one last time."

"Why not call him yourself?"

"My fingers ache." She brandishes her swollen arthritic knuckles. They might be a boxer's fists at the end of a brutal career. "And I can never keep the numbers straight. There's so many to dial for an international call."

"If I call him and have him ring you back, do you swear you'll tell him the truth?"

"Not over the phone. I want him here so I can confess face to face."

"But you promise you'll be honest with him then?"

"Yes."

"Okay, it's a deal. Now let me help you downstairs."

"No. I'll stay and go through this stuff."

I leave her there at the cedar chest, and in a state of shock—or maybe my feet have fallen asleep—I almost tumble ass over tea-kettle down the stairs. I grab my purse and barge through the front door into the fresh air. Gulping it down, I have the sensation of surfacing after a dive into a muddy pond. My gene pool. Oh, how I'd love to swim out of it!

I cling to the thought of Lawrence. I cling to him as the priest urged us to cling to the waterski rope and trust God to pull us where we need to go. But then pawing for the car keys, I feel the pyx still in my purse. The towline slips out of my hands and God's boat goes speeding off with the rope jiggling behind it.

I don't have the stamina to run back into the house and start over, haggling with Mom to eat the Bread of Life, begging her not to despair, not to die, when in my heart of hearts what I want is for her to be released and me to be free. I open the golden box and take the Host on my tongue for the second time today. A sacrilege, I'm sure. Then I get into the Honda and grip the steering wheel. Once the wafer melts there's nothing to do but mumble "Amen" and switch on the ignition.

## Quinn

The question my memoir obliquely addresses—the same one I've
been avoiding in my sessions with Dr. Rokoko—is how I sur-
vived my childhood. How did I escape? Was I the fittest? Or like
a feral boy, did I have the good fortune to be raised by a nurtur-
ing wolf? As Orestes himself expressed it, half in pride, half in
horror, "Does mother's blood run in my veins?"

Candy believes it does. She's long accused me of being as bad
as Mom. But that just raises a different question: How bad is
Mom? Sure, she can be ruthless and conniving, but no more so
than the monsters I've had to contend with onstage and off. A
case could be made that at her worst she was excellent prepara-
tion for my professional career.

Today's *International Herald Tribune* reprints an article from
the *New York Times* science section that examines the maternal
instincts of animals. Its conclusion: cannibalism, abuse, aban-
donment, and neglect are motherly coping mechanisms. Lovable panda cubs, it points out, are born in pairs, and one is always
left to die. Mama pigs roll over and crush the runt of the litter.
Penguins push excess eggs out of the nest and into the Antarctic
deep freeze. Huggable female bunny rabbits drop their babies,

then hop away, returning for just two minutes a day at feeding time. "Rabbits are a highly popular prey," the article says, "and many predators will pursue them into their burrows. To keep the fox from the nursery door, the mother rabbit shuns the room. Her absence may not make her pups' hearts grow fonder, but it may keep those hearts thumping a little longer."

Is this the explanation for Mom's cruel and contradictory behavior? For the way she alternately blessed and blasted me? Were her vacillations from icy indifference to blistering interference all part of a strategy to protect me?

As I dither over these questions at breakfast, there's a muffled concussion at the window. Another bird has hurtled against its reflection in the conservatory glass. Pigeons are forever snapping their ruby-ringed necks and bouncing off in a shower of feathers. Today a fawn-colored dove staggers away dazed, then drunkenly turns and marches back into the transparent door. It hits the glass headfirst.

I leap to my feet to save the bird from brain damage. But then the phone rings and scares the dove into flight. I answer the call with a rote response to preserve my privacy. "Two aught seven, four three five, treble six two."

"Can I talk to Quinn Mitchell?"

"Who's calling?"

"This is Candy, Quinn. You sound like a servant in a PBS drama."

I revert to—I wouldn't call it my real voice. I have many voices. Mimicry has served me not just as an actor. It has permitted me to fit in, or at least fool people that I belong, anyplace in the world. For Candy's benefit, I scrub the Britishness and adopt an American accent, Maryland specific.

"I was finishing breakfast," I say. "I had egg in my mouth."

"What time do you roll out of bed? It's six here. Doesn't that make it eleven there?"

"I got a late start. Nice to hear from you." I don't want her to feel she's called at an inconvenient moment.

"The reason I'm bothering you, Mom's not so good."

"What is it?"

"She's afraid she's dying and going to hell."

"What's your prediction?"

"She's a sad little bag of bones." On the long-distance line it is difficult to say whether Candy sounds flippant or sympathetic. "But she's feisty enough to last for God knows how much longer."

"I mean what do you make of her chances of staying out of hell?"

There's a pause. I can almost hear Candy counting to ten and tapping her foot to stay calm. "Sometimes you seem to get a kick out of acting like a heartless prick," she says.

"You're confused about male anatomy. Pricks don't have hearts."

"You can say that again."

I chuckle at her comeback.

"I'm at the end of my rope, Quinn. I can't do it alone anymore. I need backup."

"Hire somebody. I'll pay for it."

"It's not that simple. She won't let anybody in the house to help her."

"You're preaching to the choir. Mom's the one you have to convince."

"Why's it always up to me to convince her? Why doesn't some-body else do it for a change? Why not you?"

"Okay, I will the next time I call. But sometimes it's hard getting through to her."

"What do you expect? You live thousands of miles away."

The dove suddenly resumes banging its head into the door—an all too blatant symbol for my conversation with Candy. "If memory serves—correct me if I'm wrong—it doesn't make any difference whether I'm here or in Maryland. Mom won't listen to me. She won't even let me see her. Last time, I had to talk to her through the mail slot."

"She doesn't have a mail slot."

"Excuse me. That changes everything. I spoke to her through a door. That makes me feel so much better."

"Why take it personally?"

"I *am* a person. How am I supposed to take it?"

"She's upset about the way she looks."

"I'm not completely in love with how I look either."

"You'd pity her if you saw her. Sometimes I hear her praying, 'Don't take me yet, Lord. Don't take me yet.' She's guilt-ridden and desperate for forgiveness before she dies."

"Call a priest and have her go to confession."

"She wants your forgiveness."

"Assure her that she has it, full and unqualified."

"She'd rather hear it from you."

I flick my free hand to distract the dove from its kamikaze attack on the glass.

"She wants to apologize to you in person," Candy says.

"Look, she doesn't owe me an apology. Staying away all these years, she did me a favor. I've made peace with the idea that she spared me. That's her best gift—her absence."

"How convenient for you." Candy's voice heats up. "What's her gift to me? I have to deal with her every damn day."

"I sympathize. I honestly do."

"First thing in the morning, I phone to make sure she's still alive, that she hasn't fallen down the stairs during the night and broken her neck. That's every day, not twice a month."

"Are you suggesting I call every day? For what? Sometimes she doesn't bother answering. I know she's there. Where else would she be? I let it ring and ring. I redial, to make sure I have the right code. I don't mean her area code. I mean that asinine business of ringing her number once, hanging up, and dialing again. It's like trying to get through to the CIA."

"She complains she gets crank calls, obscene calls, heavy breathers. She doesn't like to answer unless she's sure it's one of us."

"Even when she does answer," I say, "it's the same story. In winter she's too cold. In summer she's too hot. If it's spring or fall, she hates the change of season."

"Think how many times I've had to listen to that."

"Look, Candy, I'd love to help." As the dove continues to knock itself silly against the glass, a migraine tightens a band from the base of my skull to the crown of my head. "My advice is for you to start taking care of yourself."

"And who'll take care of Mom?"

"Maybe if you weren't at her beck and call, she'd go into assisted living."

"She'll never do that."

"Fine. I'll hire her a live-in nurse."

"She'll never do that either. That's always your solution, isn't it? Write a check. The easy way out."

"If it's so goddamn easy, why doesn't somebody else pay her bills?"

"I'll do it if you'll clean out her earwax, clip her toenails, and wash her pissy sheets. Do we have a deal?"

"Somebody's at the door." I drop the phone, scurry to the terrace, and scare the bird away, screaming. The neighbors no doubt think I'm nuts.

When I'm back on the line, Candy asks, "What was that?"

I don't waste time explaining. Candy's and my worst arguments have always been over how to defend Mom against her poor choices, how to perk up her spirits, how to steer clear when she was on a tear. Things haven't changed one iota. The more we obsess about her well-being, the more Mom ignores us.

I try to sound calm. Imperturbable. "Appropriately individuated," as Dr. Rokoko puts it. "It's not that I don't want to be supportive," I tell Candy. "It's just that I've detached. In a healthy sense of the word."

"Must be wonderful to have that luxury."

"You need to detach and live your own life and let her live hers."

"She doesn't have a life. She's dying."

"A minute ago," I remind her, "you said there's no predicting how long she'll last."

"She asked me to say she'd like to see you one last time. She wants to see Maury too. I guess that means sending him travel money."

"This is sort of sudden."

"How many times do I have to repeat it? She wants to see you."

"Why?"

"She wants your forgiveness."

"It's not my place to forgive her. I'm not God. I don't judge people."

Candy's laughter crackles on the line. "Of course you do. If you weren't an actor, you'd have made a hell of a critic. You know all the rules. Now it's time to learn a little compassion."

"I can't possibly leave London this winter."

"Tell her yourself. I'm tired of being your messenger. She's counting on a call from you today. If you don't care about her last wishes—"

"It's not a question of not *caring*."

"Blame it on your busy schedule. But wait a few hours before you phone her. She's like you. She sleeps late and wakes up in a nasty mood."

Candy slams down the receiver.


I go for a walk to clear my head. But the descent of Holly Mount, past St. Mary's Catholic Church, then past the cemetery of St. John's Anglican Church, clarifies nothing. Though it's not raining, the wind whips a dripping mist from the cedar trees. Pitted with decay and furred over with moss, the toothy headstones are wired together by dead blackberry vines, like a display of the appalling state of British dentistry.

It's never dawned on me before that I might end up buried here. I don't relish the thought of being buried anywhere. But I do wonder about my father and why I've never visited his grave. That's the least of it, I suppose—the least of the things I've never done that pertain to him. Mom discouraged questions, Candy choked up whenever I asked about Dad, and with Maury silence on the subject seemed a matter of simple kindness.

From Church Row I spot Kay Kendall's tomb. A film addict and faithful reader of screen magazines, Mom would love the landmark. During our strained telephone chats, actors and actresses are a favorite topic. As we gossip about celebrities who live near me in NW3—Emma Thompson, David Soul, Kenneth Branagh, Helena Bonham Carter—she shows a surer grasp of their personal affairs than she does of mine. And in every reference to my career, she can't resist sticking in the knife and twisting.

"I'm praying you'll land a starring role," she invariably says, "in the next Steven Spielberg movie."

"I'm a character actor," I remind her again. "Not a star. I'll never be bankable in the States."

"You just need a good script and a hardworking agent. Before I die, I want you to win an Academy Award or an Emmy. I want to watch you on TV in your tux thanking everybody who made your success possible. I want to be mentioned by name."

"Sorry, Mom. That's not going to happen."

"Pray and you shall receive."

"Pray for something worthwhile," I say. "Pray for yourself."

"Praying for you, I am praying for myself."

"Well, while you're at it, why not pray that Maury gets promoted to CEO of a Fortune 500 corporation."

But she's relentless, remorseless. Why does Candy imagine that I can persuade Mom of anything, let alone that she's forgiven? I'm not as dumb as that dove. I know when to quit beating my head against a door.


Through air as gray and cold as a gun barrel, I head up Flask Walk toward the Heath. Despite the weather, men drink outside the pub

while women—their wives?—look on in disdain. For a few blocks
I break into a jog. I used to subscribe to the consoling illusion that
each hour of exercise adds a day to the tag end of your life. Now
I'd settle for peace in the present moment. But thoughts of Mom
dog my steps. That she's anxious for my absolution needles me
like the north wind. You don't have to be a character in a Greek
tragedy to fear you're killing your mother by freezing your heart,
forgetting the good, and festering over the bad. What kind of man
ignores a final request?

The kind, it comes to me in self-defense, who has tasted the
back of her hand, but kept on paying the bills. Mal, my wise-
acre agent, says, "Whenever anybody claims it's not about the
money, it's about the money." But despite Candy's crack that I
try to solve every problem with a check, it really isn't about the
money.

Crossing the zebra on East Heath Road, I follow the footpath
to the Mixed Bathing Pond. In a nod to political correctness, two
further ponds welcome gays and lesbians. During this season,
only swans and mallards float like shooting gallery targets on the
tea-colored water. Bundled in anoraks, fishermen hug the shore,
icons of stoic agony, religiously committed to a ceremony that
looks about as availing as a rain dance. By suffering man learns.
But what do they gain by plumbing these shallows? I've never
seen them reel in so much as a minnow.

The hike up Parliament Hill sets my heart drumming and my
head spinning. I decide I'll spring for Maury's plane ticket to
Maryland. I can't make up my mind about myself. With the tense
wait for the BBC contract, the sessions with Dr. Rokoko, the
deadline for my memoir, and now Tamzin to consider—this is a
bad time for a trip to the States.

The bald summit of Parliament Hill usually attracts kite fly-ers. But today's wind would rip a kite to ribbons. Rifling inside my Barbour coat, it inflates me like the Michelin Man and threat-ens to float me over the whorled grasses to Highgate. To steady myself I latch onto a wooden bench and gaze out at London where rooftop antennas and satellite dishes describe an oriental script against the curdled sky.

At the foot of the hill on a rugby pitch, a solitary figure—man or boy, I can't judge at this distance— practices kicking up-and-unders. Punting the ball high into the air, he chases and catches it on the fly, a prodigious achievement that I, in my fashion, at-tempt to imitate. Memories of childhood sail end over end through my turbulent brain, and I try to gather them in before they go to ground.

Mom refused to understand how scared I was to visit Maury at Patuxent. As a kid, I complained every Sunday how terrified I was of the other cons, their hard-faced wives and girlfriends. The monosyllabic guards who frisked us coming and going didn't make me feel safer. To the contrary, I was afraid they'd slap me into prison, too, in a cell beside Maury.

Mom swore she'd never let them lock me away. But if she had that power, why was Maury behind bars? And why, after his pa-role, couldn't she keep the cops from arresting him on bogus charges every time there was a crime anywhere in the county?

When they first sprung Maury from Patuxent, I was happy for him. At school, though, my classmates taunted me about my jail-bird brother and I started to feel that some taint from him attached to me. It didn't help that Mom told me to ignore them. Just as

Candy believed that everybody was staring at her leg, I thought people eyed me with suspicion and distaste.

Then one day in the ninth grade I was cramming for a science quiz when a man barged into the study hall. He wore a denim shirt and jeans spackled with concrete. I took him for someone on the maintenance staff. But he looked me over and barked, "My car's out back. Let's go."

"Where? What for?"

"You'll find out."

"I'm not allowed to leave the building during school hours."

"Aren't you the scholar." He grabbed me by the shirt collar and muscled me into the hallway. Students and teachers gawked, but said nothing. When I hesitated, not knowing whether to shout for help or go along quietly, he slammed me against a locker. "Do I have to handcuff you?"

"Who are you? What did I do?"

He flipped open his wallet, flashing a police badge. Then he frog-marched me outside to a squad car. "Climb in."

"Have you talked to the principal? Do I have permission to leave?"

"Just get in."

He made me sit in the backseat, caged by steel mesh. My instant reaction was that Maury had been arrested again. "Does this have to do with my brother?"

"I'll ask the questions. You keep your trap shut."

We sped down U.S. 1, past body and fender shops and bail bondsmen's offices, to the County Service Building, a mock colonial bunker that brooded behind wooden pillars. To be driven to the same police station where, I knew from family lore, Maury had been booked for Dad's murder was the realization of a nightmare. Now you've done it, I remember thinking. You're going to jail. Against all reason, I was sure I had to be guilty of something.

The man hauled me into a squad room. In that stark gray space fizzing with neon light, a teenage girl in a torn blouse sat thumbing through mug shots.

"Is this the guy?" the cop asked her.

She glanced up, her face partially veiled by straight blond hair.

"You said dark hair, about six feet tall, green shirt," the cop prompted her.

"Is she accusing me of something? I've never seen her before."

"Shut up and let her look at you."

Her blue eyes sized me up more bluntly than any girl's ever had. She had cute birdlike features and a mole, like a beauty mark, on her cheek. We were about the same age, and she seemed every bit as scared as I was. It astounded me that she was scared of me or of the person she mistook me for. Even after she murmured, "It's not him," I had the sense that she might have said that only out of fear.

"He fits the description," the cop insisted.

"It was a man in his twenties," she whispered.

"I'm only fifteen," I said.

"I want any shit from you, I'll squeeze your head."

He hauled me down the corridor to a different room. "Watch this smartass while I talk to a witness."

A uniformed policeman stood guard beside an immense naked man who lay handcuffed to a table. Crosshatched with cuts and scratches, the man displayed no more animation than a hassock that had split a seam. Maybe he was in shock or sedated. He didn't let out a whimper as a paramedic swathed him with alcohol.

"A fucking mess, ain't he?" the policeman said. "He robbed the wrong guys at a pool hall, and they tossed him through a plate glass window. He didn't have so much lard on him, he'd probably be dead."

The cop in the spattered jeans came and led me back to the girl. "Take a second look," he said. "Take as long as you need. Age aside, could it be him?"

"No. He's not the one. I'm positive."

"Okey-dokey. Sit tight while I drop Mister Blabbermouth back at school."

As we left the County Service Building, a man called out, "How's it hanging, Gil?"

"Like a hammer."

In the squad car, he didn't apologize, but he let me sit up front and explained about the girl. "A guy jumped her and grabbed her tits. She broke away before he did worse."

"And you blamed me?" In four short years I had gone from having a man's hand down my pants to being suspected of sexual assault. How could I not feel tainted?

"You fit the description."

"She told you it was a man in his twenties. Why search in a school?"

"A hunch. No harm done."

"Not to you. What am I supposed to tell my teacher?"

"Tell him you talk too damn much." He leaned over and flung open the door on my side.


Normally I wouldn't have confided in a soul, no more than I had confessed to anybody before Dr. Rokoko about the creep in the woods. Ashamed and angry, I wanted to punish the cop—and at the same time I was afraid of being punished. If Mom found out, she was sure to flare up as quick as a kitchen match, not caring who got burned. Still, people had seen me dragged out of school and driven off in a squad car. I couldn't hide what had happened.

My science teacher sent me to the office. There the principal listened to my story, then despite my abject begging that he not tell Mom, he said he had no choice. He phoned her straightaway, and I resigned myself to being beaten.

That evening at home, however, she caught me by surprise and was furious at the police, not at me. Next day she called in sick at Safeway and made me come with her to the County Service Building, fuming the whole time about false arrest.

Mother Courage. That was another role she gloried in. Whenever she wasn't playing Mother Discourage or Medea or Blanche Dubois, she was a defender of underdogs, a pugnacious righter of wrongs, a fearless protector of her family. That these campaigns frequently ended in losing battles didn't deter Mom. All that mattered at the moment was settling a score.

With her silver hair helmeted in a page-boy style, she marched off to war in a pair of pedal pushers and a man's shirt hanging loose at her hips. Yet no pinstriped state's attorney or swaggering sleek-suited defense lawyer commanded quicker attention. She demanded to speak to the chief of police and promptly got her wish.

A florid fellow, short-armed and thick-necked, the chief wore a starched white shirt that creaked like a bulletproof vest. In bemusement, he listened to Mom lay out her bill of charges, then inquired mildly, "Did your son notice the name and badge number of the alleged officer in this alleged incident?"

"Gil," I said. "His name was Gil. I saw his badge but not the number."

The chief lazily swung his eyes over to me. "What's Gil's last name?"

"I don't know."

"Can you describe him?"

"He's heavy-set and wore work clothes. You know, blue jeans."

"Well, that gives us something to go on. We have an officer named Gil." He instructed his secretary to call Officer Conroy.

Then the three of us waited in awkward silence. Awkward for me, that is. It's hard to remember what I feared more. That the chief would humiliate Mom, and then she'd take it out on me? Or that somehow they'd both turn against me?

The chief didn't appear to feel any stress. Not bothering to straighten the papers on his desk or lighten the atmosphere with chitchat, he stared at Mom, and she locked her belligerent gaze on him.

Gil arrived in uniform, carrying a visored cap under one arm as though it were a serving tray. When the chief summarized Mom's complaints, Gil said, "Gee, I don't get it. I've never seen this boy before in my life. And what she accuses me of doing violates our procedures. We're trained to treat juveniles with kid gloves."

"That's a lie," Mom said. "I know damn well what you do to juveniles."

Petrified that she'd mention Maury—how would it help to tell them her older son was a convicted killer?—I broke in. "He put me in a room with the girl and pressured her to identify me. He prejudged—he prejudiced me."

"What do we have here?" the chief asked. "A Philadelphia lawyer?"

"He's smart and he tells the truth," Mom said.

"I believe my men are smart and tell the truth, too," the chief said.

"There were witnesses," I said. "Kids at my school. The girl."

Ignoring me, the chief asked Mom, "What am I supposed to do, ma'am? It's your boy's word against a police veteran of . . . how many years, Gil?"

"Eighteen years."

"He's been on the force longer than your son's been on earth. Under the circumstances, what can I do?"

"Fire him," Mom flung back.

"Afraid I'm not going to do that on the say-so of a kid. Of course, if you care to file a formal complaint—"

"That's what I'm doing now. Complaining."

"—you'll need to write a letter and submit it to the review board."

"Why should I believe I'll do better with a letter than talking to you?"

"That's your choice, ma'am. Now I've got things to tend to."

"Me too," Mom shouted. "I'm missing work. I'm being docked a day's pay. I've spent half my life fighting courts and parole boards. What do you have to do to get justice in this state?"

The chief signaled that Gil should go. Then he stood up, dismissing us. But Mom wouldn't leave. And with a fascination that verged on horror, I watched her veer off into self-immolating anger. It came to me then, not for the first time and certainly not the last, that in my childhood calculus of fear this was what I dreaded most—Mom's meltdowns.

Nostrils spread, voice lowered to a menacing register, she reared back and lambasted the chief. To crack his smug veneer and leave him with a scar to remember her by, she called him a coward. She accused him of having a backbone as soft as a banana, and she doubted how hard the rest of him was.

She wasn't doing this for me, I knew. It answered some deep need of hers. If it all ended in tears, in bloodshed or even a jail sentence, that was a price she was willing to pay. She'd have piled abuse on him for hours had the chief not sauntered from behind his desk and out of the room. The two of us were reduced to silence again. Then there was nothing to do except skulk down the hall to the exit.

On the ride home, terrified that I'd become her next target, I talked to protect myself. I talked to calm my nerves. I thanked her for defending me. I told her I loved her and was proud of her. But as I gibbered away and watched her hands and prayed they'd stay fastened to the steering wheel, I recognized that for all her brave standing up to authority Mom was . . . was wrong in the head. That was the politest way of putting it. And it was the hardest thing for me to accept. It's hard even today to acknowledge that the woman whose love and approval I craved, and who seemed to me, then as now, remarkable in so many respects, is clinically disturbed and dangerous. I didn't know how to deal with it back then. I don't know now.

At 4 p.m., darkness drops over London like a stage curtain. Some people find the early winter nightfall profoundly depressing. I regard it as a good excuse to pour a drink. Back in my conservatory, I measure two inches of Irish whiskey into a coffee mug, postpone the call I promised to make to Mom, and memorize the script of what I'll say.

Then I commence punching numbers—twenty for my discounted long-distance service, followed by the U.S. code, the Maryland area code, and finally the digits of her home phone. After a single ring, I hang up and redial. Since it's the signal she insists on, you'd expect her to snatch up the receiver the instant the second ring crosses the Atlantic. But no, I have time for a leisurely sip of whiskey. Because of her poor hearing, I suppose, the rings—four, five, six—have to wash over her in vibrating waves before she notices.

"Hello," Mom warbles as if from the bottom of a dank well.

"It's Quinn."

"Where are you? You sound like you're right in the next room."

"I'm in London."

"Is it cold there? It's cold here," she says.

"It's nice and invigorating." Another sip of whiskey warms my innards. "Candy told me you wanted to talk."

"What I want to do is talk in person, not over the phone."

"Good. It's been too long since we've seen each other. I should be in the States sometime this spring. I'll stop in Maryland."

"I need to talk to you sooner." Her voice strengthens in her old habit of command.

"I don't think that's possible, Mom. Not with the schedule I have."

"What are you doing that's more important than your mother?"

If I were her director, I'd discourage this tonal shift. In one line she's sad Ophelia drowning; in the next she's the tyrannical mother ruling with an iron fist over the House of Bernarda

Alba. Like the weak tubercular son in *Long Day's Journey into Night*, I grope for an alibi. "I've agreed to write my memoirs. The publisher has me on a tight deadline."

"That's wonderful, Quinn." The truculence evaporates from her voice. "Tell me about it."

"Not much to tell yet. I'm just starting."

"I'll pray for a best seller. Do you need pictures? Candy and I were going through photographs yesterday."

"It's not that sort of book."

"Readers would love to see you as a baby. I hope you don't dwell on the bad parts. Be positive and write about all your blessings. And don't be too hard on me. I'm hard enough on myself these days and don't know how much longer I'll last."

"I'm sorry to hear that. What seems to be the problem?" With this question I'm uncorking a bottle that could be bottomless. To fortify myself, I pour a second Irish whiskey.

"I remember and I regret . . ." Mom's words trail off in what may be a fault in the connection or a bit of internal editing. "I remember, but I don't regret. I'm afraid I won't go to heaven unless I clear the decks with you kids."

"Please, don't feel you need to do that with me. I'm fine."

"You may be fine. I'm a wreck. Half of the time I don't know who I am. I look in the mirror and can't figure it out."

"We all have those days."

"The doctor calls them panic attacks. I don't see what I have to be panicked about. Just life, I guess. These spells last for days unless I pop one of my pills."

"What pills?"

"I have a whole bunch. Xanax is the best."

"You take Xanax?" Pictures of druggie old stars in decline or young ones plagued by stage fright come to mind. "Did a doctor prescribe it?"

"What do you think? I bought it on the street?"

"What else do you take?"

She recites a list—Atenolol, Senequan, Celexa, Synthroid, Restoril—as if reading labels off the vials on her end table.

"Sounds like you might be overmedicated."

"That's what Candy says. But without medicine, I can't sleep and I can't wake up. I have terrible dreams."

Much as I empathize, I have no desire to compare nightmares with Mom.

"And every day I have to get up and dress and hurry downstairs," she says, "because if I stay in bed, Candy blames it on my being depressed. That gives her another excuse to bring up assisted living. She claims I'll be happier there. But she just wants me out of the way."

"No, she loves you and has your best interests at heart."

"She loves somebody else now. Bet you didn't know that. He wants her to move to North Carolina."

"Good for Candy. She deserves some happiness."

"How much happiness do you suppose this Leonard Lawrence or Lawrence Leonard gives her? He's a dentist, almost retirement age."

"I'm glad she has someone who loves her."

"I tell her, I say, do you know the definition of a sixty-five-year-old man that's good in bed? It's one that stays on his side and doesn't snore."

With my fist wrapped around the whiskey, I believe I catch sight of fox eyes in the garden.

"Candy, all kids," Mom goes on, "think their parents have no clue about sex. They don't accept that their mother's made of flesh and blood, and that at a certain age the flesh was weak and the blood was hot. Dad and I, we fought a lot. Mostly my fault. I had a filthy temper and I'd smack him around to get a rise out of him and remind him I was alive. But after the worst fights, we had the best loving."

Alternately an Irish Catholic prude and an outspoken bawd, Mom has always had this cringe-making habit of sharing more information than anybody, especially her children, care to hear.

"Want to know something funny?" she says. "I've started thinking about Jack. For a long time I didn't, but now I do. I remember he was the one that locked the doors at night before he switched off the lights and came to bed. I haven't felt safe since he died."

"I didn't know that," I say for want of something better.

"There's lots you don't know."

"Well, one thing I don't know—and it worries me—are you eating? Candy says you canceled Meals on Wheels."

"I drink Ensure every day."

"What about meat and vegetables? What about a hot meal?"

"To hell with cooking! Men retire. Why not women? I can't be bothered fixing food."

"You don't have to. Let me pay somebody to do it for you."

She draws a weary breath. "Eating bores me. The doctor says I have that disease where you lose interest in everything."

"What disease is that?"

"He wrote the name down on a slip of paper, but I lost it. It's one word."

"Anhedonia," I suggest.

"That sounds like more than one word."

"If you'd let somebody clean and cook and keep you company, you'd feel better."

"How good am I supposed to feel at eighty? I don't want strangers nosing around, ordering me to do this, do that in my own house. The women in that line of work, they can't even carry on a conversation. Most of them—now don't accuse me of being a racist. I've lived on the same street with them for decades—most of them are black and they have a chip on their shoulder. They grump and gripe and do as they damn well please. 'Don't you like your job?' I ask them. 'You deserve a better one, like singing or dancing. Something to cheer you up.' I say, 'I'm sorry about slavery and segregation and all that. But I didn't have anything to do with it. My people sailed over on a boat from County Cork and worked for a living.'"

"Please, promise me you don't say that, Mom."

"Why not? They don't care what they say to me. Last summer when Candy went to the shore with Leonard, she hired a nurse to babysit me. First thing she said, this nurse, she says, 'Lemme see you sit on the toilet and get up off it. We don't want any dribble accidents.' I told her, 'Damned if I will. You go directly to hell. I may be old, but I haven't lost my dignity.'"

Hoping Hollywood wisdom will soothe her, I observe, "Bette Davis said getting old ain't for sissies."

"That's for damn sure. I'm not scared of dying. I'm scared of living on and on, wasting Candy's time, wasting your money and winding up in a hospital with tubes stuck in every hole of my body. Promise me that won't happen, Quinn."

"Be sure you write a living will."

"I don't need to put it down on paper for you to know what to do."

I resist a third glass of whiskey. My vision is already shaky. The fluorescent fox eyes I thought I saw in the garden turn out to be my eyes mirrored in the conservatory door.

"I'd pull the plug on myself," she says. "But then they wouldn't pay off my insurance policy, and I'd go to hell."

"Don't say that. Don't even think it."

"That's what Candy tells me. But she's got her lover boy, and I'm all alone. Yesterday, I found a snapshot of you as a little kid and I felt . . . I don't know. Like I told Candy, 'Who are you? Where did you come from?'"

"You told Candy you didn't know where she came from?"

"No, I was saying where'd you come from?"

"Well, if you don't know, Mom . . ." I laugh uncomfortably. ". . . who does? Did you find me under a rock?"

"I mean, you've gone so far and done so much, it's hard to believe you belong to me. After we looked at the pictures," she says, "Candy went off to meet Leonard, and I stayed there and finished my cigarette."

"You still smoke?"

"Why not? You afraid it's bad for my health?"

"You could fall asleep and burn the house down."

"So what? Maybe if I burn here, I won't burn in the other place." She dredges in a ragged breath. "Anyway, Candy left, and I rested my eyes. Don't worry, I stubbed out the cigarette first. Next thing I knew, it was night and I couldn't figure out where I was. Then I couldn't stand up."

"Oh God," I groan.

"That's what I said. 'Oh God, don't let me be paralyzed.' I shimmied around on my butt to stir my circulation. Then I grabbed onto the cedar chest, but I didn't have the strength to pry myself off the floor. I felt legless."

"Why didn't you call Candy or the rescue squad? You should keep a phone in every room."

"I don't like having one near my bedroom, ruining the little sleep I get. I decided to sleep right there on the floor beside the cedar chest. I was warm enough in my housecoat, and by daybreak I counted on the blood coming back to my feet.

"I laid my face against the carpet, and it was like bedding down on fur. Which reminded me of all the cats and dogs I've owned in my life. Every last one dead now. I miss them, but I wouldn't buy another pet. It'd just be underfoot, tripping me, and I couldn't bear having it die before I do. Or worse, live on with nobody to look after it. Normally I pray myself to sleep. But last night I kept remembering animals and fur until I had to pee."

Willpower weakening, I pour a third whiskey. But it doesn't dull my senses. I remain preternaturally alert as Mom plugs into my brainstem, like one computer uploading its files onto another. This unbroken flow between us calls to mind nights in my childhood when she perched on my bed—*pace* Dr. Rokoko, sometimes she stretched out beside me—and released a stream of consciousness that rivaled Molly Bloom's riverine soliloquy. I listened then, and do now, with a combination of curiosity and skin-crawling qualms.

"I headed for the bathroom on my hands and knees," she says. "Then I got tired and slithered along on my belly. In the dark I didn't have any idea where I was going. I bumped into a wall. Then I hit the door frame. Then this awful burning started and I thought I'd wet myself and was afraid Candy would find me in a puddle, like a sick cat. That'd be the last straw. Straight into assisted living!

"Then I saw crabs in my mind, and pictured how I used to boil them, and they'd scrape and scratch to climb out of the pot. They never made it. Not a one of them. They pulled each other down, like drowning people do, until they turned bright red and died. That's how I felt, like I was boiling alive."

"Jesus Christ, Mom!"

"Lying there on fire, it hit me that I was having a foretaste of hell and this is what I'll suffer for eternity unless you fly home and forgive me."

"Of course I'll fly home. You know I will. Just tell me how you are now."

"Not even a blister," she says. "Turns out I collapsed on a heating grate. The furnace kicked off before it did me any damage. I keep the thermostat on sixty to save money. In the morning my feet were fine. Now when can I count on your coming here?"


The next day I wake to dismal light. The damp roof tiles of Hampstead are as slickly layered as the scales of a snake. I think of Mom on the heating grate, and rather than pity, I feel I've been had again; she's conned me into flying to the States. Still, I book a ticket on BA and cancel the cleaning lady and my appointment with Dr. Rokoko. I leave a message on Tamzin's cell phone that I'm making an emergency visit to my mother. The entire time I have the impression that I've seen this film before. It has the formulaic shape of a trite made-for-TV movie. Failing parent urgently summons children. Together they revisit ancient history, heal old wounds, and achieve the contemporary equivalent of catharsis—closure! Soft music. Slow fade.

But the script for my family has never been that saccharine and our past can't be so tidily summed up. We're more like brooding, brawling characters invented by Euripides. My last call from Heathrow reaches Mal, who maintains he has BBC on another line. "We're close," he swears. "Very close."

"I'm not sure I'm still interested," I lie through my teeth.

"Don't throw in the towel," he says, and leaps from boxing to sex. "Before we get into bed on this deal, we just need to find out who's screwing who."

BOOK TWO

## Maury

Mom promised me a plane ticket to Maryland. It comes in the mail in an envelope with Candy's return address and a letter from her saying Quinn paid for it and I should be thankful to him. I am thankful and I look forward to flying. But then Nicky tells me to fork over the ticket. She cashes it in and buys me a seat on a bus. The money left over, she says, barely covers what I owe her.

I tell Nicky if it's a question of squaring accounts, I'll hitchhike east and she can keep all the money. But she claims my hitching days are done. At my age, either people won't pick me up or they'll pick me up and kill me. That's how it is, everybody just roaming around and ready to steal.

The day Nicky drives me to Needles to the Greyhound station, she goes over it again. The schedule. The cities where I change buses. The state lines where the time changes and I lose an hour and have to fix my watch. She hands me a map out of the glove compartment and shows me the roads that go to Maryland. Some are blue, some red, all zigzagging and crooked as the veins on the back of my hands. They have numbers so you can keep them straight, and I store them in a drawer in my head.

Nicky goes on talking it to death. How I need to keep track of my bag. How I have to eat. How I shouldn't stare at people except when I'm talking to them, and then I should look them in the eye, but not too long and not too hard. How I'd be smart not to stand too near anybody in the bathroom.

The way she talks, the trip sounds like prison. But that's okay. I know prison. To get along you go along and follow the rules.

She drops me in front of the station, says, "Bye-bye. Bring home the bacon," and speeds off. I wait there in the sun, holding my bag, my feet in the pool of my shadow that's like a circle of oil on a slab after a trailer leaves. I have this feeling I might sink in it over my head. So I step into the shade where my shadow doesn't follow.

A gizmo with a clear plastic window, like the oven in Nicky's house, has a stack of newspapers inside it. On the front page there's a prison riot. The inmates are stripped and hooded and have their hands cuffed behind their backs. Dogs on leashes bare their teeth, ready to bite. A dozen naked guys are piled together. Maybe hurt, maybe dead. They're stacked up like wood and their arms and legs jut out.

The guards, some of them women, laugh and point at the privates on these prisoners. You can't really see them because the newsprint is smeared between their legs. Still, you know what's under the eraser marks. I don't look too long because it gives me that feeling of sinking in an oil pool to see parts of their bodies rubbed out.

A little boy and his mother leave the station. She's pulling a suitcase on wheels. He's carrying a toy bus no bigger than a cigarette pack. I don't stare. I don't stand too close. But I ask where they bought the toy bus. Without stopping or looking my way, the mother says, "The souvenir shop." Then they hurry on, and I haul my bag inside.

The shop has maps and cigarettes and gum and cold drinks. There are free color foldouts of towns along the road and I take a few. There are toy buses too and I buy one that's silver.

I hold it up to my eye. Through the windshield I see the little bus has seats and luggage racks and a button-size steering wheel. It even has a door in back for the bathroom. There's no driver or passengers, and it's no trouble to memorize the layout. In case of a fire or a rollover I'd escape through a window. Whenever I go light in the head, then light in my whole body till I'm scared I'll float away, I usually stretch out and grab the floor until the feeling stops. But now I can grab the toy bus instead.

As I count the coins to the cashier, I repeat the numbers to myself, not out loud, and I don't stare too hard. When Mom worked at Safeway, she hated people who made her wait. I go fast. But there's a bad moment when the cashier makes change and tries to put it in my hand. I ask her to put it on the counter and let me pick it up. She shoots me a look. She seems to be a nice girl, so I tell her I don't like to be touched.

On the ceiling of the station, there's a speaker calling the names of cities and the numbers of buses. I trace the towns on Nicky's map, and when the voice calls my bus, it's not hard to find outside at the curb. The problem starts when the driver says I have to stick my bag into a space behind an aluminum flap underneath the bus. I argue that the bag has to be where I can see it.

"You carry it on board, you'll block the aisle," he says.

"No, it'll fit over my seat." I show him inside my toy bus where the luggage rack is.

"Whoa, man!" He ducks his head. "Don't blind me with the damn thing."

I move it away from his face.

"If the bag fits overhead, fine," he says. "If it don't, it's gotta go here."

I slip sideways up the aisle, my map, my foldouts, and the toy bus in one hand, my bag in the other. Pressing it flat, I stuff the bag onto the rack. Once I'm in my seat, I can't see it except by looking up, but that's better than having it in the hole.

The bus is just another box, but a big one. Not like a cell, more like a holding pen crowded with sweating cons. Some passengers are fat, and the skinny ones wear belts with a sack hanging in front like a stomach. Nicky has one she calls her fanny pack. But with that name shouldn't it hang down in back?

Everybody settles and the door shuts with a squeak that I could imitate but don't. Then the bus eases through Needles the way I inched up the aisle, sucking in my belly, careful not to rub against anybody. It rounds corners real slow, like the tall iron gate at Patuxent slamming shut. People have to jump out of the way quick. God help them if they don't. It'd squash you like a bug.

Outside the city, on the interstate, the land flattens under the beating sun. It reminds me of the Mexican table in Nicky's house, the one with hammer marks on the copper and crimps at the edges. Light hits it and flashes over my face.

Faster and faster, the exit ramp numbers slide back in the corner of my eye and fall into the same drawer with the road numbers in my head. You can try to remember, Cole always said, but it's dumb to try and forget. The harder you work at it, the more it sticks in your mind.

I had twelve years with Cole at Patuxent and I go to him now whenever I'm lonely. I remember his smell—he had straw-colored hair and he smelled like straw—and how strong he was and how he held me. His hands were so big, he was like one of those black guys on the basketball court that can palm a ball.

At first I asked him not to touch me. I told him it was like an electric shock. He warned the other guys on our tier, and they didn't touch me either. At fourteen, small and weak, I'd have been turned out as somebody's punk if Cole hadn't spread the word. No one went against him. He was the toughest con at Patuxent. He had killed a cop and there was no way he'd ever get paroled, so he had nothing to lose.

On the tier, there was so much noise I couldn't sleep. I heard what sounded like rats gnawing my skull, scrambling around in the box, drawer to drawer. I didn't know whether they were scratching to dig out or dig in. I told Cole, and he said it was just guys sharpening tin and plastic on the cement floor, making shanks. I still couldn't sleep.

Every day I cleaned my cell and lined things up by size and shape. That's what I did as a kid when Mom dragged me to Safeway during her shift and let me play in the aisles. I'd start at one end and straighten out the stock. I didn't bother about labels or prices or products. I fixed on shapes and sizes and sometimes colors. I'd stack the cans and bags, then mix them up and make a new design. Before Mom punched out at the end of the day, I had to switch everything back where it belonged.

Since there wasn't enough in my cell to keep me busy, I'd scrub the floor, then snap my fingers five times. I'd flush the toilet five times. I'd flick the light switch five times. Then the number changed and I had to snap and flush and flick seven times or four times or nine.

Still, nothing stopped the noise and let me sleep. It wasn't one sound after another, but lots of different sounds at the same time, like riding on this bus and hearing a radio, hearing music from somebody's earphones, hearing people talk, the horns of passing cars, and the hum of tires on the highway and the hum in my mouth. Or like when I was little and Dad screamed and Mom screamed and I found myself screaming too. You wouldn't think a single ear could hold so much. But then my head holds that box that holds the jumble of drawers that hold my whole life.

When it got to where in prison I began to hear chainsaws and burglar alarms and vacuum cleaners nonstop, I dropped to the floor and rocked back and forth. I didn't quit even after the guards threw me in the hole. The doctors asked me why I did it, and what could I say except that too many noises bring too many ideas, and the heaviness in my head gets like balancing on a cliff, scared I'll tip over.

When I was a baby, I had a blue blanket with silk edges that I slept with. I'd rub the silk and suck my thumb and doze off in no time. I knew not to expect a blue blanket at Patuxent. They'd never let me have one, and if they did, people would poke fun. So Cole suggested I rub his hair, and it was smooth as silk.

I hadn't let him touch me yet. But one day when my mind started tipping over and I fell off the cliff, he found me on the floor. Times like that my ideas are loud as words and I figure people hear them and pretend not to. They stare at me, and I know I ought to shut up but I can't.

I didn't need to explain to Cole. He understood and cupped his hand on my head. There was no electric shock, just that calmness that came over me when the doctors made me swallow a pill.

Cole lifted me onto my bunk, and his hand went from my head to my neck and he hugged me the way Candy tried to do when we were little. I loved her, but it hurt to have her touch me. I liked to be near her, just not too close. The best was when she was in her wheelchair and I was behind it, pushing. She squealed for me to go fast, and I'd grab the plastic grips like the handlebars on my bike and start running. It was as hard as pumping a bike uphill. Then we'd zoom downhill, with Candy laughing and me careful not to step on cracks in the sidewalk. Mom called us a hell on wheels. But it was heaven to me, with Candy's hair blowing against my face, soft, real soft, in a touch that tingled and didn't hurt.

That's how it was with Cole. It tingled, it didn't hurt. If I didn't like what he did, he stopped. He never yelled or got rough. He fought other guys, punched them till they bled, but never me. He taught me how to stay alive in prison. We lifted weights together, spotting each other on the bench press. I needed muscles, he said, to protect me when he wasn't around. It was like I was the son and he was the father. Not Dad, but how I wish Dad had been.

Cole laughed when I told him this. "Hope to hell your daddy and you never did what we do."

"Never," I said. "We didn't talk. He didn't teach me things. He chopped the head off a turtle."

People on the outside don't believe it, but you get to feel at home in prison, even get to like it. I didn't tell that to Mom and Candy. They shuffled in every Sunday, and we sat in that box in the visiting room and talked over the telephone. Most times, they talked and I listened. Or didn't listen and just looked at what inmates had scratched with their fingernails on the glass. It didn't seem possible that it could stop a bullet if you could make a mark on it, a little picture, with your fingernail.

When Mom had Quinn in her belly, it grew bigger by the week. Candy was excited that she'd have a sister or a brother and said you could feel it somersaulting in Mom's stomach. She wished I could feel the baby kick. But I was just as glad not to.

At the end of the hour, they pressed their palms on one side of the glass and told me to lay mine on the other, so we were touching, yet not touching. Mom always cried and Candy did too, both of them believing I was sad to be locked up and aching to go home with them. But all I ever wanted was to get back to Cole.

Some nights we stayed awake while the sky in my cell window turned from black to gray. "Don't you ever sleep?" I asked, and Cole said, "I'm going to be dead a long, long time. I'll sleep then."

He told me he had been in the army and fought a war. I don't know which one. Not the war they have now. An earlier one. He had traveled the country, worked different jobs, had a wife and kids. "Then I fucked it all away," he said, "drinking and doing drugs. Wasn't anything I didn't smoke, swallow, or shoot up."

"Is that how you killed the cop? By mistake when you were high?"

He found that funny. "'Less you're crazy, which I'm not, you don't shoot a cop by mistake. I caught the son of a bitch in bed with my wife. I told him to climb off her before I killed him. I was carrying a .357 and didn't want a slug to go through him and hit the wife too. With me doing life, the kids figured to have it hard enough without being orphans in the bargain."

His wife and kids never visited. What was the point? he said. Smarter for them to start over in a new place with somebody else. He didn't say if he had other family alive. They didn't visit either. On Sundays he'd buy a pill from a black guy and nod off.

He didn't hound me, like the doctors, to describe what I did to Dad. He told me he'd listen if I wanted to talk about it. But there was nothing to say. That drawer in the box in my brain was nailed shut.

"You must've blacked out," Cole said.

"I don't remember any color except red. There was blood everyplace."

"Yeah, sounds like you blacked out."

While Mom kept on pushing for my parole, I was planning to commit an offense that would bury my case at the bottom of the pile. But Cole warned me not to. Years down the road, there'd be younger, tougher cons on the tier, he said, and he'd be too old to chase them off me. Then where would I be? He told me to go while I had the chance.

Afterward, I visited him regular, just like Mom and Candy, and later on Quinn did me. We talked on the fake telephone. We touched hands on the bulletproof glass when we said good-bye. I was ready to keep coming back. I had nothing better to do. Cole's the one that broke it off. "Look," he said, "it's time you found yourself a woman."

I never did. I had no idea how or where to find one. Not that I had any interest in hunting around. No interest in men either. It's Cole I miss—his big hands, his straw-smelling hair. Nobody else.

That evening, the bus looks to be on fire. The window is cool, though, when I lean my cheek against it. The sky's a flag with red and white stripes and a scatter of stars. I feel the hum of the tires on the road, and I hum along with them, but low so nobody hears. Around Phoenix, cactus stands up tall on the scrubland. Some are as high as telephone poles, and have branches, left and right. Some have melted into green candles that have burned down to nothing. That's how hot it is outside where the AC doesn't reach.

Once it's dark, I think about dinner and practice for it. Nicky warned me to slow down and in my mind go over ordering and eating. She offered to pack food in a bag. Maybe I should have let her. Restaurants are risky. I don't like to eat except in places that have pictures on the menu. I like to see what I'm ordering. And I like to sit in the right spot in case there's music that might make me dizzy. Nicky said if I practice, I'll be okay. So eyes closed, I watch myself in Wendy's, eating at a table between a door and a window.

The bus hiccups, gears downshift as we chug into the mountains, and I shift the sound in my mouth. It'd be so easy for the tires to lose their grip and send us crashing into the ditch. The grinding sound of the gears bites into my chest, and I squeeze my toy bus, imagining myself at the button-size wheel steering us safe along the cliff edge.

We pull into a parking lot that has gas pumps, picnic tables, bathrooms, and fast food. It's not Wendy's or any other place I know, but I'm too hungry to care. Passengers cross the pavement, puffing clouds when they breathe. It's cold in the mountains but warm inside, and after I order my food, I pick a good table in the meat-smelling heat and watch that the bus doesn't leave without me.

When I look down at what I'm about to eat—I don't lean my nose too close like that time Mom pushed my face into the soup—I suddenly remember my bag that Nicky warned me to keep an eye on. It's in the bus, on the luggage rack where I can't see it. I shovel in a big bite and race across the parking lot. Then I remember the map and the foldouts and the toy bus, and have to run back to get them before hurrying to the big bus. My bag is where I left it, and I'm happy, just tired and hungry.

Once everybody's back on board and we're on the road, moonlight pours through the windows and sparkles on wrists and fingers where people's watches and rings are. I hear them sleeping, and I smell their clothes, their breathing, and the food they ate. The rerun air from the bathroom vent smells of every ass that ever sat in there. One minute I'm shivering, the next I'm sweating. I pull the darkness over me, then throw it off. Somehow I dream, but don't sleep.

I'm still hungry and remember Mom's hamburgers and how she chopped onions and cooked them inside the meat. I remember when I went to prison she gave me the chain from around her neck, the same one Candy wore to the hospital when she caught polio. A Miraculous Medal of the Blessed Mother. But the guards took it away from me so I wouldn't choke myself to death. Or do like that inmate who wrapped a wire around his dick, tightening it until it dropped off.

I dream Mom's face and her eyes, one blue, one brown. That time I fell and cut my forehead, she drove me to the emergency room. The doctor rolled me in a blanket, the way the guards pin your arms and legs before they throw you in the hole for your own good. As the doctor stitched me up, Mom stayed beside me, saying, "*Shhh-shhh.*" But I couldn't stop screaming.

Or was that the day Dad died? All of us crammed into the kitchen, the butcher knife in my hand.


By morning we're out of the mountains and in winter. It's brown outside, with dead grass, not sandy desert, stretching on and on. Trees along a creek bank have trash instead of leaves on their limbs. The tires hiss on the road, and there's rain on the roof. That evening when the car lights click on, the highway looks like it's swimming with snakes. I lean my cheek against the cold glass and watch folks at the end of the workday drive home to dinner. I wonder whether Mom still fries hamburgers with onions inside. I wonder what she has to give me.

After another day and a night, the rain in Maryland turns to sleet, then snow. That makes me happy. By the time the bus slides into the station, Mom and Dad are waiting for me. Mom's hair is cut in bangs above her eyebrows, and Dad has his head shaved. This is strange not just because Dad's alive and I know he's dead, but because he's younger than me. The two of them flash big smiles, like I'm the father, home at last to make everything better. It's not until I notice Mom has a skinny leg that I recognize it's Candy, and that Dad's Quinn. I hope my smile's as big as theirs. And I hope they don't hug me.

## Candy

Waiting for Maury, we sit on the icy parking lot at the bus station in Quinn's rental car, a metallic Chrysler with a chrome grill like a shark's mouth. Because of my leg—or is it because he's a scofflaw?—he hogs a handicapped slot.

"I guess you couldn't get a bigger, more expensive car," I tease him.

"I asked for something sleeker. But the agency only had Detroit pig iron."

"What do you drive in London?"

"I don't drive. I take taxis or the tube."

"Oh yes, the *tyube*." I try a British accent.

"You'll never guess who was on the plane," he says, then doesn't give me a chance to guess. "Michael Jackson."

"I don't believe you."

"It's true. I cleared customs right behind him. He wore a mask. Homeland Security didn't ask him to lift it to let them look at what's left of his face. They were too busy searching everyone else's body cavities."

"I don't believe you," I say again.

Joking around like this allows us to reconnect after yesterday's bad start. I guess we were shocked to see each other. Quinn complimented me on how nice I look, and I said the same about him. But he's aged and has his hair cropped real short.

Still, it's more than the changes over time that caught me off guard. As it hit me how much my hopes depend on him, and how even when he was a kid I regarded him as a rescuer, he hurt me by insisting he'd stay at the Hilton, not at my place. Then soon as he checked in, he announced he was ready to wrap things up today and fly back to London tomorrow.

I had to remind him that Mom doesn't play by anybody else's rules or schedule. Foggy from her meds, she crawls into bed right after dark and doesn't resurface until late morning. Then she's in no mood to deal with anything or anybody until the afternoon. Today when I phoned to tell her Quinn had landed, she declared that she couldn't cope. Not now. Maybe later.

I didn't dare let on to Quinn that I had spoken to Mom. I said we'd postpone visiting her until after Maury arrived and the three of us had a chance to talk things over.

Obviously put out, Quinn lifted his chin. Nobody in the family has been favored with such a regal jaw. It must come from his real father. He didn't even ask why Maury caught a bus after he paid for a plane ticket. All he wanted to know was what Mom had on her mind. I claimed I had no idea.

Now as we wait, he keeps the engine running, the heat on full blast, and the radio tuned to NPR. To hell with the environment and the price of gas.

If I were alone, I'd wait in the bus station despite the winos and welfare mothers, the smell of buttered popcorn and poopy diapers. But in his black leather gloves, navy blue cashmere overcoat, and tasseled loafers, Quinn wouldn't fit in with the Greyhound crowd. He's such a, I don't know, a dude, some belligerent kid in butt-crack blue jeans would be sure to smart off, and since Quinn can't bear to let anybody else have the last word, there'd be trouble.

NPR broadcasts a report about electronic spying on American citizens. The wiretappers are based a few miles up the road at Fort Meade, and while some maintain it's illegal, I don't mind that the government might be eavesdropping. Nobody else listens to me.

A cold steel claw seems to scoop into my guts. It's a sensation I associate with childhood Sundays when Maury and I were stranded at church, never knowing when Dad would pick us up. He and Mom frequently skipped Mass, but never let us miss. She lolled at home reading the morning newspapers. He dropped us at Mt. Calvary, then holed up at a tavern where he played poker and drank. Sometimes we had to cool our heels for hours, and I fretted that Maury might trip into one of his moaning spells. I also worried what shape Dad would be in when he showed up.

Then a lot depended on whether he hightailed it straight home or drove back to the tavern with us in tow. When I warned him Mom would be furious, he called me Little Miss Muffet and told me to mind my own business.

Early on, I accepted my fate as the responsible daughter—the one who told the truth and nobody paid attention to. In grade school, soon after I learned to add and subtract, I drew up a budget and proved how if Mom and Dad quit smoking and cut down on drinking, they'd save enough money to buy a new car. In another family this kind of practical good advice would have been admired. But my reward was a slap from Mom that set my ears ringing.

During those awful Sundays at the tavern, there was an arcade game that Maury and I played called the claw machine. You paid a quarter, and a three-pronged scoop popped open, twitching like a fiend's hand in a sci-fi film. It was supposed to grab the goodies from a tray below it. But the watch or tube of lipstick you reached for always slipped through the metal fingers. A trinket as light as a key chain was too heavy to lift, and the hundred-dollar bill wrapped around a golf ball might as well have been an anvil.

Still, I was as mesmerized by the game as Maury was by fans and air conditioners. I kept playing it until it felt like the pronged talon was eating my guts. I stayed at it hoping if I won just once the pain would stop.

When I described those days to Quinn, he said they sounded like a scene from Tennessee Williams. They captured, according to him, "all the nickel-plated promise, wistful yearning, and crushing disappointment of childhood." But this wasn't a stage play; it was my childhood we were discussing.

As for my life now, I'd like to believe that nothing worse can go wrong. The family situation has bottomed out. But every time I assume it's as bad as it's going to get, Mom throws a screwball like she did yesterday. Why couldn't she carry her secret to the grave?

More to myself than to Quinn, I mumble, "They tell you everything happens for a purpose."

"Who tells you?"

"Priests. Nuns. I'm not positive about God's purpose, but I know Mom. She always has a plan. Look at us."

"What about us?" Quinn asks.

"She had each one of us for a reason."

"I view us more as accidents, sports of nature."

"No. She had Maury to kill Dad. Me to look after her. And you to become famous and rich and support her."

"Candy, I'm gobsmacked."

"You're what?"

"I'm shocked. You sound as cynical as people accuse me of being."

I can't help grinning. It's not often I hold my own with Quinn, much less surprise him. "In this family, Maury's the only innocent one, the only one without an agenda."

"What's yours?" he asks.

"Square Mom away and move to North Carolina. Did she tell you about Lawrence?"

"She did, and I'm happy for you. If you love him, look after him and yourself and let Mom do whatever she wants. Bottom line, that's what she'll do anyway."

Though we haven't spoken face to face for years, I have watched Quinn in movies, and I find myself studying him now, uncertain what's real and what's a role he's played before. He kills the engine, then the radio and removes his gloves. I remember a film where he tugged off his gloves like this before informing his wife that he was divorcing her for a younger woman.

"We all make choices," he says. "Mom made hers. You're a kind, generous, and loving daughter and you chose to live near her. Maury and I chose to get as far away as possible."

Wait a damn minute, I want to shout. I didn't choose. I never decided. It was one damn thing after another until I was trapped. "You talk about choices," I tell Quinn. "Do you really think Mom *chose* to do what she did alone?"

He unbuttons his overcoat. It's stuffy in the Chrysler. On the roof, there's the ping of sleet. "She wasn't alone," he says. "You stayed with her. So did I for twenty-one years. We all went through a hell of a lot."

He's skating close to a line that I'm reluctant to cross—the final reckoning of the damage. What Maury did stole Dad's life and destroyed his own. The degree to which it robbed the rest of us is something I don't like to dwell on. But that doesn't mean I don't have regrets. "Sometimes I wish I was the one that grew up in prison," I tell Quinn, "and got chased out of the nest to California."

"I understand," he says, and even though he can't possibly, it feels good to have him reach over and rub my neck. "You're pretty enough to have gone to Hollywood."

"Fat chance. Honestly, I don't envy Maury. I'll be punished for saying that."

"Not by me you won't," Quinn says.

Reassured by his manicured hand, I recall when he was a baby how lovely it was to cradle him in my arms. Then there came the lovelier time when he was old enough to hug back, and his chubby arms tightened around my neck.

Since I raised him I always expected to love him like a mother. But my emotions about Quinn are all over the map. I'm like one of those girls that gets pregnant in her teens and gives her baby up for adoption. Then decades later they reunite, and the mother doesn't know how to feel. Sure, there's love. But he's a grown man and there's something else close to sexual guilt. But what do I know? I never had a baby of my own. Maybe this jumble of love and guilt is normal. Maybe it's what Mom craves—a grown child's caress. She's had damn little affection from me or anyone else lately.

"Let's go look for Maury," Quinn says.


Passengers have started streaming out of the bus station. The two of us struggle against the tide, me limping through the slush in my boots, Quinn tiptoeing in his tasseled loafers. When Maury spots us, his jaw drops like he doesn't believe we're here, even though I promised him we would be.

He's in blue jeans and white tennis shoes with Velcro tabs and a Windbreaker too flimsy for a Maryland winter. Suntanned and powerfully built, he has calm gray eyes that give the impression there's very little going on in his head. It breaks my heart that he carries a canvas gym bag, like a kid at a Little League game, not a fifty-three-year-old man on a cross-country trip. His other hand clutches a map, a couple of travel brochures, and a toy bus.

The three of us hang back grinning. Maury actually appears to be grimacing. "What's wrong with your hair?"

I assume he's speaking to me and touch my forehead, afraid my bangs have blown haywire. Quinn guesses Maury means him and makes a motion like he's running shears over his scalp. Maury pats his own head with the hand that holds the map, the brochures, and the toy bus. To passersby we must look like deaf-mutes signing.

On the ride to my place, Maury sits in back with his bag on his lap. Quinn offers to open the trunk and stow it there, but Maury wants to keep it where he can see it. Quinn and I ask: How was the bus ride? Is he hungry? Is he sleepy?

His reply, "I'll sleep a long time when I'm dead," drains the air out of the conversation. Maury's never been comfortable with questions one right after the other. So Quinn and I let him set his own pace, talking if he cares to, staying quiet if not. On Ritchie Highway, we're behind a tractor trailer that throws a rooster tail of ice when Maury pipes up, "And Mom?"

"She's at home," I tell him. "She doesn't go out in this type weather. She's afraid of falling."

"Do I sleep there?"

"No, my place," I say. "We'll visit her tomorrow."

In the rearview mirror I notice that he's nodding at the news. "And my boat?" he asks.

He's lost me. But Quinn has no trouble following. "I'll bet it's still up in the attic."

Maury continues his nodding, timing it to a musical beat even though the radio carries a stock market report, not a song. Over the years it's slipped my mind how nerve-racking it is to be around him. I'm scared Mom'll soon get her fill and send him packing again.

I own a townhouse. As Lawrence jokes, there's no town and hardly a house, just a one-story, two-bedroom condo abutted on both sides by identical units. When I moved away from Mom, this was all I could afford. But it's served me as well as a mansion. Still, I'm queasy to have Quinn here. It's not London and how I picture his home. Maybe it's better he's staying at the Hilton. Suddenly I feel defensive about Maryland and everything in it. I know people consider it an uninteresting stretch on the interstate, just a sliver of nothing much. But I'll miss it when Lawrence and I move.

Maury drops his bag in the spare bedroom and returns with the toy bus bulging in his pants pocket. He looks like he's wearing a truss. "And Quinn?" he asks.

"Present and accounted for," Quinn calls from the kitchen.

"Where's he sleep?" Maury says.

"At a hotel. He's jet-lagged. He'll be drowsy when we're wide awake."

"Is there anything to drink?" Quinn shouts.

"Nothing alcoholic, if that's what you mean."

"That's spot-on what I mean." He strikes a pose in the kitchen doorway, still in his cashmere coat, like he won't be here long. "When are we supposed to meet Lawrence at the restaurant?"

"The reservation's for six-thirty."

"Why don't we go there early?"

"Why?" I ask.

"Come on, Candy, don't make me spell it out like I'm on methadone maintenance. I need to clear my sinuses with some firewater."

Minutes later we're back in his rented Chrysler, caught in rush-hour traffic, which in this neck of the woods lasts from late afternoon until long after nightfall. Quinn has tuned in NPR again, a program of Latin folk music whose hypnotic beat strangely puts a stop to Maury's head bobbing. He balances the bus on his knee and steadies it so it doesn't roll down his leg to the floor.

Why did I ever dream that having the boys home together was the answer to my troubles? The notion that we'd make common cause and convince Mom to go to assisted living, that they'd like Lawrence and he'd like them, now strikes me as insane. I debate whether I dare ask Maury to leave the toy bus in the car, not in his pocket or, God forbid, on the table. And would Quinn be insulted if I begged him to be kind to me by being kind to Lawrence because I love the man and don't want to lose him?

Propped on stilts over the South River, the restaurant is a popular summer hangout, specializing in crabs. It's been here since we were kids. It has a swimming area and a diving board fenced off from sea nettles and speedboats. On each rotting fence post there's a sign streaked with seagull droppings that warns that the water is polluted.

On this wintry night the restaurant is dank and almost empty. Waitresses wearing sweaters over their nylon uniforms lounge at the bar with the cook and the bartender, and watch a poker tournament on ESPN. I asked Lawrence to reserve a table with a view of the river. We have our pick of a dozen, each one topped with souvenir placemats, rolls of paper towels instead of napkins, and wire baskets full of condiments. There's not much to see outside except pellets of ice sizzling into water as black as a skillet.

Next to our table stands a fish tank that contains no fish, just snails, slimy seaweed, and a miniature man in a diving suit. Right off the bat, Maury rivets his eyes on the diver, maybe imagining that it'd make the perfect addition to the toy bus, which I'm disappointed to see him set in the condiment basket.

When Quinn excuses himself to go to the bathroom, Maury delivers a line that cracks me up. "Don't stand too close to anybody." Quinn and I laugh, but Maury is startled and stares off at the chain of bubbles that links the diver to the surface. He begins to gurgle in his throat, imitating the sound of the bubbles.

"You look good," I tell him.

"You and Quinn look old."

Leave it to Maury to lay it out straight. He's inherited Mom's brutal frankness. Maybe they're both Ass Burgers. "Well, none of us is getting any younger," I say.

"Mom must really look old."

"Please don't tell her that. It'll hurt her feelings."

On his return from the men's room, Quinn pauses at the bar, shooting the breeze with the waitresses, charming the cook and the bartender. They may not recognize him or know him by name, but they sense he's *somebody*. Under his cashmere coat he's wearing a black shirt, buttoned at the collar, and no tie. Although in all honesty he's not as handsome as Maury, he has striking looks and just two speeds—off and on. With strangers or an audience, he's always on.

He brings a bottle of white wine and three plastic glasses to our table. "It's a passably good pinot grigio—as long as you don't mind drinking it out of plastic."

I let him pour me a bit. Maury asks for a Coke, and it comes in a giant frosted root beer mug. At Quinn's instigation we lift our drinks and click them together. "What shall we toast?" he asks.

"It's about us tonight," I suggest.

"To the three of us then," Quinn says.

Maury's eyes swing between us like he's following a tennis match. To the waitresses across the room he may resemble a good-looking cowboy in a cigarette ad. But up close, he seems perplexed and a fraction slow. In the past—in the present for all I know—women were attracted to him. But I've always assumed that he's asexual. A-everything.

Eager to involve Maury, words pour out of me like bubbles from the tiny diver's mouth. Ever since childhood, there's been a safe that I'd love to unlock inside my brother. What's he thinking? How does he feel? That's what TV reporters ask the plane crash survivor, the dead soldier's wife, the condemned inmate. What's it like to be in your skin, in your skull? Did Dad's murder and twelve years in jail numb him out? Or was it the numbness that allowed him to do what he did in the first place? But of course I say none of this.

"Can I have another Coke?" Maury asks.

"Sure." Quinn waves to the waitress. "What are you looking at?" he says to Maury, who's squinting through the bus windshield.

"The seat where I rode and the rack where I kept my bag."

With Maury preoccupied, Quinn and I are free to trade glances. I'm afraid he'll roll his eyes and crack a joke. It's not like I've never made fun of Maury myself and laughed at Quinn's fooling around.

But tonight we have serious things to talk about. "We need to discuss assisted living," I say.

Maury lowers the bus from his eye. "What's that?"

"It's where Mom'll have care around the clock," I say. "She'll have her own room and three nutritious meals a day."

"Sounds like Patuxent," Maury says.

Somebody chuckles, and I'm prepared to be annoyed at Quinn. But the laughter's from Lawrence, who's brought Maury's second Coke. "Am I interrupting family business?"

"Not at all." Quinn clambers to his feet and shakes Lawrence's hand. Maury keeps his hands on his lap.

Lawrence kisses my cheek. "Hi, hon. Scoot over and let me have that chair."

Quinn and Lawrence are right away on a first-name basis, and Maury . . . Maury is on his own basis. He gazes out the window where white streaks fall like chalk marks on a blackboard. The sleet has changed to snow.

"It's not supposed to accumulate," Lawrence promises us.

"I wish it would," Quinn says. "I haven't seen a heavy snowfall since I moved to London."

"I love snow," Maury says.

That's all I need. A blizzard to maroon us in this restaurant. It shouldn't matter that Lawrence isn't as tall and handsome as my brothers. But I wish he hadn't worn a Banlon sweater and Sansabelt slacks that make him appear paunchier than he is. Lawrence has a basically good body and is healthy from playing thirty-six holes every weekend. While he doesn't have Maury's shoulders or Quinn's cheekbones, he's going a distinguished gray at the temples. If only he wasn't so eager to please and didn't have an aggravating habit of talking like a political candidate.

"Am I happy to meet you for the first time under these circumstances?" he asks Quinn, and promptly answers his own question. "Of course not! Would I rather your mother was hale and hearty and we could meet in London? That goes without saying! Do I hope that day comes soon? You bet! But am I glad we got this chance to talk? Obviously I am. I like your mother. She's a pistol."

"Yeah," Quinn agrees. "Loaded with live ammunition."

Just when I fear Lawrence will behave like a dork all night, Quinn acts like an idiot himself. The waitress takes our order, and he asks about each item on the menu, "Is it fresh?"

"Sir, all our fish is fresh. We buy it off boats from the bay."

"Are you telling me these Alaskan king crab claws come from the Chesapeake?"

"No, they're flown in from Seattle. But they're real fresh."

"You mean frozen."

"Yeah, frozen fresh."

"Frozen is the opposite of fresh."

"No, spoiled is the opposite of fresh."

"Is anything here fresh *and* unfrozen?"

"I'll ask in the kitchen."

She goes off, and Quinn says, "Do you suppose the poor girl spent her childhood eating lead paint off a windowsill?"

"In winter it's tough to find unfrozen fish," Lawrence says. "During the off-season these waterfront restaurants have to think outside the box."

Maury jerks his head around. "Outside what box?"

"Just, you know, normal business practices."

"Aren't boxes normal?"

"Sure they are," Lawrence says. "That's a nice bus you have."

I give his thigh a gentle squeeze. I love my brothers, but not like I do this kind man.

After a second bottle of wine, Quinn loses the last traces of standoffishness and starts talking nonstop. He doesn't ask anything of Lawrence and me except that we listen. Though to my mind this one-way traffic's not much of a conversation, it amuses Lawrence, who's exposed to Quinn's high-voltage energy for the first time.

He describes a Neil Simon revival he did last summer in London with an American actress famous for a TV sitcom. It worried her when several minor royals visited backstage after the show. She whispered to Quinn that she didn't know how to act.

"I noticed that at the first rehearsal," Quinn says. "But she meant she didn't know how to act around royals. I said, 'Just do what I do.' So when Princess Beatrice swanks in, I kiss her hand and damned if Miss Airhead doesn't do the same. Lays a big wet smacker on the girl's knuckles."

I've never heard this one before and chuckle. But then he recycles an old tale about being a pallbearer at Dad's mother's funeral. On the trip from the undertaker's parlor, he lost track of the other cars and drove to the nearest Catholic church. Sure enough a requiem mass was in progress, but Quinn didn't realize until it was too late that he had crashed the wrong funeral.

Lawrence lets out a belly laugh, and Maury glances up from his plate, his cheeks crammed with food like a chipmunk's. This makes me laugh. Quinn probably assumes it's for his story.

I find myself musing how much he's like Bill Clinton. Quinn's leaner, harder-looking, and doesn't have the ex-president's thatch of white hair. But both of them have this charisma, as everybody calls it, that's combined with a little-boy vulnerability. You never forget—they never let you forget—that the smartest kid in the class hailed from a hard luck family. Dead father. Messed-up mother. Black sheep brother. Now, successful as they are, they don't hide their broken parts, and they make sure every woman knows they're needy.

"You're a funny guy," Lawrence tells him. "You could be a stand-up comic. How'd you wind up in acting?"

Simple as flipping a switch, Lawrence taps into one of my brother's favorite anecdotes. At the university, the drama department held an annual speech contest. When Quinn won first prize as a freshman, they invited him to audition for a play. Naturally, he landed the lead role.

"That's something out of Hollywood legend, " Lawrence says. "Like discovering Lana Turner in a drugstore. What was your speech?"

"I advocated the abolition of professional boxing," Quinn says. "The irony is, I loved boxing. Mom and I used to watch the *Friday Night Fights*. But instinctively I knew my audience—a bunch of bleeding heart professors and lily-livered students. So I described how seeing the Emile Griffith–Benny Paret match convinced me the sport should be banned. I led off with a couple of zinging lines." He falls into a stagey voice. "'In my living room last night I witnessed a murder. It was the most sick-making spectacle I have ever seen.'"

Alarmed, I sneak a look at Maury. But mention of murder doesn't appear to have registered.

"Hey, hold on a sec," Lawrence breaks in. "You couldn't have watched the Griffith-Paret fight. That was before you were born."

Suddenly, as so often in my life, I feel like I'm the one on the spot. Embarrassed for Quinn, furious at Lawrence for bringing this up, I hunch my shoulders and wait for a blow to fall. But I shouldn't have worried. Quinn handles it like a minor speed bump.

"I never claimed I saw it live," he says. "Mom and I watched it on one of those *Fights of the Century* shows. Believe me, it was just as gruesome to see Griffith punch Paret to death on tape."

"Did they catch him?" Maury asks. "Did he get life?"

But the waitress brings the bill and his question gets lost in the good-natured debate over who'll pay. Quinn, as I'd have predicted, wins and swears to Lawrence that he'll let him pick up the tab when we have dinner in London.

As we leave the restaurant, Maury's at my side, and I forget for an instant and give him a hug. He shivers, like a horse shuddering off flies. To cover my mistake, I say, "We need to buy you a warmer coat."

The falling snow doesn't stick to the parking lot, but it glitters in everybody's hair, like confetti at a party. Maury's delighted by this, but then remembers he left his bus in the restaurant and rushes back to fetch it.

"What's he need it for?" Lawrence asks.

"The return trip west," Quinn says, and is rewarded with the last laugh of the night.

Feeling the wine, I almost warn him what Mom's about to tell him tomorrow. But I catch myself. For all I know he won't be upset; he might be happy to learn he's only half-related to us.

Quinn climbs into his rented Chrysler and heads off to the Hilton. The three of us bundle into Lawrence's Volvo. I'm tired, and my leg aches. I don't mention this to Lawrence for fear he'll advise me again to get tested for post-polio syndrome. If I have it, I don't want to know—not unless they discover a cure.

On the drive Lawrence is subdued as he digests, along with the dinner and wine, the fact that in addition to the world's most difficult mother I have two wildly mismatched brothers. Or is he wistful that with Maury in town we won't be spending the night together? He treats me with extra tenderness as he walks me to the door of the townhouse and says, "This is like kissing good night outside the Tri Delt house."

"I wouldn't know about that. But a kiss is a kiss."

He extends a hand to Maury, catches himself, and digs into his pocket for the car keys. "Sweet dreams, you two."

Alone with Maury, thrown back on ourselves like when we were kids, I'm in danger of plunging feet first into one of my pity parties. On nights like this as a little girl I used to sneak out of bed after everybody was asleep and fix a batch of Jell-O. I didn't like Jell-O myself. But the rest of the family did, and I made it as a surprise for them in the morning.

Doing for others in a Christlike spirit—that was what the nuns urged on us. But even back then I realized I was guilty of a martyr complex and believed that I deserved whatever disappointment I brought on myself. I feel different now. I deserve Lawrence and his love. I deserve a life of my own, just like Maury deserves forgiveness for murder and Quinn deserves understanding for his aloofness. But in the end, whether or not we get what we think we have coming, we need to wake up in the morning, brush our teeth, and buckle down to work.

Maury's in the spare room, rocking and moaning. I trust he's in bed, not spread-eagle on the floor. I tap on the door, and the noise dies. "I laid out towels for you in the bathroom," I tell him. "The blue ones."

After a long pause he says, "Okay."

"If you wake up before me, there's milk in the fridge and instant coffee and cereal in the cupboard."

Another pause. "Okay."

I don't linger. I know he's eager to get back to rocking and moaning.

I could call Lawrence. Some of our best, most intimate talks have been by telephone. But it's late, and he has been on his feet all day playing Doctor Drill and Fill. So to hear a cheerful human voice I dial the weather and listen to a recorded announcement. "Intermittent snow. No accumulation. Cold."

# Quinn

Unsteady on my pins, I stroll from the lobby to the bar at the Hilton. Neither spot looks inviting. The public areas of the hotel are penitentially bright and deserted except for sleepy employees. At eleven o'clock on a Saturday night, regardless of the weather, people in London roister through the streets, just getting started. Here in Maryland they're ready to call it a day.

With nothing better to do, I retreat to my room. The wine-induced euphoria that helped get me through dinner *en famille* has diminished to a dull throb behind my eyes. I open the minibar and collect a few Chivas Regal miniatures. Headache or not, I splash Scotch into a toothbrush glass and top it off with club soda.

Although a maid has turned down the bed, the curtains remain open on the room's only window. Maybe the hotel management is proud of the view—a baleful stretch of interstate. Snowflakes spool yellow gauze around streetlights that look as lethal as surgical instruments. Thirty-six hours after my homecoming, and already I feel a yoke settling on my shoulders, the familiar weight of childhood. Back then I had no choice of roles. There was just the part I was fated to play. Now I want to believe I'm free to choose my character; I can even change my lines.

I shut the drapes. It's not that easy to drop the curtain on tonight. I feel awful about Candy, so fragile and eager to please. What she asks is simple—a late shot, a last shot, at happiness. How can I begrudge her and Lawrence that? Why couldn't I get out of my own way and grant them what they need? Pay attention and listen—that's all they expected.

Instead, I talked a blue streak, I talked bollocks. Here I am hoping to play Greek tragedy, yet when I hit my mark, I act like a sad tramp trapped in theater of the absurd. Uncertain whether the stage directions call for laughter or tears, I shamble around like a baggy-pants vaudevillian. To Lawrence and Candy I must have sounded as bad as a moron hogging the mike at a comedy club on amateur night. If for some reason I felt compelled to talk about my fuckup at the funeral, I might at least have been honest. It hurt. It wasn't funny.

Before her death I had crossed paths with my paternal grandmother a grand total of two times. What I recalled of her was a hornet's nest of black hair restrained by barrettes. So my first shock at her wake was to see a wizened white-tressed woman in the casket.

Then came the second shock of encountering relatives who presumed to know me when I didn't recognize a single one of them. I can only compare the experience to traveling in a foreign country and running into fans who've never seen me except on a movie screen, and who've never heard my voice except dubbed into the local language. These people don't know me. At such moments I barely know myself. I'm some ghost they've imagined, a shadow they've projected.

Yet the weight of my grandmother's corpse was real. And there was no denying the meaty presence of the other pallbearers. After we carried the casket to the hearse, the rest of them scattered to rented limos, and I climbed into my car alone. In an hour or two, I kept telling myself, this would be over. These relatives, these strangers, would recede into oblivion. Then one chapter of my life would end and a new one would begin.

Along with a cast of University of Maryland drama students, I had been selected to travel to Europe and perform plays on American military bases. At the end of the summer, when the others flew back to College Park, my secret plan was to stay in London. Like a Cuban baseball player, I had plotted every detail of my defection. Letting on nothing to Mom or Candy, I had contacted an English agent. Confident of my talent, confident I'd soon be self-supporting, I had no nagging sense that I was leaving anyone or anything of value behind. That was the advantage of not having a father. I was free to reinvent myself, free to be my own father.

The disadvantages . . . well, they're what I edited out of the cartoon narrative I told Candy and Lawrence. I would never admit to them how lonely it felt to slink into that church, hide in a rear pew, and discover that the requiem mass was almost over. Up at the altar, between rows of lighted candles, the casket looked like the one I had carried. But I recognized nobody around me. After the final blessing, I skulked forward to take my place among the pallbearers, and a man grabbed me by the elbow. A gesture of condolence, I thought.

He squeezed harder and hissed, "What's your problem, buster?"

I looked at his face. I looked at the rest of the congregation. Then I turned to the priest. He at least wasn't angry. But by his baffled expression I knew I had blundered into the wrong funeral.

"Sorry," I murmured. "I've made a mistake."

"Damn straight you have," said the man who had grabbed my arm. He pushed me up the aisle, past disgruntled onlookers, and out to the church portico. I attempted to explain, but he was in no frame of mind to listen. He'd have welcomed any excuse to throw me down the marble staircase. So I hurried to my car.

I didn't speed away though. I sat there, and as the church emptied, I studied every face, still futilely hoping to spot a familiar one, a forgiving one. Then I slipped back inside, thinking the pastor might know where my grandmother was being buried.

In the sacristy, he stopped polishing a chalice and seemed prepared to use it as a club. But when I mentioned my grandmother's name, he remembered her as a parishioner, and said she had moved to a nursing home. Her funeral was scheduled for the chapel there.

He offered directions, but there was no chance I'd make it on time. As in a nightmare, I was late and I was lost.

Replenishing my toothbrush glass with Chivas Regal, I let the words "late" and "lost" reverberate and end up thinking about Maury. If I feel like odd man out, how about him? What does he feel? On the surface, he appears to be completely shut down. It's possible he's smothered all emotion to protect himself from people and to protect people from him. At dinner, whenever he wasn't making a weird noise in his throat or staring into the toy bus, he sat there like a statue, a monument to an event that neither he nor anyone else can understand.

It comes to me how little I know about him or the killing. When, at age ten, I asked Mom about that day, she grabbed me by the hair and slammed my head against a wall. I never asked again.

*It's always about you, isn't it?* Through a fog of jet lag, wine, and whiskey, I recall the line that girlfriends have often flung in my face.

I start off fretting about Maury and wind up fixated on myself. Better to quit maundering and get ready for bed.

I'm at the sink, wrist deep in warm water when the phone rings. I hope it's Mal, with word from the BBC. But at this hour, in this place, I figure it has to be Candy. I pick up the bathroom extension, and there's a British accent. "Quinn Mitchell, please."

"Speaking."

"You sound *sooo* American." It's Tamzin.

"That's what happens to me at home. I become a ventriloquist. Or a ventriloquist's dummy."

"Quite a gift."

"It's almost midnight," I say. "It must be dawn there. Why aren't you in bed?"

"I *am* in bed. Soon as we hang up, I'll fall asleep. I was worried about your mother. How is she?"

"Fine as far as I know." I lower the toilet lid and myself onto it. "She hasn't deigned to see me yet."

"I was afraid she was dying."

"Sorry to upset you. She's just old, and my brother and sister and I have to decide whether she can live independently any longer."

"That's sad. I was reading Anna Akhmatova and—"

"Anna who?"

"A Russian poet. She wrote some lines that seemed suitable. Shall I read them to you?"

"In Russian?"

"In translation. Like to copy them down?"

"I don't have a pen." I neglect to add that except for toilet paper, there's nothing to write on.

"Well, listen and let me know what you think. 'This woman is ill. / She is all alone. / Her husband is in the grave, her/son in prison: pray for her.'"

Has Tamzin Googled my family history? In a spasm of pedantry, I correct one error. "Her son's out of prison now. Otherwise, the quote's a keeper." Then after a pause, "I miss you."

"I miss you too. I was thinking about our trip to Venice."

Suddenly I wish I were anywhere except the bathroom. The last place I care to discuss that weekend is perched on a toilet lid.

"The city was incredible," she says. "The sex was incredible."

This snaps me to my feet. I picture Hugh Grant doing his boyish, abashed, head-bobbing number. But the mirror over the sink frames a middle-aged man in his undershirt.

"Do you ever do phone sex?" Tamzin asks.

"You mean calling a hotline and talking to a tart?"

"I mean talking to me. Talking dirty."

I almost say, I'm too old for that. You're too young. Instead, I tell her I prefer her in the warm moist flesh.

"I'll be thinking about you at the library tomorrow," she says. "Is there anything I should look up for you?"

There's so much I yearn for and wish Tamzin could supply. How do I apologize to Candy? How can I understand Maury? But I tell her, "Mothers seem to be the order of the day. What you don't often read is something about child abuse from the maternal point of view."

"I'll call if I find a good quote."

"Call regardless. Now go to sleep."

"You too."

*     *     *

In the morning I waste the better part of an hour wheedling a pot of weak tea and a couple of soggy buns from room service. When I pull back the drapes, the window is curtained by clouds, and the interstate is clotted with cars whose headlights waver like insect antennae. The fog compounds the anxiety that feeds my impatience. Why not phone Mom and get this over with? Ask what she has in mind? What's this adagio my family is always dancing?

But while I dither, Candy calls with news that Mom has granted us an audience later in the day. "First, Maury and I are going to Mass," she adds. "Then I'll bring her Communion at the house."

"Meet you there."

"Oh please, Quinn, come to church with us."

"I haven't been to Mass in years."

"All the more reason to go today. It'll be good for the three of us to be together."

"We were together last night."

"Do I have to beg? There's little enough in my life to be proud of. Are you going to deny me the pleasure of being seen in church with my famous brother?"

I join them at Holy Comforter. Not the grim, faux-Gothic church we attended as kids, but a new one near Candy's townhouse. In this splendid A-frame of stained wood and tinted glass seating is in the round, and the floor slants toward the altar. No pew has an obstructed view. I've performed in plenty of provincial theaters with smaller capacity and poorer acoustics.

Today the house is packed. Not just with oldsters on the brink of death and children preparing for First Communion, but yuppie couples and smartly dressed singletons. The choir sounds semiprofessional and the musical accompaniment—a piano, a guitar, and a tambourine—worthy of a supper club. Since my recent churchgoing has been restricted to marriages and funerals in fusty bone-chilling Anglican chapels, this is a pleasant surprise, even though the First Reading does appear to have been orchestrated by Candy to chastise me.

"They became vain in their reasoning," intones a woman in a purple pleated robe, "and their senseless heart was darkened; professing themselves to be wise they became fools."

Grimy as the state of my soul is at present, there was a time—and it lasted well into my adolescence—when I believed in God and Catholic theology every bit as avidly as Candy does. I could recite the complete Baltimore Catechism and I regarded its boiled-down answers as divinely revealed verities. *God made me to know, love, and serve Him in this world and to be happy with Him in the next.*

I had no trouble embracing the dogma of the virgin birth of Christ, His resurrection from the dead, and the transubstantiation of wafer and wine into His body and blood. The concept of original sin—the evil that even children do—struck me as self-evident. Given Dad's murder, how could I conclude otherwise?

Certain Catholic tenets gained no traction with me, however. I never had the conviction that I was a child of God, secure in my Savior's love. Worse, I doubted that good works guaranteed me grace. Everything from my humblest hope to my grandest aspirations depended upon a miracle. In this respect, my belief system resembled the bingo parties and games of chance that the church organized to raise cash. With every moral choice I made, I felt I purchased a lottery ticket and prayed that I'd win. Heaven was a jackpot I never counted on.

Even maternal love, which most people regard as freely given and freely accepted, struck me as a long shot. Mom's love was always contingent, changeable. As for other kinds of love, maybe if Dad had lived he would have shared his gambling savvy and provided wise counsel about cutting the odds and scoring with women. But the first time I fell in love, I had nobody to depend on and cried out to all the angels and saints for help.

Deirdre Healy was the eldest of a clan of daughters who boasted the classic features of the Breck shampoo girl—faultless complexions, lustrous russet-colored hair, and green eyes. At sixteen, she had a plush body and suntanned cleavage that couldn't be restrained by her modest one-piece Jansen swimsuit. My memory is of her tugging at its straps and elasticized leg holes to tuck her exuberant flesh out of sight.

The Healy sisters congregated daily on a diving platform at a beach not far from the restaurant where we ate last night. While Deirdre sunned herself, her sisters whooped and screeched as teenage boys, in the universal courting ritual, heaved them into the water. I couldn't comprehend this. Why would any girl be attracted to a cretin who manhandled her into the South River? I kept my distance and cloaked my desire for Deirdre in an elaborate pretense of indifference.

But she quickly tired of waiting for me to make the first move and took the initiative. She grabbed me with astonishingly strong hands and hurled me into the drink. Before I had a chance to surface, she jumped in on top of me.

Had I drowned there and then, I'd have died happy. Her skin was slippery with suntan oil. Her swimsuit felt as if it would have peeled off as easily as the fuzz from a ripe peach. Afraid there was no future for us on dry land, I would gladly have remained underwater with her in my arms forever. But after frisking around for a few minutes she climbed back onto the diving platform, and I followed.

Deirdre Healy went to a Catholic girls' school in faraway Frederick, Maryland. Her parents had rented a cottage at the shore for the summer. Since she was a temporary resident, I figured it was possible that she hadn't heard about Dad's murder. So I impersonated a normal kid.

Or almost normal. My consuming passion for Deirdre verged on religious fanaticism. Like an anchorite in the desert subsisting on locusts and honey, I worshipped her. I recited the Rosary every day, praying that she would love me in return. This was another instance of my counting on a miracle when what was called for was direct action. But I had no confidence in myself. It took a mighty leap of faith for me just to peck her on the lips at the height of the Fourth of July fireworks.

Then after the last rocket's red glare, she led me to a screened-in gazebo where we watched shooting stars. In an orgy of intimacy, she let me lay my head on her lap. To be cushioned by her plump crossed thighs was veriest heaven—until she asked, "Is it true that your brother murdered your father?"

The question hollowed me out, and pain poured in. "Yes," I admitted.

"And he's in prison?"

"He's out now. He doesn't live in Maryland." I wanted to assure her that she was safe; we didn't have to worry about him.

"Tell me about what happened."

Her small voice sounded sincere, curious, not accusatory. So in a first for me, I opened up, imagining that Deirdre might open up too. No double entendre intended. I would have been happy had she opened her heart.

On a different level, I suppose I believed that telling her the little I knew about the murder might make me not only sympathetic, but interesting. Not every boy had such a tumultuous backstory, and even fewer had my precocious knack of self-dramatization. I put everything I had into this performance, and confided in Deirdre with all the untutored artistry at my disposal.

When I finished, instead of applause or follow-up questions, she asked me to move my head. "My legs are asleep," she said.

I craved feedback, and when none was forthcoming, I felt crushed. Maybe with time, over the course of a summer of repeat performances, I could have persuaded her that just because Maury was a killer didn't mean I was undeserving, and just because my nuclear family was damaged didn't make me radioactive. But at the first whiff of rejection, something inside me clicked off. I abandoned her fragrant lap and left the gazebo. I can't lie and claim that I wasn't available for a curtain call. Had she said a word, had she whispered my name, the ice in my heart would have melted, and I would have raced back to her. But she didn't and I kept on walking.


At points during Mass, Candy nudges my elbow, reminding me when to sit, stand, and kneel. She should save her signals for Maury, who stays on his knees, head bowed, throughout the service. Even when the congregation rises, clasps hands, and recites the Our Father, he kneels and doesn't offer anybody a sign of peace. But as parishioners press forward for Communion he joins the queue while I hang back. Is it conceivable that in prison and in the desert all these decades he's been a sacrament-receiving Catholic?

They line up before a female Eucharistic minister, a well-padded matron with a champagne-colored permanent. When I was an altar boy, Monsignor Dade stressed that a priest alone had the power to handle the Host with his canonically blessed fingers. These days everybody does it. Everybody except Maury, who clasps his mitts behind his back, sticks out his tongue and accepts the wafer on its quivering tip.

Candy, who carries what appears to be a gold pillbox, whispers to the woman that she wants one for herself and one for the road. Then they return to the pew, my sister in a trance every bit as profound as my brother's. I don't know what to make of them. God only knows what to make of the three of us. A murderer, a limping old maid, and a . . . what *am* I? A cynic, someone not quite committed enough to identify himself as an agnostic. Here we are in church again together. If we got anything from Mom, I guess we got this. Much that she tried to smack into us has fallen away, but this remains.

After Mass, I ask Maury if he'd like to ride with me, thinking Candy might welcome a break. He cocks his head, considers it, then says no. Candy says nothing at all. Bearing the consecrated Host, she maintains a sacerdotal silence.

In separate cars, we cruise through countryside that has morphed into indistinguishable housing developments with baronial names—Kingwood, Queens Arms, Deer Run. Between the residential areas, strip malls blight a landscape that I recall as open fields, aromatic with honeysuckle and mown grass. Not that I'm the nostalgic type. My childhood and Maryland itself undermine any tendency to romanticize. If I feel anything now, it's not regret over leaving the state. It's uneasiness at the idea of being sucked back in.

Because Candy drives slowly, I soon outdistance her, and despite the fog and the absence of familiar landmarks, I have no trouble finding my way. To my surprise, Mom's neighborhood—I never think of it as mine—has undergone a sea change of a different sort. It's gotten better. Tidy yards, flowerpots planted with winter perennials, glinting motorcycles, and foreign cars all suggest prosperity and conscientious upkeep. Although no one is out on this misty morning, it's easy to imagine the rainbow community holding a block party in summer.

Only Mom's house, blistered with age, brings down the aspirational tone of the street. It hasn't had a lick of maintenance since my last visit. The lawn is as stubbly as my shaved pate. The general state of dereliction distresses me. Where does she spend the money I send? Why not invest some in upkeep? Yet I recognize the real question is how I can let my mother live in these conditions.

Then again, what choice do I have? I can't conceive of her leaving this house any more than of her flying to London for a holiday. She's welded to its ruin and to everything—rancors as well as rare joys—that transpired here.

Once Candy and Maury roll in, the three of us process single file to the front door, a priestess and her acolytes. Candy knocks, pauses, and knocks again. As we wait, the fog encloses us in a cocoon, a portentous stage effect for some mysterious ceremony. Candy repeats the knocking code, and I begin to fear we'll have to break the door down.

Finally a quavering voice asks, "Who is it?"

"Us," I shout to save Candy from violating her vow of silence.

The door swings wide with a creak, and an unrecognizable crone lists before us. To gussy herself up for the occasion, Mom has skid-marked her mouth with bright red lipstick. Only her eyes betray the person imprisoned inside this shrunken effigy. My shock at her disintegration is something I have to hide. It would be ignoble not to. Orestes' baffled line at seeing his mother after many years wells up in me: *I loved her once and now I loathe, I have to loathe—what is she?*

As Candy bears the Eucharist into the house, Maury attempts to sneak in behind her without being noticed. But Mom won't let him pass. She kisses him on the mouth.

Then holding her blouse at the collar and shielding her breasts with an arm, she kisses me on the lips, too. This has always been her contradictory style—a wet kiss on the mouth and a crossed arm to avoid body contact. "Hello, stranger," she says. "Welcome home, wanderer. I'd have rolled out the red carpet, but that'd just swell your head bigger."

When the door shuts behind us, air is in short supply and the living room is as rank as a wolf den. My brain brimming over with the *Oresteia*, another line comes to me, *I know the ancient crimes that live within this house.* But in fact it doesn't seem like a killing ground or a murder scene. It's simply our home. And as with so much of the past, it's a bewildering mess.

Amid the disarray, there's a neatly tended shrine on an end table. At the foot of a crucifix, photos and holy cards fan out—a gallery of saints and family members. Among the snapshots of Candy, Maury, and me, I spot one of Dad beside a Sacred Heart pierced by seven swords. That's a change. His aura used to be everywhere, but his likeness nowhere visible.

Mom twitters on about how well Maury and I look, but Candy shushes her and breaks out the pyx. Mom sits on the sofa, I take the rocking chair, and Maury squats on the floor. Candy stays on her feet, speaking with a gravity I've never known her to possess. "The peace of the Lord be with you always."

Her voice, her words, soothe me, just as they did in childhood when she echoed Mom and urged me to "Go to your happy place." Candy was it—sister, mother, happy place all in one. I never had any reason to doubt her love, yet it dawns on me that she might have questioned mine. Too often I've taken her for granted.

"My brothers and sisters," Candy says, "to prepare ourselves for this celebration, let us call to mind our sins."

For me the list is long and I suppose ingratitude and arrogance are my worst offenses. I love the people in this room and I blame them. I regret that we're not closer; I can't wait to get away from them.

Candy prays the confiteor. For an altar boy this was the Himalayas of the Latin Mass. As a third grader, I spent a month learning it by heart. Now, in English translation, it sounds to me like the first of twelve steps in a self-help program. "I confess to Almighty God and to you my brothers and sisters, for what I have done and what I failed to do."

Muttering *mea culpa, mea culpa, mea maxima culpa,* Mom drums the fallen breasts that I'm not sure ever fed me. Ranged in front of her, the three of us don't appear to pray with and for her, but *to* her, as if to one of those Irish mummies trapped for centuries in peat moss.

"I myself am the living bread come down from heaven," Candy declares. "If anyone eats this bread he shall live forever."

The words bring a peculiar glitter to Mom's eyes. Does she pray to live or to die? I lower my gaze to the folded hands in her lap, the fists that launched a thousand slaps. I suspect she still packs a wallop and don't believe she'll check out peacefully.

My knees crack as I stand for the Lord's Prayer. Maury uncoils from the floor as smoothly as a column of smoke. I reach over to Mom, and Candy holds her other hand. Then Maury catches me off guard by latching onto my free hand. The electricity that he says surges through him whenever he's touched now shoots through me, and I am moved against my will, against my rational judgment. That cornball hymn, "May the Circle Be Unbroken," pops into mind. Having cried on cue for crowds in their thousands and movie audiences in the millions, I shed a few genuine tears in front of my family. All this religion has laid me wide open.

As Mom accepts the Eucharist, she mumbles, "The Body of Christ," then works the wafer around in her sawdust-dry mouth. There's not enough saliva to dissolve the bread. She chews it until finally she manages to force it down with a harsh swallow.

Sinking back into the rocking chair, I shrug off my topcoat. But while Mom returns to the sofa, Candy and Maury remain on their feet.

"We'll let you two talk," Candy tells Mom in the pastoral manner she's adopted. "Maury's dead set on driving around to some of our old haunts."

"Your old what?" Mom asks.

"Places he remembers."

"There's nothing left," she says. "It's all gone. Everywhere looks like everywhere else."

But Maury is already at the door. Candy, I see, has planned to leave me alone with Mom. I have no say in the matter. They bolt into the Sunday gloom.

"Why don't you hang up your coat?" Mom says.

"It's okay where it is."

"It'll get wrinkled on that chair."

"It's cashmere. It doesn't wrinkle."

"Oh, cashmere," she mocks me. When she crosses her legs, I notice how stick thin they are. Her blue-veined wrists are worse—just twigs.

"How are you, Mom?"

"Exactly like I look. I'm not going to get better. But you, you look terrific. Except for your hair. What happened? You cut it for a role?"

"I cut it because I'm going thin on top, and this is better than a comb-over."

"I remember when you had thick blond curls."

"Now Maury's the one with movie star hair," I say. "He looks younger than me."

"Yeah, no matter how old he gets, he'll always be a little boy." She cants her head, as if weighed down by the thicker eyeglass on that side. "Sorry I don't have anything to offer you. Not unless you're in the market for a cigarette."

She fumbles a pack of Kents from the end table and lights up. With smoke pluming from her nostrils she looks more like her old self. "Can I ask you a question?"

"Shoot," I say.

"Do you have a girlfriend?"

"Why? You worried I'm gay?"

"No, I'm worried you'll never get married and give me grandchildren."

"You've got bigger stuff, better stuff to worry about."

"No, I don't. Even after I'm dead, I don't want to think things have petered out here. I'm afraid Candy and Maury got scared off marrying and having kids."

"Yeah, I have a girlfriend," I tell her. "It's too soon to know where it's going."

She sucks down a drag, then shapes the ash at the end of her cigarette. "Mind if I ask another question? When you strolled in with Candy and Maury, that definitely raised eyebrows in my mind. Did you go to Mass with them?"

"I did."

"Did you take Communion?"

Is there any point in lying? Who am I protecting? And from what? "No, I didn't."

She sighs and recrosses her bony legs. "Have you lost your faith?"

"Not at all."

"Then why not receive the sacraments?"

"Technically, I'm not in a state of grace."

"Technically?"

"Okay, *actually* I'm not. Now if I confess my mortal sins, will you grant me absolution?"

"Save that for a priest. Your sins, I mean. Not your sarcasm. I'm worried about the state of your soul."

"From what I gather from Candy, you're worried about your own soul."

"Naturally I am." She taps the Kent in the vague direction of an ashtray. A live cinder goes dead as it falls to the carpet. "At my age who wouldn't be?"

"I'm confident you'll do beautifully on Judgment Day."

"I don't count on it. That's why I pray so hard. What the hell, these days I pray for the church. I never thought it'd come to this— me praying for its soul instead of depending on it to save mine. You must have heard about the scandals here."

"They've had trouble in Ireland too," I say.

"Priests! Ireland!" She spits out the words the way she would a nasty shred of tobacco. "I had a bellyful of them hanging around my parents' house on St. Patrick's Day."

"Thought your family didn't go in for Irish holidays."

"We weren't professional Irish, if that's what you mean. We didn't wear green derbies and drink green beer and sing 'Danny Boy.' None of that malarkey. Like my mother said, 'If Ireland was so great, why'd we leave it?'"

"To keep from starving to death," I suggest.

"It wasn't hunger that brought us here. It was to escape the English. Now you're living with them, like a traitor."

"I thought we were talking about your soul."

"It's your soul that's in question. My father boasted he'd kill an Englishman before he died. Now it's up to you."

"Yeah, murdering a limey, that'll put me in a state of grace."

She uncrosses her legs. She can't seem to get comfortable. "But priests, getting back to them," she says, "they'd drink a couple of jars and get tight as ticks and start talking smut. Many's the time one of them touched me where he shouldn't have. They were always after me to sit on their laps. The nuns warned us girls never to sit on a man's lap unless we put down a magazine first. But with the priests I knew, you'd need to put down a phone book. Now they've gone in for little boys," she says, more animated by the moment. "Doesn't shock me a bit. When it comes to men, nothing does."

"The way you talk I'm surprised you're still a Catholic."

"It'd take more than a few bad priests, even a bad pope, to shake my faith."

"With that attitude, you shouldn't have any trouble at the Pearly Gates. What worries me is your health and happiness here and now."

She screws up her face like a jeweler with a loupe discovering a fake diamond. "Is that why Candy ran off with Maury? So you can nag me about assisted living? Are you trying to make me sell my home and move into a roach nest?"

"I'm here because you asked me to come."

"Assisted dying is what it amounts to."

"If you'd rather live at home, Mom, that's your choice. But what'll you do if Candy moves away with Lawrence?"

She peers at the ash on her Kent. "I'll be dead by then."

"Let's hope not. Let's hope you live a long, long time."

"Why? So I can be Candy's matron of honor?"

"Wouldn't you like to see your daughter married?"

"Don't patronize me."

"Mom, Mom. You've been through a lot in your life. You spent so many years looking after us, why not let us take care of you?"

"What a bunch of crap. You don't intend to take care of me. You'll pay a team of darkies to do it. A goddamn waste of money. There won't be a cent left for you kids."

"Don't worry about leaving me money."

"I'm not. It's for Candy and Maury. I've been laying aside a little for them each month. Now you want me to piss away my nest egg."

"Wait a minute. You've been saving what I send you?"

"Part of it."

I don't know whether to laugh or howl. Whether to shit or go blind, as my foulmouthed mother often sums up her quandaries. During the most vigorous bull market in history, she's been parking cash in a savings account that probably draws no interest.

"That money was for you," I say.

"Once it's in my name, I'll do what I damn well please with it. If you don't like it, quit writing the checks."

Her sheer ballsiness is breathtaking. "Look, I didn't travel all the way from London to argue with you," I say.

"Good, because I'm not up to fighting either. I'd like you to look over the stuff Candy and I found in the cedar chest. There may be things you'd be interested in keeping."

"Shall we do it together?"

"No, you go ahead. I'll finish my prayers and my cigarette."

My overcoat, draped over the back of the chair, describes the outline of a torso, like a chalk drawing at a crime scene. I feel as deflated as the coat. Still, I smile and plant a kiss on the crown of her head. Her hair smells not of the rankness that permeates the house, but almost refreshingly of cigarette smoke.

Upstairs, I step into the room that used to be mine, then mine and Maury's after his parole. The walls, formerly covered with movie posters and baseball pennants, are bare, and the floor space is crammed with beds. Two twins from Candy's room have been squeezed in along with the ones Maury and I slept on. Leaning over them to a window, I look out at the backyard. The rusty stanchions of the clothesline jut up from bare earth like a pair of crucifixes. The emptiness between them begs for a third cross.

In what Mom calls the library, the cedar chest is the size of a child's coffin. The lid lifts not on a corpse, but on something almost as painful to me—fossils of family history. Photographs, Christmas and birthday cards, my grade school and high school reports, playbills from college, clippings from British reviews. Everything ready to be sorted, discarded, or salvaged. Whatever I wish.

And what I wish fervently at the moment is to vanish. I want to get out of here and back to Tamzin and my snug conservatory. Instead, like a forensic coroner at a mass grave, I suppress my personal revulsion and sit next to the cedar chest and concentrate on learning what the dead—and under this rubric, I include the boy I used to be—have to teach the living.

Mom seems to have saved everything except my fingernail parings and navel lint. There's the blue-beaded bracelet I wore home from the maternity ward, a hank of my blond baby hair, and an envelope of teeth, yellow as kernels of corn, that the tooth fairy exchanged for dimes. Whatever bizarre freight of emotion these mementos carry for her, I'm tempted to declare that they mean nothing to me. But that's not true. Otherwise I wouldn't fear that if I saved this midden heap and shipped it to London, the past would own me. Yet how can I discard it without insulting Mom and showing that I don't value what she treasures?

I browse through a few letters, full of false bravado, that I mailed soon after I settled in England. Then there are the curt notes that I've taken to enclosing along with Mom's monthly check. Each one includes less and less of myself. It's only the hand-drawn cards I did in grade school that suggest the true depth of feeling that used to connect us. Every Christmas and Easter I composed a spiritual bouquet, reckoning on sheets of loose-leaf paper the number of Masses, Communions, and Rosaries I dedicated to the salvation of her soul. How can she have any doubt that she's well fixed for eternity?

Deeper into the cedar chest, I dig down to another sheaf of newspaper clippings. They're not about me. Yellow with age and as delicate as antique lace, they deal with Maury and the murder. I handle them with care. No, with caution. I'm not convinced I'm supposed to read them. This information—the headlines about the "Boy Killer," "The Bad Seed"—has always been off-limits.

But then another possibility presents itself. Maybe Mom decided the time has come, and that's why she sent me up here—to find material for my memoir.

I break out in a sweat, a cold one, yet remain clearheaded as I read on. Under the clippings, a buckram folder contains the paperwork from Maury's original booking and a transcript of his confession, neatly typed at the County Service Building hours after the killing. Are these relics of his childhood the equivalent, in Mom's mind, to my baby teeth and hair? What did she save for Candy—her leg brace? It hits me that at last I'm getting an answer to the question that years ago got my head slammed into a wall.

My mother and father were arguing in the kitchen. I remembered all the things he did to me, and I got really mad. I waited outside the kitchen door, thinking what to do. I opened the door and went in where they were hollering. I told them to stop. My father saw me and I knew by his look that he'd punish me for sticking my nose into his business which I had been brought up never to do. There were knives in the kitchen drawer and I took out the biggest one, the butcher knife. He ran at me, and I held the knife in front of me to keep him away. But he didn't stop and his belly bumped into the knife. I pushed it into him. I don't remember how far. I was crying and my mother was screaming and my father fell on the floor and blood came out of his mouth. Mom grabbed the butcher knife and said we better call an ambulance.

This sounds more or less like my brother—in the same way that stage dialogue sounds more or less like a fictional character. What's missing are Maury's verbal tics and some indication of the off-kilter cadence of his voice. The confession doesn't suggest anything of the impression he made the same day on the psychiatric staff at

Clifton T. Perkins Criminal Mental Health Clinic. They concluded that he displayed symptoms of "morbid ideation," "thought disorganization," "easy distractibility," "sensory integration disorder," "attention impulse disorder," and "manic behavior." The transcript of his admission interview almost makes me weep.

**Staff:** Where are your parents?

**Patient:** Mom's at home. Dad's probably in hell.

**Staff:** Why did you kill your father?

**Patient:** Do I have to say what I already said?

**Staff:** Not if you don't feel like it. Does it bother you to talk about it?

**Patient:** I get dizzy.

**Staff:** Why?

**Patient:** I don't know.

**Staff:** Were you dizzy when you stabbed your father?

**Patient:** Yeah. Everything was spinning.

**Staff:** Could you describe yourself? What kind of boy you are?

**Patient:** I try to be polite and clean.

**Staff:** Anything else? Anything you like or dislike?

**Patient:** I don't like people that cuss and yell at me. I stay away from them.

**Staff:** Did your father do that?

**Patient:** Yeah, a lot.

**Staff:** And your mother?

**Patient:** Less than my father.

**Staff:** What do you think is going to happen to you?

**Patient:** I don't know. I guess I'll stay here or go someplace else.

**Staff:** Where?

**Patient:** Maybe reform school.

**Staff:** Why do you think that?

**Patient:** I don't know. Maybe when I'm twenty-one they'll put me in prison.

**Summary:** Maury believes that he is a normal child, that he is no different from any other boy, except it takes him a little longer to do his homework. He says that he will never marry because that brings too many problems.

**Predisposition:** Passive-aggressive personality

**Impairment:** Severe

**Prognosis:** Guarded

There's a loud thump; Mom groans on the stairs. She sounds hurt. I pitch to my feet, spilling papers off my lap. But before I have a chance to rush to her, she crawls into the room on her hands and knees.

"Sit down," she wheezes. "There's something I better tell you."

# Maury

When we're out of Mom's house, the stink stays inside and Candy and I stand next to her car catching our breath. There's cloud everyplace, from the top of the sky down to the ground, and we add our clouds to it, like the puffs of cigarette smoke from Mom's mouth. I don't like looking up the street where the houses disappear and dark windows and black roofs float in the air with nothing underneath them.

Candy unlocks the car with the clicker on her key ring. It chirps like a frog. I make the sound myself. Before they bulldozed the creek, I caught frogs behind the house. Turtles and lizards too. Never a snake. I saw them, but I knew Mom wouldn't let me bring them in the house. She believes they're all poison. Now in winter they're sleeping, warm underground. Or else they're dead.

In the car a good smell comes off Candy and off the little green cardboard Christmas tree that swings from her rearview mirror. "Where would you like to go?" she asks. "What would you like to see?"

"All this cloud, there's nothing to see."

"The fog'll burn off."

"Burn?"

"It'll lift. Go away. I'm glad to drive you wherever you want." She revs the engine and starts driving before I make up my mind. The cloud rolls over the hood and onto the roof. "There must be places you'd like to visit," she says, "even if everything has changed."

"Yeah," I say.

"Yeah, it's changed? Or yeah, there's places you'd like to visit?"

"Yeah, it's changed."

"What changes have you noticed?" she asks.

She's staring at me instead of the road. It's a thing Nicky does that scares me. Even in clear weather in the desert, you can't tell what's ahead. In this cloud, there could be a car, a wall. "Dead," I say, afraid what we'll bump into.

"Dead?" From Candy's voice I know I've made a mistake.

"There's more dead people than when we lived here."

"But we're still alive. So's Mom."

"Why does it smell that way in her house?"

"What way?"

"Like cats." I worry how deep this cloud is.

"Mom's cats passed away a long time ago."

"I still smell them."

"Maybe it's because she's been sick."

"And she'll die like the cats?"

"We hope not. Mom's different from a cat. She has a soul." Candy talks like she did giving Communion to Mom. "She'll be in heaven, and we'll join her there when we die."

"I won't."

"Why not?"

"I'll be in the other place."

"Oh, Maury, that's not true."

"Yeah, it is. Because of what I did."

"That was a long time ago. You were punished and forgiven."

"Still . . ."

"Do you go to Mass and Communion in California?" She keeps tunneling into cloud where we could crash head-on into anything.

"Whenever there's a Mexican to drive me."

"A Mexican?"

"They're the only Catholics around."

Stopped at a red light, Candy doesn't notice it turn green. She's staring so hard at me, she doesn't see it go yellow, then red again. A car behind us honks, and Candy zips across the intersection. More horns blow, and a truck just misses smashing us.

"I better watch what I'm doing." She laughs like it's a joke. But I hear in her voice that it's not funny. "Now where shall we go?" she asks. "Your choice."

"Patuxent."

"You're kidding. Why would you want to do that?"

"To see Cole."

"Who's Cole?"

"A friend."

"An inmate?" The joking has gone out of her voice.

"Yeah."

"I didn't realize you were in touch with anyone at Patuxent."

"I'm not."

"Then how do you know he's still there?"

"You kill a cop, they never let you out."

Candy brushes a hand at her hair. When her bangs flip off her forehead, she looks like Mom, only younger and prettier and with a skinny leg in her boot.

"After being cooped up at Patuxent for a dozen years, it surprises me you want to visit," she says.

"You visited."

"That was to see you. Somebody I love."

I don't tell her how I feel about Cole. "If it's too much trouble, don't bother."

"It's not too much trouble." Her hand is at her hair again. "If that's what you want, that's what we'll do."

She tugs the wheel and the tires squeal and we tunnel back through the cloud. It hits me that Cole could be dead. I don't mention this to Candy. It's too late. Now that the idea is in my brain, I have to learn whether he's alive or not. Your problem is you don't think, Nicky always says. But my problem is I can't stop thinking about a thing once I start.

I don't recall how old Cole is. Not like Mom, but he's way up there and doesn't have long to go. All the years he's been locked up, I figure he'd rather burn than be buried in another box. But it could be he doesn't get to choose. That's how it is in prison. They say, and you do what they say, or else it's into the hole.

If he hasn't shaved, his mouth'll be as whiskery as Mom's. But I bet there'll be glass between us. So no touching. Just looking and pressing hands against the glass, like me looking through the car window where trucks rip by so fast I'm afraid they'll suck me out onto the highway.

I change from the window to looking at Candy, and she says, "This used to be farmland, with people selling vegetables beside the road. On the drive home from Patuxent, we'd buy fresh corn and tomatoes. Do you remember that, Maury?"

"I wasn't in the car."

"I mean the times when we visited you."

"Yeah." A fire flickers from drawer to drawer in the box in my head, and I follow it, hunting for Cole and a place to be with him. But passing cars and trucks set off a racket, and in the side mirror headlights burn out of the cloud like the point of Mom's cigarette. My mind can't find a safe spot.

"Do you remember visiting me when I was in the hospital?" Candy asks.

"I remember the little girl in the machine."

"Yes, an iron lung."

"Did she ever get out of it? Or is she like Cole, in for life?"

"I don't know, Maury."

By the time we're on the parking lot at Patuxent the cloud's gone, just like Candy promised. Or maybe it was never here to start with. The sun feels nice, but it makes a pool under me on the pavement, and I step away. The lockup building stares back at me through two tall chain-link fences.

They're easy to climb, these fences, till you hit the barbed wire on top. I saw a guy tangle himself up there trying to escape. Guards hollered for him to climb down, and when he didn't, they said they'd shoot, and when he still didn't, they shot him. He hung there a long time, his clothes snagged in the wire. They had to take a ladder and cut him down, just like I cut the tree branches from the fence at Nicky's house. I don't want to think about any of this. But like Cole, whether he's alive or dead, it sticks in my brain.

"Ready?" Candy asks, locking up with the frog chirper.

We go into the gatehouse through a glass door so thick it shuts with the sound of the safe where Nicky keeps her money. For a minute we're locked between one glass door and the next. It's so tight, I have trouble breathing. Then at a buzz we move through a metal detector into the big room where everybody waits. I make the buzzing noise to myself. It's Sunday and there are as many people here as in church this morning. It smells like feet and dogs, and I'd never lie down on this floor.

A guard drags a police dog on a leash, telling it, "C'mon, checkup, checkup." And it snuffles at shoes and bags and up and down your legs. These people don't mind. They come every week, they're used to a dog with its nose in their privates. But when the teeth and wet tongue get near Candy, she flinches.

A black guard in a booth talks through a microphone and matches our names against the visitors list. When I ask for Cole, he looks at me. He looks so long, I have to look away. I'm scared he thinks there's a mistake and I belong back in jail.

"Ole Cole," he says, "he ain't too popular these days. Ain't had visitor one since I been on staff. You kin?"

"He's a friend," Candy talks for me.

"Cole's visitor list, it's years, it's decades, out of date," the guard says.

"My brother traveled a long way," Candy tells him. "He traveled from California to visit his friend."

"Ain't up to me. His name's on the list, and I'll let him through. But inside they might could decide no and send him back."

"Can I go in with him?" Candy asks.

"No, ma'am." There's a radio in the booth and it's singing that rhyming music about ditches and bitches and ass and grass. "Nobody gets in 'less his name's down here. And yours ain't."

"I'll be in the car," Candy tells me, smiling—maybe because she's glad to wait outside. Now I'm not sure I want to go in. But people behind us are pushing and the guard whistles through his teeth, waiting. "Stay as long as you like," Candy says.

"It's an hour, max," the guard says.

The ground in the yard is frozen. Under my feet there's an echo, like from an escape tunnel some con is digging. The wind that blew away the cloud pushes at me. But it doesn't have the sand in it that stings you in Slab City. My shadow pours out ahead of me. Every blade of grass is dead, and there's not a tree or bush to hide behind.

The building swarms with the smell I lived with when I was a boy. Bad food and bad gas and bad men. People talk about jail and think bars. But the worst is the smell and the banging steel doors. The noise shakes the cellblock, and that shaking is in my voice when I tell a guard at a desk my name and Cole's.

The belt around his belly has holsters for handcuffs, a walkie-talkie, and a nightstick. No gun. I don't know whether he believes I belong here or not. His questions come down so fast I can't keep up. They come down like snow, the first flakes melting and making wet spots. Then flurry after flurry, they pile up, and my head is as full as the glass ball at Mom's house where a blizzard buries the miniature town.

The guard says Cole's sick. Been sick for years. The guard doesn't let on from what. He might be sick from anything. In prison they've got diseases, and you can catch them. Or they catch you. I don't ask. Probably the guard wouldn't tell me. Probably he doesn't have to unless I'm a blood relative. He knows I'm on Cole's visitors list, but tells me he doesn't have to let me in.

"I came from California," I say what Candy said to the guard at the gate. "I came on a bus." I pull the plastic bus from my pocket.

He laughs. "Must have been a tight fit."

"I sat in the sixth row." I hold it out for him to look at.

"I get the picture. Lemme call upstairs and ask the supervisor do we make an exception for you."

Ten minutes. I count them on the clock on the wall. I don't do it out loud. I watch the red hand circle and the black hand jump, and I count to myself. Then the guard says I'm an exception and orders me to empty my pockets and put everything, including the bus, in a locker and he'll hold the key.

A different guard leads me through steel doors, downstairs to a tier that I never knew about. It smells like soap and the purple medicine Nicky paints on me when I cut myself. None of the men look really sick. Still, they're cuffed to beds. One or two call out to me.

"Hush up," the guard tells them. Then he whispers, "Buncha skull-fucked toads."

The last bed in the line is behind hanging sheets, and the inmate is tied with wires and tubes, not cuffs. They snake into his arms and up his nose and between his legs. Stuff drips in and out of him. Mostly out, so that his face has that collapsed look of a cantaloupe that's gone bad. He has less hair than Quinn, just baby wisps above his ears. It doesn't smell like straw. Still, I know by his eyes that it's Cole.

I lean down and look at him and he looks at me. His eyes are full of water like you'd see on a rainy street. It's hard to say whether he recognizes me. To remind him who I am, I do what he used to do. I spread my fingers over his head. His scalp feels paper thin. I could crush it with one squeeze. But I hold on, remembering him holding me, teaching me, being my father. Nothing, not even the water in his eyes, budges.

"I don't know as I'd do that if I was you," the guard says. "They claim you can't catch it. But why run the risk?"

"Sleep," I whisper to Cole. "You're going to sleep for a long time."

When I'm ready, we walk back past the men cuffed to their beds.

"How long you known Cole?" the guard at the desk asks.

"Since I was a boy."

"Do you know his family? Anybody we could notify?"

"He had a wife and kids, but they never visited."

"We need to decide what to do."

"You mean burn him or bury him in a box?"

The guard gives me a look. "That's not my department."

"I know he'd rather burn, not end up in a box."

"Like I say, it ain't up to me. Unless you're kin, it ain't up to you either."

When I fetch my belongings from the locker, I say, "I'd like to leave him something."

"What?" The guard eyes my plastic bus.

"Money for cigarettes and candy."

"He's finished smoking, and all his food drips through that tube in his nose."

I hand him ten dollars.

"It's your money, man. I'll take it," he says, "and when Cole passes, I'll toss it in the kitty for the Christmas party."

He has to write up a receipt that I sign so no one accuses him of stealing. But he writes the date wrong and has to do it over again. Then carrying the pink slip of paper, I cross the yard, and the wind blows it out of my hand. The paper flaps in the dead grass, and I chase it. Like a butterfly, it lands here, lands there. Nicky's afraid of anything with wings, even moths. I catch them without hurting them and set them free. But Nicky stomps them flat. Which is what I do with the receipt. Stomp it. A corner of it flaps at the side of my shoe, one wing still flying. I fold it in half and stuff it in my back pocket.

In the gatehouse, I spot a guard at the glass door spying on me, probably wondering what I stuffed in my pocket. I look over my shoulder like I left something behind, like pieces of me have broken off.

Candy's in the car, and the windshield mists from her breathing. She switches on the engine, and the glass starts to clear. I bet the mist is gone before I get there. I walk slow to make sure I win.

"Did you have a nice visit with your friend?" she asks.

I nod that I did.

"Was he happy to see you?"

I nod.

"What's wrong?"

"Nothing. I'm good."

"If you'd like, Quinn or I'll bring you back for another visit." She pulls out of the parking lot. "Maybe you two'll stay in touch now."

There's water in my eyes. It doesn't stand still like in Cole's. It trickles down and tastes salty in my mouth.

"Oh, sweetie, I'm sorry," Candy says. "It must have been sad after all these years." Then she does that scary thing of taking her hand off the steering wheel and not watching where she's driving. Her fingers flutter in the air like the blowing scrap of pink paper.

# Quinn

"Why are you crawling?"

I rush over to Mom, but she rejects my help, and wades on hands and knees through the papers that have fallen from my lap. Maury's legal file crackles under her like ancient parchment. In her frayed housecoat, with her thin yellowish hair straggling down, she could be a character, half-wraith, half-clown, from a Samuel Beckett play, grumbling, "I can't go on, I'll go on."

She slumps against the cedar chest and jabs her glasses back up the bridge of her nose. "Damn! Forgot my cigarettes. Run downstairs and get them, hon. An ashtray too."

"Not until you tell me what's wrong."

"Nothing's wrong—" She strains to catch her breath. "—except I lost the spring in the legs. Easier to do the stairs on all fours. An old woman's no better than a baby. Now what about those cigarettes?"

"The last thing you need is a cigarette."

"Don't preach to me. I've had a raft of that from Candy. Just get my Kents."

I do as I'm told. It's a chore reminiscent of childhood, an encore performance of my original role as Stepin Fetchit. Mom was always ordering me to bring her a Coke, peanuts, potato chips, chocolate-covered pecans—all the sweets and savories that I was forbidden to sample except with her permission. She warned me these were treats for the weekend, but only if I behaved. She warned me they'd ruin my teeth and my complexion. She warned me she'd blister my bottom with a hairbrush if I disobeyed her and sneaked a bite. The most I might hope for was an occasional nibble of the ambrosia she gorged on.

When I recounted this to Dr. Rokoko, he refused to believe me. He dismissed the story as a fabrication, another of what he refers to as my "burlesque shows," a blatant play for his sympathy. It took me the better part of a session to persuade him that I had raised the subject only to demonstrate how well trained I was as a child—and how happy!—to serve the household goddess. And here I am a grown man doing it again.

When I return, Mom is examining a photograph of herself as a schoolgirl. "Ever notice how women as they age, their eyes get smaller and smaller? I don't think men's do."

She flicks aside the snapshot like someone slinging cards at a hat, then lights a Kent. I reassume my seat on the folding chair. She shucks off her slippers, and her feet are not a pretty sight. Cracked and discolored, her toenails might be mistaken for the talons of a raptor.

"Your toenails need cutting," I say. "Do you have a clipper?"

"Don't be silly. Candy does that."

"Why don't we give Candy a break and let me take a turn?"

"We've got better things to do." She drags on the cigarette. "Tell me the truth. What did you think of Leonard?"

"His name's Lawrence. Leonard's his last name."

She bridles. "You know who I'm talking about."

"A nice man. Smart, considerate, good company. I'm happy for Candy."

"They're virtually living together. I don't understand how she squares that with being a Catholic. A Eucharistic minister, no less."

"Maybe like you said, it's virtual between them."

"Aren't you the comedian! Me, I don't feature Lawrence as the masculine lover-boy type. You know, he does all the cooking."

"The best chefs are men."

"Do you cook?"

"I don't have enough sexual confidence."

She chuckles, and in an effusion of her distinctive brand of maternal affection, says, "You're such an asshole. Have you looked in the cedar chest?"

"Yeah. You saved everything, didn't you?"

"Of course. You were my beautiful baby. My best shot at the big time after things bottomed out with Candy and Maury."

"Is that what I was?" Despite myself, I'm moved. Moved, among other things, to wonder what she has in mind. I'm not sure I was meant to see Maury's file. I scoop the papers from the floor and re-insert them in the buckram folder. Mom sucks at the Kent and says nothing.

"This is fascinating stuff," I say tentatively. "But I'm surprised by how Maury sounded. Maybe the cops didn't quote him word for word."

"Maybe. But he'll surprise you, Maury will. I ever tell you about the time—he couldn't have been older than four—he came home holding his hands behind his back? Said he had a present for me. I asked him what and he showed me a fistful of maggots. He'd been rooting around in a garbage can and decided they'd make swell pets."

Mom shakes with laughter, then with coughing. It racks her so badly, I'm afraid she'll choke. Scrambling down onto the floor, I pat her shoulders. Her bones are rickety and I'm afraid to pound harder.

"Poor Maury," she wheezes. "I shouldn't make fun of him. In his way, he was a love, just like you and Candy. When we first bought this house, other places down the block were still being built, and the carpenters sort of adopted Maury. In the morning I'd open the front door and he'd run outside and I didn't see him again until suppertime. He was gaga over that gizmo, the one with the bubble in it, that says whether a board is level or not."

I bide my time while she gathers momentum toward wherever she's going. She proceeds at her own pace, and there's no pushing her. You just have to enjoy the garrulous ride.

"I sewed him a little apron," she says, "with pockets for nails and a hoop for a hammer. Damned if he didn't learn how to use tools. When he sets his mind to it, he catches on quick. The carpenters let him have some scraps of plywood, and he banged them together and made a box for my jewelry. I keep it in the drawer of my night table."

"I suppose he's more capable than he seems."

"I'm getting a crick in my neck." Mom pats the carpet on the other side of her. "Move around here."

Again I do as I'm told, and together we lean against the cedar chest. "What do you remember about your grandparents?" she asks. "I mean my parents."

"Not much." The truth is nothing at all.

"By the time you were born, my father was on his last legs from kidney failure. The doctor ordered him to pee in a bottle for them to test it. But Daddy said the hell with that and peed wherever he pleased. He'd do his business right out in the front yard. He was a maverick. I guess I inherited his orneriness."

"You? Ornery?" I josh her.

Lost in reverie, she gazes at the ceiling, where light reflected from the windshield of the derelict car in her driveway shimmers and dances. This hopscotching through family history is part of the flow that used to bind us together. There was, there still is, a powerful current between us as her words surge forward and, at the same time, eddy into whirlpools of the past. Whatever her faults as a mother, she's always had a voice that echoed in me like a blood fable.

"The night my father died," she goes on, "I stayed at my parents' house and ironed the suit he was supposed to be buried in. I hung it on a hook in the room where I slept. Only thing is, I never dozed off. I stared at that suit so long, it looked like he was in it, and his arms and legs were moving. I had to climb out of bed and touch it to prove to myself it was empty. After he was in the grave, we gave his clothes to Goodwill and I never much thought about him again. My mother now, she was a different matter."

"How's that?" I obediently hit my mark.

"I dream about her all the time. Do you dream?"

"Very little," I lie.

"Maybe you have to be old. Or maybe you have to have had a mother like mine. She lied about everything. Even now I don't know the whole truth. She told me she sailed over from Ireland as a young woman, met your grandfather, and married him. It wasn't till she died and I went through her papers that I found out she changed her name, first and last, the minute she set foot in the USA."

"She wasn't the only immigrant to do that."

"I have a hunch she was running from something. A husband or the law back in County Cork. Maybe she was mixed up with the

IRA. On top of changing her name, she knocked a decade off her age. Claimed she was twenty-five when she was pushing thirty-five. She didn't have me until she was past forty. Nearly as old as I was when I had you. It's a miracle it didn't kill her considering medical care back then."

"What woman doesn't like to pass for younger?" I say.

"Well, it makes you wonder what else she lied about," Mom says. "Learning she had a different name and a different age, I started to rethink everything about my mother. But after she was dead, it was too late to ask. I decided I couldn't really blame her for doing what she had to do to get to America and get a man."

"Right." Clasping a hand to the nape of her neck, I knead the stringy tendons. "Otherwise, you wouldn't have been born. And if you weren't born, where would I be?"

"That's my point. Sometimes people do things that start off wrong, then end up okay. So while you might regret what you did, you can't completely wish it never happened."

She stubs out her cigarette and drops it in the ashtray. Suddenly a tremor seizes her. I feel the shaking in my hand. She's crying.

"What's the matter?" I ask.

"You're going to hate me when you hear the truth."

"Did you hate your mother when you found out her real name and age?"

"Yes, a little."

"But you got over it." I continue to try to soothe her with my hand.

"What she did wasn't as bad. I lied about something far worse."

"How bad can it be?" I ask, thinking, Here we are down on the dirty floor surrounded by family dregs—pictures of a dead father, a girl in a wheelchair, a boy in prison, legal briefs, and psychiatric reports. What could conceivably be worse than what's already gone wrong? As the possibilities pour through me, I fear I might start shaking too.

"I won't ask you to promise not to hate me," Mom says. "But I want you to hear me out to the end."

Without lighting another cigarette, she inhales, and there's a rasping noise of old smoke ravaging her lungs. "You were born left-handed. I noticed that straightaway when you were a teeny baby and I tied a sock over your hand."

Immense anticlimax fizzles through me. Is this what she's been tediously circling?

"In those days," she adds, "lots of mothers believed it was bad to raise a southpaw in a right-handed world."

"Well, it's not exactly a tragedy."

"I asked you not to interrupt," she barks. "Your real father was left-handed, and I didn't want you to be like him."

A master of double and triple takes, I'm able to project a reaction for the benefit of spectators in the last row. But at the moment I'm frozen in wooden-faced disbelief. "My *real* father?"

"You're not Maury's and Candy's full brother. You have different fathers."

Along with incredulity, with absolute shock, a curious exhilaration, very close to giddiness, wells up inside me. Absurdly, I feel free. I feel I've been reborn. Yet while this news seems the answer to everything, I insist, "You need to tell me the rest."

"You know how babies are made." Her nostrils flare in warning.

"Look, I'm the one who should be upset. Not you. I'd like some background."

"About what?"

"Who's my father?"

"What's the difference? You never met him and you never will. His name wouldn't mean a damn thing to you."

"Yes, it would. It'd mean I know my name."

"Your name's Quinn Mitchell. Leave it at that."

"Didn't it dawn on you that I might like to meet him?"

Her eyes go frantic. "He has to be dead by now. He was older than me. He'd be near a hundred. Promise you won't look for him or his family."

"How can I when you won't tell me his name?"

"Tom Trythall. There! Satisfied?"

"No." She's so quick to confess, I question how much trust to place in the name. The previous configuration of the family, painful and convoluted as it was, may be preferable to the facts I'm dragging out of her. Still, I insist, "You have to explain. I want to know everything."

She removes her glasses, and the asymmetry of her eyes diminishes. "Your father . . . Jack, he'd go off on benders that lasted days. When a woman sits at home and the man is gone, the loneliness is terrible. Rumors spread. Then I met Tom and he was sweet to me. It started off innocent enough, just talking over coffee. But we got to like each other, and I figured since people were already gossiping . . . well, what the hell, why not?"

"Did you love him?"

"I thought I did at the time."

"Did you tell him you were pregnant?"

"Yeah. But there was no future for us. He had a wife and family. And me being Catholic, I didn't relish a divorce and living the rest of my life in sin. I didn't see any solution except to play the hand I was dealt."

"Did Dad . . . did Jack know?"

"Put it this way, he suspected. Now next thing you'll ask is whether that's what we were fighting about the day he died."

"It hadn't crossed my mind. But since you brought it up . . ."

"Look, Jack and I argued at the drop of a hat. This was just one more thing." She thrusts her glasses back on and glares at me.

"What became of Tom Trythall?"

"After the murder, he pleaded to get back together. That's a man for you. Raring to go like nothing had happened. But I was finished. I had no time and no more interest in that type of love. Even if I'd wanted to be with him, which I didn't, there was always a mob around—cops, lawyers, nosy neighbors. And I had to think about you kids."

"You never had any more contact with him?"

"A couple phone calls. I don't know whether I should tell you this"—which naturally ensures that she will —"but he hounded me to get rid of the baby. Get rid of you. I told him to go to hell, and not just because it's a mortal sin. I couldn't bear not to have you. I was sick the whole nine months. It was like a snake had curled up inside me and was eating its way out. But I never considered an abortion." She clamps a hand to my arm. "Was I mistaken, sweetheart? Would you rather not have been born?"

The question demands a prompt, emphatic answer. I should sing out, Of course not, you did the right thing. But after my euphoria, the giddiness is giving way to an inner earthquake, a great seismic shift as of continental plates grinding into new alignment.

"Do you hate me?" she breaks the silence. "Why don't you say something?"

"I don't know what to say."

"You at a loss for words!"

"I need time to think."

"At least say you forgive me."

Having served since childhood as her sounding board and more often as her whipping boy, I'm now expected to grant absolution. I do so, yet ask, "Why are you telling me this now?"

"I don't want to die with it on my conscience."

"Haven't you confessed it to a priest?"

"More than once. He told me it wasn't fair for you not to know."

"Fair?" I'm at a loss as to how the term applies in this case. Then it occurs to me that Candy may have known all along. Does this account for her bristliness at what she perceives as my princely advantages? Does she imagine that because of my lack of Mitchell blood, I started off on a pedestal and from that launching pad I winged upward to success?

"What are you thinking?" Mom asks.

"I'm thinking how awful it must have been for you to keep this secret for so many years."

"Sometimes I worry Tom's family will squirm out of the woodwork," she says, "and hit you up for money or embarrass you."

"I'm not that easy to embarrass."

She dries her eyes on a cuff of her housecoat. "So you don't hate me? If my mother did this to me, I'd kill her."

I nudge her shoulder with mine. "I'd never tangle with you."

"Who are you kidding? You're a tough customer. Always have been. When you were little, you were so defiant, you wouldn't even cry when I whipped you. Candy, she'd start bawling soon as she saw the stick. But you wouldn't give me the satisfaction."

"What did you do then?"

"What do you think I did? I beat you harder and harder until you gave in and wailed."

"I rest my case. You're the heavyweight champ."

Downstairs, there are three knocks at the door. The signal. The code. Candy and Maury are home. Mom presses a nicotine-stained fingertip to my lips. "Don't mention a word about this. Neither of them knows. Go down and tell them I'm taking a nap."

BOOK THREE

# Candy

As Maury advanced through the system at Patuxent, he eventually lived on an open tier. "Open" meaning he had privileges and spent most of the day out of his cell, mixing with the prison population. The Sunday before Christmas, as a special treat, inmates of his status threw a party for their families. Instead of herding into those cramped stalls of bulletproof glass, we huddled in an echoey hallway on furniture that was bolted to the floor. There we snacked on food the cons had pitched in to buy, and washed it down with Kool-Aid. As I sipped mine from a paper cup, I was always reminded of those religious nuts who poisoned themselves in the jungle and I had to swallow quick to keep from gagging.

Recorded carols played over a loudspeaker, and some couples paired off and smooched, petted and felt each other up. Mom claimed to be scandalized. But they were the lucky ones. For the rest of us, it'd be hard to say who looked more sad-sack, the inmates stuck with unhappy wives and squabbling kids, or the ones that didn't have families and stayed to themselves, glassy-eyed from the jailhouse hooch they secretly brewed.

Like a college boy giving a tour of his dorm, Maury showed us his cell. There, too, the furniture had been bolted to the floor, and the toilet was made of brushed aluminum and didn't have a seat. It stood right next to the head of his bunk. How he had to have hated that!

From those Christmas parties I remember that Maury had a friend, an older guy, big and rawboned and not bad looking, with dishwater blond hair. Nobody visited him, and he hung out with us, shooting the breeze about how well Maury was doing in group therapy. He almost seemed like a caseworker, not a con.

That has to have been Cole. But when I ask Maury on the drive home, he doesn't care to talk. Heaving his broad shoulders one last time, he quits crying and just sits there. I'm so upset, I feel like crying myself. The day has turned topsy-turvy, and as usual I don't have a clue how to reach anybody in this family.

The moment Quinn opens the door at Mom's, Maury makes a beeline for the kitchen. Pipes groan as he splashes water from the spigot over his reddened face. Quinn glances at me, baffled either by Maury's behavior or by what Mom has told him.

"You okay?" I ask.

"Tip-top. Mom's taking a nap. You and Maury have a good time?"

"He visited a friend at Patuxent. I stayed in the car."

He arches his eyebrows, an expression that's exaggerated by his high forehead. I can't guess whether he's surprised or sympathetic. Maybe he doesn't know himself. Maury blunders out of the kitchen half-blinded by the paper towel he's dabbing at his eyes.

"Shall we wait here until she wakes up?" I ask.

"She's finished for the day." Quinn collects his coat from the chair and drapes it over his shoulders like a shawl. "Let's go to your house."

I had hoped to spend the afternoon with Lawrence. But I appreciate that Quinn might need to discuss what Mom said. We set out in separate cars, and once again he leads in his big, blunt-nosed Chrysler.

The patio in back of my townhouse has been a mess since last summer. I spend so much time at Lawrence's, I've neglected the place. Lawn chairs are stacked haphazardly, dead leaves clutter the grill, and a garden hose snakes across the fieldstones. In the shade beside the fence chunks of rust-colored ice lie scattered like iron filings at a pit mine. Quinn doesn't need to see this. He's had more than enough bad housekeeping at Mom's. I shut the curtains.

"I'm tired," Maury announces, and vanishes into the guest room and closes the door so that we barely hear him moaning.

Quinn wanders into the kitchen. I don't know why there rather than the living room that I've tried to make cozy with throw pillows and crocheted blankets. He shrugs off his coat and flops on a chair at the Formica-topped table.

"Coffee?" I suggest.

"You're positive you're not hiding any alcohol?"

"Not unless you're up for vanilla extract."

"It may come to that. I'll have coffee if it's not too much trouble."

"No trouble. It's instant. I bet you drink latte or cappuccino."

"I drink Irish whiskey."

"You're outta luck."

I spoon up the Maxwell House, microwave the water, and fetch half-and-half from the fridge and sugar from the cupboard where I stash it away from the ants. The entire time, Quinn stares at the tabletop like it's a mirror. I don't know what he sees, but I see a man who's had a lousy day.

Plunking the cup in front of him, I lower myself onto a chair and ease my leg out straight. He grins at some private joke. " 'They fuck you up, your mum and dad.' "

"You'll hear no argument from me," I say.

" 'They may not mean to, but they do. They fill you with the faults they had and add some extra, just for you.' "

From the rhyme, I gather he's reciting a poem. Does he always have to depend on a script? His memory bank is chock-full of quotes, but they don't tell me anything more personal than Maury's strangled silences do.

"Say hello to your left-handed half-brother," he wisecracks. "I assume you're up to date on the revised family genealogy."

"I have a pretty good hunch."

"And it never dawned on you that I might have been grateful for a heads-up?"

"There's only so much of Mom's dirty work I'm willing to do. She begged me to call and blindside you with the news—like it wasn't her responsibility and this was something I could deal with long distance. I told her to count me out."

He samples the black instant coffee and grimaces. Spooning in sugar, he says, "So I had to fly all the way from London to learn I'm a bastard."

"And to visit Mom and help me decide what to do with her."

"At this moment, I don't think you want to hear what I'd like to do with her."

"I don't blame you. I'd be mad too."

"It might interest you to know that I'm under the court-mandated care of a shrink for anger issues."

"What do you mean?"

"I mean I had some public outbursts this winter. Fights that made the newspapers."

"That's terrible, Quinn. I never thought you were the type. Has counseling helped?"

"Hard to say. The analyst is of the opinion that my rage is misplaced. But what am I supposed to do? Slug Mom?"

With no cream or sugar, my coffee tastes as bitter as bile. "You did shove her once."

He shakes his head; he doesn't recall.

"She was hitting me," I prompt him. "Who knows why? You were a teenager. I must have been about thirty. She was slapping me in the face and you pushed her away and held her back. You were my hero."

"What did she do then?"

"Kicked you in the shins."

"What the hell's wrong with her? She'd probably claim the poem has it ass-backward, and it's kids that fuck up Mom and Dad."

"Not that it helps, Quinn, but I was damned upset when she told me you had a different father. No daughter likes to learn that her mother has round heels. But honestly, you can't blame her for wanting some love after all that Dad dragged her through. He could be a real bastard."

"She told me that more often than not she's the one that slapped him."

"He didn't have to hit her. He hurt her in other ways."

Quinn doses his coffee with cream and more sugar, still hoping to make it bearable. "When she was winding up to throw me her beanball," he says, "she warned me I'd hate her, I'd never forgive her. I told her not to worry; it wouldn't change a thing. I didn't admit what I already feel about her."

"I'm not sure I want to hear it. No matter what, she's our mother."

"Yeah. O dear Mother Night."

"Stop it, Quinn. I know you're hurt. But this doesn't help."

"I can't quit asking myself what else she's lied about. You know her, the way she lets out bad news piecemeal. She never just makes a clean breast of things."

"Now, you know she wouldn't stand for any talk about breasts," I try to joke him out of his mood. "She warned me to keep my legs crossed. 'If you get pregnant, don't bother coming home. I'm not raising any bastards for you.'"

"And here she was raising one of her own. Me!"

"When I asked about the facts of life, she acted like it was a mortal sin. I mean, asking was a sin. Doing it was out of the question. She advised me never to get completely naked in front of a man, not even my husband, because that ruins the romance. I suppose she thought I should wear a sock or a glove on my wedding night."

"She's like some bog-trotting nun," Quinn exclaims. "All she ever told me about sex is you sort of roll around. If that's how she and Dad did it, God knows how we were conceived."

Now we're both laughing. Like a lot of our conversations that lurch back and forth between kidding and almost crying, the point is in danger of being lost. After I've had another bitter sip of coffee I ask, "Seriously, Quinn, are you all right?"

"I don't know. At first it didn't sink in. Now I feel like I've had a collision with a chainsaw. Mom just keeps hacking away—cutting you off at the ankles and the knees until you don't have a limb to stand on."

"She promised me she'd tell you who your father is."

"She did after a little coaxing. Said it was someone named Tom Trythall."

"Never heard of him."

"Maybe he worked with her at Safeway. The butcher, the baker, the candlestick maker," he mutters. "It could be anybody. And why should I believe she told me the right name? It's a family tradition. She admits her mother lied about everything including her name."

"Why would Mom lie about this? She could simply have kept it to herself."

"Same reason she does everything," he says. "Her never-ending need to run the show. Before she told me about Trythall, she suggested I check out the cedar chest. There were piles of photographs and birthday cards and baby teeth."

"I know. We looked through them a few days ago."

"Then you must have seen the folder with Maury's confession and case records."

"No. We stuck to the pictures."

"Maybe she went back and slipped it in for me to read."

"Well, she did mention that you're doing your memoirs."

"So she's what? Lending me a hand with my research? Come on, Candy, level with me. What's going on here? How long have you known Dad wasn't my father?"

"Only since last week. But I always thought there was something different about you. You weren't like other kids. You weren't like Maury or me." I take his manicured hand in mine. "You were smarter, better looking, more lovable."

"All because of Tom Trythall, the missing link." His eyes crinkle at the corners as they do on camera when his character grudgingly breaks into a fake grin.

As I totter to my feet and clear off the coffee cups, my leg throbs. "Will you do me a favor? I'd like to see Lawrence. Some weeks we're so busy at the office, Sunday's the one day we have to spend together. Would you mind keeping Maury company tonight while I go to his place?"

"You don't trust Maury on his own?"

"It's not that. I don't want him to feel deserted. You could sleep in my bed. Or on the couch."

"I'd rather take him out to a restaurant, then back to the Hilton. My room has two king-size beds. And there's a minibar. You go to your happy place, I'll go to mine."

As I pass his chair, I lean down and kiss his cheek. "Thanks."

On the road to Lawrence's house, I drive faster than the speed limit, faster than my cautious nature normally allows. But after a day with Mom, Maury, and Quinn, I feel liberated and lighthearted. Although I didn't own up to it with Quinn and have difficulty admitting it to myself, I feel strangely relieved that he and I didn't have the same father. When he left home and became so successful, it was like a reproach. If he could do it, why couldn't I? Now I think I'm not inferior. I'm simply from different stock.

When I first visited Lawrence's farm, it stunned me that such properties still exist in the overbuilt corridor between Washington and Annapolis and Baltimore. I had never seen anything like it except in *My Weekly Messenger*. Required reading for every parochial-school kid in the fifties, the *Messenger* was a comic book of Bible stories and uplifting articles that carried an ongoing serial about a family that fell on hard times in the city and retreated to the country where life was cheerful. They renovated a broken-down farmhouse and raised chickens and a cow, and Mom and Dad and Buddy and Sis bonded through hard work and prayer. They grew vegetables, produced plenty of fresh milk and eggs, ate hearty meals, and said grace before and after each one. Gradually the worn-out father and frazzled mother regained their health and love, and the kids became happy again.

Because Mom lived in constant fear that our house would be repossessed and we'd wind up on the street, I prayed that we'd move to the country and farm our way to recovery. I kept the idea to myself, however. After she slapped me silly that time for drawing up a budget, I didn't dare say a word about my secret dream.

Then miraculously, half a lifetime later, I met Lawrence and that dream came true. Crunching over the gravel road onto his land, I spot his house, a rambling white brick colonial on a rise above the river. Big trees grow out front, oaks and maples, bare in this season, and a barn shelters his Volvo and a sit-down lawnmower. The lights are on upstairs and down, and the brightness makes me feel warm and welcome. I'm home.

I let myself in, and Lawrence calls from the kitchen. "Is that you, honey? I'm fixing crab cakes."

I hurry to him without taking off my coat. As in those dreams where I dance or run or swim with no thought of my bad leg, I'm graceful, flawless. Hugging him from behind, I kiss his neck and his ears.

"Whoa!" he says. "Careful or I'll lose track of how much Old Bay I've added." He's stirring the crab meat in a bowl. "How many can you eat?"

"I'm starving."

"I'll cook us two apiece." He lights the flame under a frying pan. "Now five minutes on each side and—"

"I can't wait that long." I'm nibbling his ears.

"You must have had a good day."

"No, a hard one. Now what I want is a hard man." I giggle at my own bawdiness.

He switches off the flame and swivels around in my arms. He's wearing an apron I bought him, one with Michelangelo's *David* on the front. He looks like a body builder, not the type of man to hesitate in this situation. A guy who'd just tear off his fig leaf. But Lawrence isn't accustomed to this kind of talk from me.

"I'm so happy to be here," I say. "I'm so happy you're in my life."

"What a sweet thing to say."

"I mean it. I love you."

We waltz into the living room, onto a throw rug in front of the fireplace. After he presses the button for the gas and sets the artificial logs ablaze, Lawrence unties his apron. Then we undress each other, a couple on the wrong side of fifty, fleshy and sun-freckled, well past our prime, making a spectacle of ourselves. But I'm not apologizing. I'm grateful.

Of all the things he might do at this moment, Lawrence acts as if he has been eavesdropping on Quinn and me. He rolls me off my back and up onto his chest. A minute later I'm under him again, then back on top of him, and it's all I can do not to whoop with joy at the goofiness of what's going on. For once Mom has told the truth. A man and a woman can roll around, yet remain locked together in love.

# Quinn

After Candy leaves, I try to decide how I feel. What does it mean to have grown up fatherless, then suddenly discover that you've had a stranger for a father all along? For forty years I lived in the shadow—yes, even Dad's absence cast a shadow—of a dead gambler. Now I'm confronted by another shade, a murkier absence. Tom Trythall, if that's his true name, hardly seems an admirable sort—a guy tomcatting around on his wife and family. Still, I'd like to know more about him. I'd like to see him or his picture.

It doesn't strike me as implausible that he shared the same curiosity. How could he have resisted looking in on his son? His love child? I imagine him driving past the house or cruising by school hoping to catch a glimpse of me. Later, he might have noticed my name on a movie poster or spotted me in a late night TV rerun.

On an impulse, I unearth the local telephone directory and thumb through its pages. Several Trythalls are listed, and I'm debating whether to dial them one by one when Maury saunters into the kitchen. His hair is cowlicked where he slept on it wrong.

"Did you get some rest?" I ask.

"Not much."

"Did Candy's and my talking keep you awake?"

"No."

He sniffs the scent of coffee, fishes a cup from the sink, rinses it and spoons in some instant. Then while his water boils in the microwave, he rolls open a drawer where Candy stores plastic bags. There are dozens of them, and they expand and breathe like living organisms when Maury pulls them out and dumps them on the drainboard. Methodically he separates each bag, wads it tight and stuffs it into another bag. His goal appears to be to compact them into the smallest possible sphere. But when the microwave pings, he imitates the sound and abandons his project, forcing the loose bags back into the drawer.

Seated opposite me with his coffee, he says, "I do this for Nicky every morning."

Does Maury fix her coffee? Or compact her plastic bags? I don't ask.

"Did Candy tell you I cried?" he says.

"No. She mentioned you visited a friend at Patuxent."

"He's dying. He's in a bed with tubes and wires in him."

"Sorry. I'm sure that made you sad."

Not that he looks sad. His granite face, the ledge of his jaw, call to mind a laconic cowpoke idling over coffee at the end of an exhausting day. But the soundtrack is out of sync and stutters along, with no transitions. "Did Mom tell you something and give you something?" he asks.

"No, we talked about the past."

"She phoned that she's got something to tell me and something to give me."

Worried about the surprises she might spring on him, I say, "Keep in mind that she's old and you can't always count on what she tells you."

He nods and gravely sips his coffee. "Did you know that snakes lay eggs just like chickens?"

"I don't believe I did."

"I used to find them in the woods. Snakes. Never eggs."

"Look, Candy's out for the night. Why don't we eat at a restaurant, then go to my hotel? What kind of food do you like?"

"The kind in pictures."

"Pictures?"

"On the menu. I like to see my food."

My spirits plummet. I had my heart set on a drink and a bottle of wine. I'd settle for the lowliest tavern as long as it has liquor. But I don't want to disappoint Maury. We stop at the International House of Pancakes, where he accepts the waitress's offer of coffee. Afraid more caffeine will destroy my chances of sleeping, I order orange juice and a club sandwich. Meanwhile Maury consults the laminated menu and its multicolored photos like a millionaire poring over his stock portfolio. He asks for a stack of hotcakes with syrup and seasonal berries. In Maryland at this time of year a seasonal berry should be something you'd pick from a holly bush. But his plate arrives smothered in raspberries and strawberries, probably flown in from Mexico.

While this IHOP may bustle at breakfast or lunch, it's dead at this hour. Half the dining room is roped off and unlighted, and we have an enormous corner table to ourselves. Maury positions the hotcakes directly under his chin and digs in.

Toying with my sandwich, I admire his appetite, if not his table manners. "Challenged" is how he would be referred to in polite circles. But I'm the one that's challenged—challenged to comprehend him and explain him to others. I have no idea what transpires inside Maury's head. Nor could I hazard a guess what he makes of me. Does he know what I do for a living? Does he know where I live? If I told him that we have different fathers, would he be as upset as I am?

"Do you remember a man named Tom Trythall?" I ask.

A speared raspberry drips syrup from the tines of his fork. "Was he in Patuxent with me?"

"No. He's a friend of Mom's. He might have worked with her at Safeway."

He shakes his head. "Can't help you." He devours the berry.

"Do you remember things from when you were a boy?"

"Sure. I have it in the box in my head. Most of it."

"My first memory," I say, "is of Mom and Candy holding me up at Patuxent to look at you through the glass."

"I remember that," he exclaims, delighted.

"I remember wearing your clothes as a kid. I remember liking to wear them," I lie.

Were Dr. Rokoko present, he would lambaste me for show-boating—speaking purely, or impurely, because it soothes me to say these things. Whether it soothes Maury is questionable. His expression, as he eats, remains as marmoreal as a statue's.

The truth is, I hated wearing Maury's clothes. They didn't fit, they were out of fashion, and although I never let on to Mom, I regarded them as a punishment, a hand-me-down hair shirt. They stigmatized me as surely as a prison uniform. I didn't understand what crime I was paying for. I worried it was for a future wrong I was destined to commit.

While I go on ruminating, Maury shovels in his hotcakes. I finish the orange juice and shove aside the half-eaten sandwich. Neither of us speaks again until we're out of the IHOP and in the car, where he delivers another nonsequitur. "Remember the bear?"

"The what?"

"The fighting bear at the carnival."

"Oh yeah."

The summer of his parole, Mom packed us off to the county fair, me barely thirteen, Maury in his late twenties, the two of us ill-matched and ill-suited for a good time on the town. Amid the 4-H exhibits and games of chance, there was a boxing ring, with a mangy bear on a stool in the corner. "Fight the bear," a barker cried out. "Survive a single round and win fifty bucks."

Muzzled and declawed, the animal didn't look ferocious. It looked, in fact, like a moldy, cheaply upholstered piece of overstuffed furniture. But it was huge and its pugilistic strategy was irresistible. Wrapping an opponent in its furry arms, it shambled around the ring, then flung him to the canvas. Match over. Prize money lost.

Maury watched several bouts with keen fascination before declaring that he was ready to fight the bear. Though he shied away from human contact, he showed no reluctance to mix it up with a hairy hugging animal. He climbed into the ring, paid the barker a dollar, and watched unruffled as the bear rose onto his hind legs and lumbered forward. Without waiting for a signal, Maury embraced the beast, and like a ballroom dancer hell-bent on leading, he whirled it in a circle. I knew he was strong from his years of jailhouse weight-lifting. What surprised me was the balance and light-footed grace that kept him upright. Minute after minute he and the bear didn't wrestle so much as pirouette around the canvas.

In the end, the spinning was what did Maury in. Dizzy, he lost his footing and staggered. One knee buckled, then the other. He never lost his grip; he kept his arms locked around the bear. But he slid down the front of it, as if its fur were finest silk.

Maury was eager to pay a dollar for another dance. But the barker refused, aware that in that crowd of college boys and country bumpkins screaming for blood nobody would settle for more ballet.

"I won," Maury maintains now.

"You sure did."

"They should have paid me fifty dollars."

"You deserved it," I agree.

When we reach the parking lot at the Hilton, he asks, "Am I spending the night with you? Because if I am, I need my toothbrush from Candy's."

"We'll buy you a new one."

The hotel gift shop has toothbrushes in a blinding array of designs and colors, and the choice falls to me. I grab one at random while Maury obsesses over a red turtle on a key chain. It's a Maryland terrapin, the university mascot. When I pay for both items at the cash register, the girl asks whether we're going to the game, and Maury flashes back to the bear. "I won."

"Let's hope we win," she says.

"I should have won fifty dollars."

"Well, good luck," she says.

In the elevator, confronting his warped funhouse image in the panel of numbered buttons, he clings to the rubber turtle as if to an amulet. The floor jerks beneath us, and he says, "The rope is made of steel. It's too strong to break."

I'm past due for a drink and pray that the coffee at IHOP doesn't keep Maury awake and moaning all night. Do I dare pour him a Scotch?

The maid has folded down the covers on one bed and deposited a foil-wrapped chocolate on the pillow. It's the same size as the terrapin, and Maury's entranced by it.

"Eat it," I tell him.

He sits on the sofa, peeling off the foil, while I crouch in front of the minibar. "Like something to drink?"

"Water," he says.

"You don't drink alcohol?"

"It hurts my head."

I toss him a bottle of Evian, and since there's no more Chivas, I make do with a miniature of Johnnie Walker Black. I swallow my medicine neat tonight, and although I vow to pace myself, I'm soon empty and return to the minibar for a second and third dose.

"Want to watch TV?" I ask.

"It hurts my head," he repeats.

Back on the sofa, I stare at the blank TV screen, which showcases us like a couple of strangers waiting for a train. "Why don't you take off your Windbreaker?" I suggest.

He sets down the turtle, which, I notice, he has neatly wrapped in the candy foil. Under his jacket, he wears a long-sleeved T-shirt that's stretched taut across his muscled chest. It occurs to me that anybody watching us in the elevator might have pegged me in Armani and Maury in his Midnight Cowboy getup as a gay guy with a piece of rough trade.

Dr. Rokoko would undoubtedly view this errant thought as evidence of my sexual hangups. That's often the therapeutic theme he harps on—the latent content of my dreams, my eroticization of violence and fear of intimacy. But as I say in self-defense, how could the secret kinks in my psyche compare in significance to the overt scars of my life?

The stone-faced fellow beside me killed the man I believed until today was my father. Now that I'm told that my father's someone else who might still be alive, everything's changed and nothing has. I'm not going to get to relive my childhood, no more than Maury and Candy will. Mom's our mother and the hard lessons she hammered into us have left their marks. Still, mysteries remain, and late as the hour is, I can't let them drop. Though Tom Trythall's name rang no bells, as the Scotch begins to work on me, other questions seethe and surface.

"Today at Mom's I read the police transcripts of your case," I tell Maury. "You know the ones I'm talking about?"

He chugs the bottle of Evian and shakes his head no. "I don't have to read them. I was there."

"Do you mind talking about this?"

He pauses. The silence draws out into the sort of pregnant beat that would annoy a theatergoer. "I've never talked about it before."

"You talked to the police."

He screws the blue cap onto the bottle, unscrews it, then screws it back on. I suppress an urge to snatch the bottle from his hands.

"The police station had lights," he says. "The blinking kind. I wanted to lie down and rock. The police wouldn't let me. They dragged me off the floor and yelled questions till I couldn't breathe."

"What did you tell them?"

"Not much. They grabbed me and said to look them in the eye. I didn't like that and the way they stared at me."

"Did they hit you?"

"No, just grabbed and shook me and wouldn't let me lie down. When I moaned, they made me quit."

"How?"

"Tied a rag over my mouth."

Almost imperceptibly at first, then faster and more emphatically, Maury starts to rock, settling into the rhythm of my questions. There's a cadence to our give-and-take that's at odds with the tense, pressurized watchfulness in his eyes. Whenever possible, he replies in monosyllables, a simple yes or no, as if despite the chaos of his life, he longs to believe in a binary universe.

"If this hurts," I say, "we can stop."

"It's okay when you go slow. The cops went fast."

"What did they ask you?"

"Why I did it."

"They didn't ask *whether* you did it?"

"No. They told me I did it. Then asked why." He balances the Evian bottle on the arm of the sofa, next to the foil-wrapped turtle. Then he pulls the bus from his pocket and lines it up with the bottle and the turtle. "I said Mom and Dad were fighting and screaming. I wanted them to be quiet."

"And when they wouldn't do that, you did what?"

"I begged them."

"In your confession you said you took the butcher knife from the drawer."

He begins to fiddle with the bottle, switching it to the rear of the turtle.

Though afraid of pushing too hard, I nudge him. "You said you were holding the butcher knife and Dad bumped into it with his belly."

He shakes his head from side to side, and since he's also rock-ing back and forth, he resembles a ship pitching and yawing in a tormented sea, a man both agreeing and disagreeing. "There's a box in my head," he says. "It has drawers. That one doesn't open."

"The drawer where Dad is?"

"The one where he dies."

I could crowbar the drawer open. But what is it I delude myself that I'll discover inside? Like the temptation to telephone all the Trythalls in the book, my cross-examination of Maury smacks of demented self-indulgence. As with the research for my memoir, it's an excuse to delay moving on.

"Sorry," I tell Maury. "Mom's never talked to me about this, and I've always wondered."

"Well, why not? He was your father too."

This brings my Scotch-fueled interrogation to a stop. "It's late," I say, then glance at my watch and notice it's not even ten o'clock. Still, I'm wasted from the whiskey and the long day. "What time do you normally go to bed?"

"Anytime." He bounces to his feet and pockets the turtle and the toy bus. In the bathroom, he refills the Evian bottle at the sink, then brushes his teeth and scrubs his face. Finally he pries off his jog-ging shoes and stretches out fully clothed on the bed that hasn't been turned down.

"Wouldn't you be more comfortable if you undressed and got under the covers?"

"I'm good." He's on his back, gazing at the perforated sound-proof ceiling as though at a sky adazzle with stars.

By the time I've finished showering, Maury still has his eyes fixed on the ceiling. I slide under the sheets of the second bed, and like him, I trance in on the constellation of pinpricks. I don't bother switching off the light and he doesn't ask me to. We lie there, I lost in thought, Maury's mind God knows where.

The moment is reminiscent of the final phase of my yoga class in Belsize Park, when we recline on our mats, in theory scoured of all earthly cares. I'm usually fizzing with impatience and planning what I'll do next—call my agent, my accountant, Tamzin. Now rather than pleasant cessation I experience the urgency of unfinished business. Something more begs to be said. An explanation. An apology. A summary account. I feel I should do something for Maury. But what? Invite him to London? Buy him his own trailer in California?

He breaks the silence. "I'm glad we did this."

"I am too. It's good to spend time together."

"I'm tired just thinking about the day. Mass, then Mom, then Patuxent with Candy, then Cole, then pancakes, then talking with you."

I wait for him to go on. When he doesn't, I ask whether I should turn out the light and he says yes.

In the dark, I'm aware of the dense timbre of his breathing, the space he occupies, the unexpected weight he exerts. It's been decades since we slept in the same room. But it all rushes over me in this anonymous Hilton—the almost audible vibration that Maury exudes, like an electrical appliance endlessly cycling through its functions. As a boy it kept me awake nights wondering what constancy of effort, what act of the will, was required to stitch him together. I still marvel that he's managed to achieve a unitary self.

Me, I've splintered, dispersed. Becoming nobody. Anybody. Everybody. Depending on the part I'm hired to play. I used to believe that if I landed the right role, or even the wrong one under the right circumstances, these fractures would heal. But the longer I live, the less convinced I am that I'll ever cohere.

"Quinn," Maury speaks up, "are you saying your prayers?"

"Why do you ask?"

"You're so quiet."

"I was half asleep."

"Do you ever pray?"

Again I ask why he wants to know.

"Because in church you didn't go to Communion," he says.

There's nothing I'd like less at the moment than to discuss the state of my soul. Not after Mom's inquisition on the same subject. Could this be the reason I've been summoned home? To coax me back into the Catholic fold? "I pray in my own way," I tell him.

"What's that?"

"I think things over. I regret what I've done wrong. I plan to do better. Look, it's late. Why don't we talk about this tomorrow?"

"That's okay. I understand."

Maybe he does. Maybe in his fashion he has me pegged far better than I have him. But it's too late and I'm too tired to keep going over it. I try to lull myself to sleep, as I sometimes do, by musing about women. Ones I loved, ones that didn't love me or that should have loved me more. From a certain point of view my life seems a calvary of females who've fallen short.

To counteract that melancholy thought, my mind jumps to Tom Trythall and struggles to bring him into focus. Over the years, with effort, I've started to imagine Dad as a character from a Sam Shepard play, a monster out of the American West. Now I have another father to define and instinctively I turn to literature, not life. Is there a character that might resemble him, that might resemble me?

· · ·

"Quinn! Quinn! Wake up," Maury says. "You're dreaming."

Switching on the table lamp between us, he kneels at the edge of my bed. His hand hovers above my head, as if he were a priest about to confer his blessing. I don't expect him to touch me, so it's a shock when he tightens his fingers on my scalp. "Is that better?" he asks.

"I'm fine."

"You had a bad nightmare."

"No, I wasn't asleep. I was thinking."

"You were groaning and grinding your teeth."

I don't argue. I lie there and let him hold on, reminded of the night in the gazebo when I laid my head in Deirdre Healy's lap and spilled my guts about the brother who now consoles me.

"You're okay," Maury says, and returns to his bed and kills the light.

"Sorry I woke you."

"I haven't been asleep yet."

"The coffee?" I suggest.

"I never sleep much. I don't like to dream. But you go right ahead."

As if following his instructions, I subside into sleep and uncapturable dreams, and don't wake until morning, roused by what sounds like an alarm clock. It's the telephone. Maury's bed is empty. In the bathroom the shower is drumming. "Hello," I croak.

"Are you all right?" Tamzin asks. "You sound sick."

"I don't know yet."

"I waited until nine your time. Did you have a hard night?"

"Is there another kind? My brother and I ate dinner at the International House of Pancakes. Then I drank all the Scotch in the hotel minibar."

"That bad, eh?" She's laughing. "Well, here's some good news. I found the quote you asked for."

I swing my legs over the side of the bed. A filament of sunlight outlines the closed curtains.

"You wanted something from an abusive mother's POV," she reminds me. "There's not much. Mothers in books are generally portrayed as nurturers, caregivers."

"The assignment was more or less a joke. Hope you didn't waste a lot of time."

"I'll invoice you for my hours." She's having me on—taking the piss, as the British put it. "I think a passage from Faulkner might suit your purposes."

"What are my purposes?"

"Your memoirs, darling," Tamzin teases me. "Listen to this and tell me whether it fits. It's from *As I Lay Dying*. The mother's dead and in a monologue from her coffin, she remembers beating her children: 'I would look forward to the times they faulted, so I could whip them. When the switch fell I could feel it upon my flesh; when it welted and ridged it was my blood that ran, and I would think with each blow of the switch: Now you are aware of me! Now I am something in your secret and selfish life, who have marked your blood with my own for ever and ever.'"

I don't know what to say.

"You think it's OTT?" Tamzin asks.

"No, it's not over the top. Reminds me of home."

"I hope you're kidding."

"I'll tell you about it sometime—how I became the man you see before you today."

"But I don't see you. When will I?"

"Things have gotten complicated. My mother decided yesterday was the perfect time to inform me that I have a different father from my brother and sister."

"You're not serious. *She's* not. Her mind must be going."

"She's as sharp as ever."

"Oh God, Quinn, are you all right?"

"I'm tempted to have you find a quote that'll tell me whether I am. But I'm finished with that."

"Finished." Her voice gets very small.

"Not with you. With other people's words. I have to see this through without a script."

Maury steps from the bathroom, fully clothed, right down to his Windbreaker. Maybe he showered in it.

"My brother's hungry. I have to go to breakfast. We'll speak later."

"Please," she says, "call me." Then she adds, "I love you."

Maury throws open the drapes, and sunlight sparkles on his wet-slicked hair. Although he seems to stare at the interstate with the same stolid fixity as he stared last night at the ceiling, he notices what I haven't. The light on the phone is blinking. Candy has left a message to call her at Lawrence's office.

"I've spoken with Mom," she says. "Today's Maury's turn. If you'll drop him off, I'll pick him up."

"Don't bother. I'll stay with him."

"No, she wants to talk to him alone."

"Do you suppose each of us has a different father?"

"That's not funny, Quinn. Listen, tell Maury that Mom has my number at work. Or if it's after five, he should phone me at home."

"Does he have the key to your place?"

"Yes, I gave him a spare."

"If you don't mind, I'll borrow it. I don't plan on hanging around the Hilton, waiting for them to refill the minibar. Better to go cold turkey at your townhouse."

"Has it been awful with Maury?"

"Not at all. I had a nightmare and he comforted me. I need more of that in my life."

# Maury

"Let's go back to the pancake place for breakfast," I say.

"Wouldn't you rather eat somewhere else?" Quinn asks. "Just for a change."

"I don't like change. I like things the same. I like what I ate last night and I'd like it again today."

"Okay, let's do it."

But when we get there, it's crowded and clanging with too many noises for me to imitate and we can't sit at the same table. The waitress tells me they don't have berries today, and I don't like it here anymore.

Quinn orders French toast, which is fried bread dunked in eggs and served with strips of burnt bacon. He takes two bites and shoves his plate away. He's quiet and drinks more coffee than I do. I bet he's remembering his nightmare. The way he screamed, it had to be the bad kind that lasts into the next day. I know the type and sometimes have them when I'm wide awake.

Without hair and with that morning puffiness around his eyes, Quinn looks old. Older than me. And that's how I think of him— as a big brother, the guy we go to for help. When I got paroled, he was just a little kid, twelve or thirteen. But he knew how to live in the world, like Cole knew how to live in prison, and I watched him and learned.

Back then, he was always talking. He joked and jabbered and made the rest of us laugh. Now he doesn't talk so much, except for his questions last night. They spun in my brain, like when you flip a bicycle upside down and spin the tire till the spokes blur into a circle that makes your eyes ache. You want to turn away, but you can't. Quinn asked so many questions I couldn't keep them straight and after he fell asleep, the blurry wheel went on spinning in the dark.

"Candy asked me to drop you at Mom's," Quinn says. "When you're finished there, call her and she'll pick you up."

"Finished what?"

"Whatever Mom has in mind."

Without the berries on top, I don't care for the color of my pancakes. They have the brown look of clay and taste like dirt until I pour on the syrup. Then they taste like sugar. "What's Mom have in her mind?" I ask.

"Oh, you know Mom. She's always thinking." He smiles, handing the waitress his card. "Didn't you say she had something to tell you and something to give you?"

"That's what she said on the phone."

"Well, you'll soon find out. Mom has Candy's numbers. If she's not at work, call her at home."

"Where will you be?"

"Candy's house. Which reminds me. Lemme have the key."

"Aren't you coming with me to Mom's?" The key is in my jeans, in the pocket with the toy bus and the rubber turtle. I stand up and squeeze my hand in there.

"She'd rather talk to you alone, like she did with me yesterday."

"What did she tell you? Maybe it's the same thing she'll tell me."

"We'll compare notes later."

After the waitress brings back his card and Quinn signs, we step outside and my shadow on the parking lot is blacker than the black-top. I'm relieved when Quinn lets me into the car until he switches the radio on. No music, only talk about terror and war and weapons. Listening to that, I can't keep straight what Mom might have to say.

The sunlight on her house is silver gray, the same color as the unshaved whiskers on my chin. The place needs painting and reshingling. There's rust dripping down the boards from the roof. My guess is the rain spouts are plugged with leaves. I could un-plug them and paint and fix the wood. And Mom's wreck of a car in the driveway, I could fix that too. It'd be no trouble to change the tires and oil and start the engine running again. But in this family nobody asks me to do the jobs I know how to do.

"I'll walk you to the door," Quinn says.

"I see it from here."

"You know, Mom won't answer unless you use the code."

"Three knocks, then one."

"You're set."

My feet are in my shadow until it floods under the shade of the front porch. I feel Quinn's eyes on me. I bang on the door, and his eyes bang on the back of my head. Then Mom opens up a crack, and I hear the car drive away. She tilts her head like an owl in a tree, leading with her big eye, the left one. She holds shut the collar of her housecoat and the sweater she wears on top of it. There's a broom in her other hand, and without unchaining the door, she sticks it through the crack, straw end first.

"That spiderweb in the corner of the porch," she says. "Up there between the post and the roof. I've been after Candy for months to sweep it down. I'm afraid the spider'll bite somebody."

"The cold kills them in winter."

"Don't count on it. Anyway, the sight of it makes me nauseous. Knock it down."

It's a tent caterpillar nest, not a spiderweb. I stab the broom at it. The gray sack splits open and out spill bits and pieces, dark as the overcooked bacon on Quinn's plate. It's baby caterpillars, all dead. I sweep them off the porch under the rosebushes, and Mom lets me in and leans the broom in a corner of the hallway.

She sits on the couch and folds her feet in her slippers up under her housecoat. I sit where Quinn sat yesterday, in the rocking chair. The smell is everyplace, and my hair is sticky like it has strings of caterpillar nest stuck in it.

"Are you enjoying your visit?" she says.

I tell her I am.

"I guess it's different in California."

I tell her it is.

"Me, I'd miss the change of seasons."

I tell her I do, too, even though I don't, except for snow.

"Do you have friends out there?"

"Nicky's my friend."

"Man or woman?"

"Woman."

"You oughta get married, a handsome fellow like you. Find a

gal to look after you. Have a family. It's never too late for a man."

"I'm friendly with the Mexicans, too. They take me to church."

"Careful who you chum around with." She lights a cigarette. That helps the smell. "Speaking of church, it wouldn't surprise me if Candy married Lawrence soon. What do you think?"

"About what?" Her questions spin the bicycle tire, blurring the spokes in a bright circle.

"Think he'll make a good husband?"

"I don't know what makes a good husband."

"Me neither." Mom laughs and coughs into a Kleenex. "We sure as hell never saw one around this house, did we?"

"I need to check on my boat."

"Your what?" She squinches her face, and the glasses slide down her nose.

"The boat I built in the attic. Is it still up there?"

"Damned if I know. It's been years since I risked that ladder."

"Be right back."

"Can't it wait? We've got things to talk about."

I head for the staircase, and she says, "I never did understand how you intended to haul it from the attic. It'd be like pulling a model boat out of a bottle. Something's bound to break."

On the second floor, I yank the cord that lowers the ladder. The spring groans loud like Quinn did last night, and the steps creak as I climb. I push open the hatch and switch on the bulb. It's hard to see through the dust. I want to hide here from Mom, like I did in the old days, staring up at the slanted roof and the shiny nail points. But the nails are rusty now and the boat is rotten down to its keel and ribs, like a cow skeleton in the desert. One touch and the last of the wood'll collapse in a puff. If I wanted to haul it from the attic, all I'd need is a broom. It'd sweep away as easy as the dead caterpillars. I close the hatch and go downstairs to listen to what Mom has to say.

She's flat on the sofa, a pillow under her head and another one on top of her chest with her arms crossed over it. She did that at Patuxent when Quinn was in her belly—crossed her arms over the big bump that Candy said moved from the baby's kicking.

"Sit beside me, sweetheart."

"I like the rocking chair," I say.

"No, I want you near me."

I do what she tells me, crouching at the edge of the sofa like I did on Quinn's bed last night. But I don't cup my hand to her head.

"It's been so nice having you home," she says. "Normally I don't have company."

"You have Candy."

"She's busy with Lawrence. Once they marry, they'll move away and play golf. You know what that means?"

I shake my head that I don't. I've seen golf on TV. I like the sound of the club hitting the ball. Nicky tried, but couldn't teach me how to keep score.

"They won't take me with them," Mom says.

"They told you that?"

"Not in so many words. But I wouldn't go even if they asked me to. I'm too old for North Carolina. I don't know a soul down there. I intend to die in my own house. Candy's been babysitting me long enough. She deserves to have her own life."

Half my butt has fallen asleep. The other half hanging over the edge starts to ache.

"That leaves me all alone," Mom says.

I begin to think this is the thing she called me to Maryland to tell me. I see what I have to do. "I'll talk to Nicky," I say. "She has space. You could live in her house. Or we could rent a trailer."

She jabs her glasses back up her nose. "I don't feature spending my last days in Slab City."

"It's nice in winter."

"Thanks anyway, sweetie. That's not for me."

"Then what'll you do?'

"Candy and Quinn plan to dump me in assisted living. If it's not bad enough dying in a roach nest, it costs money. I'll have to sell the house and waste my savings. There'll be nothing left for you. I told you I have something to give you. But if I go to assisted living, it'll eat up your money."

The bicycle tire is spinning faster. "You oughta live with Quinn in London."

"Fat chance! All his fancy friends around, he doesn't want to be stuck with an old woman that looks like death warmed over. Doesn't it burn your ass to lose the money I saved for you?"

"That's all right."

"I wanted to leave some for Candy too. Now she'll miss out."

"Lawrence is a dentist. He makes money."

"It's good for a married woman to have her own."

"Give her mine."

"What a love you are. But there won't be a penny left." One of her hands slips off the pillow and onto my arm. I pull back, but she holds tight. "You've always been so generous. Even as a little boy you shared everything with Candy. And you loved and helped me. I didn't have to ask. When I was in trouble, you protected me. You knew what to do then. You know now."

"No, I don't."

"Sure, you do. I need to die so Quinn can fly back to London and Candy can marry Lawrence and you can have the money that belongs to you."

"I don't want the money."

"Don't just think of yourself, dammit." Her different-colored eyes flash at me, and her fingernails dig into my arm. "Have some sympathy for Candy. Have some mercy on me."

"I don't understand."

"Yes, you do."

"I'll fix your car and paint your house, and we'll live here together."

"No, you're better off in California with Nicky. And I'll be better off once you take this pillow and press it over my face."

"I can't do that." My head starts to float with what she says.

"Why not?"

"You're my mother."

"You killed Dad."

"This is different." I feel like I need to get down on the floor.

"You killed your father but you won't kill me?" she shouts.

"I can't. I love you."

"Then do it for love."

I stand up and almost tip over.

"Sit down," she says real loud so that her big voice and her skinny body don't match.

"My head is messing with my brain."

"Trust me." She pats the sofa. "Sit down and let's talk this over. There's nothing to be scared of. I'm dying already. Let's just get it done with. I'd do it myself, but then they won't pay my insurance and I'll go to hell."

"I'll go to hell if I kill you."

"You can confess."

"They'll throw me in prison. This time I won't get out."

"I mean confess to a priest."

"They'll blame me." She keeps patting the couch beside her, and I keep backing away.

"Nobody'll blame you. I'm old and sick and they'll think I died in my sleep."

"No, they'll accuse me of killing you for your money."

"Who'll accuse you?"

"The cops."

"You don't have to tell them a damn thing."

"They're smart and they've got tricks. This time they'll gas me."

"No, no, no. Listen to me, goddammit. You're making me cuss. You're making me lose my soul. Is that what you want? You want to condemn me to hell?" she hollers. "Okay! I'll do it myself and you'll have that on your conscience because you're too selfish."

She mashes the pillow over her nose and mouth. Her arms shake, and she moans like I do.

"Stop!" I grab the pillow, but she won't let go. I lift her clean off the couch. She weighs nothing and has no strength so she loses her grip and falls to the floor. I bend down to help her up, but she comes at me like a sidewinder, hissing, "You son of a bitch. Gimme back my pillow!"

I run to the front door. She's on her feet now, following me. Her glasses hang cockeyed off her nose, and her fists clench to wallop me. I keep on going outside, through the rosebushes and onto the dead grass in the yard. The pillow is still in my hand. Mom hobbles onto the porch in her slippers and housecoat. The door slams behind her and she hollers, "You goddamn killer retard. Now look what you made me do."

Up and down the block, her yelling brings people to their windows and doors. Their worried faces turn our way. Next thing they'll be dialing 911 because Mom's screaming bloody murder. Then she runs at me, stepping right out of her slippers. I let go of the pillow and hurry into the trees left over from the woods where I caught frogs and lizards. Those that aren't dead are underground for winter. The creek is underground forever. But I know a path and a place to hide at the tree where I had a house, a little box that Dad nailed to the branches. It's gone now, and the hammer marks on the oak have healed over into scars, so the tree looks wounded. I catch my breath and as soon as I'm sure Mom isn't after me, I run on out the other side of the woods.

## Candy

As a girl, I dreamed about becoming a nurse. Because of Maury. It never dawned on me to become a doctor. Girls didn't do that in my day. But being a nurse, I believed, I'd learn what was wrong with him and how to cure it. The closest I've come is working in a dentist's office, which at least led me to Lawrence. God works in strange ways.

When by the end of the day Maury hasn't called the office, I drive to the townhouse where Quinn's in the kitchen opening a bottle of wine with a brand new Screwpull. The label reads pinot noir, which I know means black, but the wine is ruby red. He pours himself a glass and drinks it off in a single gulp.

"Thought you were going cold turkey," I say.

"The road to home is paved with good intentions."

He sets out a glass for me, and I signal him to pour an inch. That's my limit. Since I have to pick up Maury I'm afraid to drink too much.

The kitchen's fluorescent lights don't flatter Quinn. He looks haggard, like this might not be his first drink of the day. His black-and-gray outfit, which I guess is fashionable in London, gives him the grim appearance of a funeral director.

"How was work?" he asks.

"Work's the easy part. I get to be with Lawrence."

"That's nice." Deep weariness dulls his voice.

"What about you? How'd you spend the day?" I ask.

"Hanging out at the mall. Judging by the crowd, it's a regular elephant burial ground for retirees. They loll around the fountain listening to the slow drip. I browsed at Barnes & Noble, had a latte at Starbucks and made up my mind not to spend my golden years in Maryland."

"Do actors retire?"

"Not if they can help it. In England there's a tradition of dying onstage. Literally. But if you don't get parts, it's as bad as being dead already."

"You get parts," I say.

"That's another thing I did today—I called my agent. I'm up for a role in a BBC special. A trilogy of Greek plays."

"Great!"

"Maybe not so great. There's been some complaining that Aeschylus might be too depressing. Probably they'll perk up the script by putting kittens and puppies in the House of Atreus."

Now I have no doubt Quinn's been drinking.

"It won't be long," he says, "before I'm cast as an aging uncle or doddering grandfather."

"Doesn't sound bad to me. I'd like to be a grandmother." I don't add the obvious—that I'd love to have been a mother. "At least you've got that to look forward to. You could have kids, then grandkids."

His response is to pour himself a second glass of wine.

"Ever think of that?" I prompt him, even though, honestly, I've never imagined him married with children. I can't picture him in a domestic setting.

"Recently I haven't done much thinking about the future. I've been preoccupied with the past."

"I know you're writing your memoirs. But you have to live in the present."

"The past is the present, isn't it?" he asks in a voice that convinces me he's quoting somebody. "It's the future too."

I tip the wine to my lips and have to resist the urge to chug it down. This is something I hadn't counted on—that Quinn might come home and fall apart, rather than rescue me.

"I have a young girl working for me, doing research," he rambles on. "I asked her to find a literary quote about mothers who abuse their children. One from the woman's point of view."

"I thought this book was going to be about your career."

"Who knows what it'll be about? Now it's piles of notes and scenes. My researcher, Tamzin, that's her name, turned up a passage from Faulkner. The gist of it is a woman speaking from the grave, confessing how she beat her kids to brand them as her property forever. Do you think that's what Mom had in mind?"

"Why go over it again? Half the time she doesn't even remember hitting us."

"But you remember. I do. I bet Maury does."

"I wouldn't say she abused us." I'm having trouble hiding my irritation. I take another taste of the wine, and it's warm, almost body temperature. "She was a single mother with no money and a bunch of stress and sometimes she lost her temper. That's all."

"That's enough, isn't it? I mean, it's worse being knocked around by your mother than your father."

"A man would pack a harder wallop," I remind him.

"But you don't expect it from your mother. Anyway, for me it was never about how hard she hit or how often. It was *why*. What was so wrong with me?"

"Listen, Quinn, nothing was wrong with you. It was just her and her moods. It's too late to change the past. We need to discuss what to do with her now."

"You think packing her off to assisted living is the answer? That's supposed to solve everything?"

"Not everything!" My voice cracks. I lean toward him across the table and start over again quieter. "But it'll solve the one thing we have to deal with here and now."

"You want to talk about here and now? Okay, here and now, I love Mom and I hate her." He leans across the table, too, his head nearly touching mine. "I blame her and I forgive her. I'm grateful for what she gave me and I regret everything I never had."

"Jesus, Mary, and Joseph!" I explode. "This is me, Candy, your sister you're talking to. Not your researcher. Not your shrink."

Quinn's face goes in an instant from agony to absolute blankness. Unlike Mom, whose expression shows every step of anger from mild exasperation to total fury, he kills the light in his eyes and brings down the curtain.

I hold his hand. "Let's not fight. In this family, you're all I have. The only one I can talk to. I'm sorry about how you feel."

Again his response is to refill his glass, then mine. Because he's pouring left-handed, the bottle shakes and a few drops splash the Formica.

"I should call Mom," I say. "She must be finished with Maury by now." But the moment I reach for the phone, somebody bangs at the front door. So I go to answer it. A black man in sweat pants and an XXL Redskins jersey has his beefy arm around Mom's scrawny shoulders. She's shivering in her housecoat and hugging a pillow to her chest.

"Is this you momma?" he asks.

"My God, yes."

"Found her in the yard, in her slippers and such. Said she's locked outta her house."

Mom appears to be frozen speechless until she sees Quinn step out of the kitchen. "It was a mistake," she whimpers. "A misunderstanding."

"I live next door to her," the man says. "Lucky I do. She coulda caught pneumonia wandering around outside."

"I wasn't wandering," Mom protests. "I was hunting for Maury."

"Where is he?" Quinn asks.

"He ran off and I couldn't find him."

"Ran off?" I ask.

"We had an argument." She shrugs off the man's arm and shuffles into the house.

"She oughta hide a key under the doormat," the man says. "Case of an emergency."

"Thanks for your help," Quinn says.

I take Mom's hand—it's like ice—and lead her to the kitchen. She can't stop shivering. Or maybe shaking with rage. "Goddamn Maury," she fumes. "He gets a bug up his ass and there's no reasoning with him." Then she spots the bottle of pinot noir, and that steams her more. "Are you two drinking in the middle of the day?"

"It's evening," says Quinn, joining us. "Have a glass. It'll thaw you out."

"Damned if I will. I had to deal with your father drunk at all hours. Now it's my kids." She removes her foggy glasses and polishes them on the pillowcase.

"What's the pillow for?" Quinn asks.

"I grabbed it when I went after Maury. I was going to slap him silly."

He chuckles. "That's not your style—a powder puff. Where's the hairbrush or that stick you used on me?"

"You're lucky I don't have it now," she snaps, but without her glasses her eyes are watery and mild.

"What were you and Maury fighting about?" I ask.

"It wasn't a fight. More a disagreement. I asked him to do me a favor. He turned me down flat and slammed out of the house."

"Did you say something mean?"

"I said, 'Do me a favor.' That's what I said."

"What favor?"

"That's between him and me." She thrusts the glasses back on and looks her normal belligerent self.

"Where did he go?"

"Into the woods. Damned if I'd chase him there and twist an ankle in a snake hole."

"I'd better look for him," Quinn says.

"No, I'll do it," I say. "I've got a key to Mom's house. You two stay here where it's warm."

"Don't believe a word he tells you," Mom calls after me. "And bring my cigarettes when you come back."

"Anything else, Your Highness?"

"You two are crocked. How many glasses have you had?"

As I limp out to the car, my leg aches, my heart hammers off-key, my breath comes quick and shallow. The state I'm in, it's a miracle I don't swerve off the highway and into the homebound lane of traffic. Still, I'm glad I'm the one looking for Maury—and not just because Quinn's drunk and shouldn't drive. I'm afraid of what Mom said to Maury. I'm afraid the favor she asked of him is the one she's hinted at with me.

On Mom's street the other houses look lived in—lights in the windows, jungle gyms and sliding boards out front, new cars in the driveway. But hers has that zombie stillness of a "silent neighbor," one of those pretend houses where the power company stores its meters and equipment. All that's missing is a Keep Out sign with the red stick figure of an electrocuted man.

I pray Maury will be waiting, shamefaced, on the front porch. He's not. I check the broken-down Chevy Nova in case he climbed into it to escape the freezing wind. He's not there either. I leave the sidewalk and cross the lawn. The ground plays tricks on me, and I stub my boots on tufted grass.

I hesitate at the edge of the backyard thicket of blackberry and honeysuckle vines where Maury burrowed caves as a kid. In this season the dead vines drape like spiderwebs from the trees. I don't relish stumbling around in there any more than Mom did. So I stand at the edge and shout, "Maury, it's me. Everything's okay. You don't need to be scared."

I'm the one that sounds scared. Scared of the shadows in this creepy place. Scared Maury may have hurt himself. Scared of what Mom asked him to do.

"No one's mad at you," I yell. "Come on out now."

I'm put in mind of many occasions when Maury hid from Mom and Dad in the woods, his feelings bruised by something they said, or more likely, the seat of his pants warm from a whipping. After they calmed down, they'd send me to tell Maury the coast was clear. He never believed me at first, and I'd have to plead with him. Half the time, I wondered why he'd ever leave his burrow. Better to live in those caves of vines than in the house.

"Mom's at my place with Quinn," I call to him. "She's not mad at you. She didn't mean it," I add, even though I fear that she did.

I holler and wheedle until a back porch light blinks on at a neighbor's house and a woman cranes her neck around the door and glares at me. "I'll be inside, Maury. I'll wait for you there."

Maybe he picked the front door lock. They learn that in prison, don't they? But when I let myself in, there's no sign of my brother. I shout his name and search the ground floor—living room, dining room alcove, and closet. When I flick on the kitchen light, roaches scatter, then regroup. Mom makes so little use of the place the roaches have lost their fear. They're just shocked to see a human being. I haven't set foot in here for years and I don't linger now. This is the last spot Maury's likely to hide.

I have a brainstorm and head for the attic. It's hard for me to climb the ladder, and I nearly fall as I push open the rusty-hinged trapdoor. Then I teeter and have to catch myself a second time when I see his boat's there but not him. The dry-rotted boards are as pale as skeleton bones.

Decades of summer heat and winter cold have turned everything to sawdust. A single spark and the attic would burst into flames. Something else for me to lose sleep over. Another problem for Mom to ignore. I back down the ladder, and the hatch bangs shut behind me.

Off-limits in recent years, Mom's bedroom is where I go last and stay longest. I glance under her bed. No Maury. Nothing but balled Kleenexes and carpet fuzz. I check the bathroom, but he's not in his old refuge. The tub's empty except for a scampering silverfish.

Back in the bedroom, every object is recognizable from my childhood. Rosary beads and holy cards on the night table. The windup clock, its numbers nearly invisible with age. A tarnished silver mirror whose backing has flaked off in a salt-and-pepper pattern.

One thing's different, though. There's a battery-powered tape machine, the type they don't manufacture now that everything's gone digital. Beside it is a stack of tapes—Dick Haymes, Tommy Dorsey, Frank Sinatra, and the Maguire sisters.

Sadness shoots through me at the thought of Mom lying here alone at night listening to songs from the forties, tunes that she and Dad danced to. In self-defense I whisper the line she's often lashed me with: *It's your own damn fault.*

But her fault for what? For being lonely? For growing old and nostalgic? For preferring to live in the past and in her own head? How would assisted living change that? Only dying will.

I limp downstairs and sob on the phone to Lawrence.

"Would you like me to drive over and wait with you?" he asks.

"I can't sit around. Maury's not in the woods. He'd have heard me. He's not in the house. I've got to go look for him."

"We'll look together."

"I don't know where to start."

"Try places he's been in the past few days," he says. "Church. The bus station. That restaurant on the river."

Lawrence's steadiness is a balm to my soul. But I tell him I'd rather search for Maury on my own.

"Let me help you, honey," he says.

"It'll be quicker this way." I need to keep Maury to myself until I find out what went wrong between Mom and him.

• • •

Since the church is close by and Maury could have reached it easily on foot, I drive there first. But if he counted on sanctuary, he's out of luck. The soaring A-frame is locked, and except for votive candles not a single light is on inside. I circle the building on foot to make sure he isn't crouching next to it out of the wind. I don't bother ringing the rectory doorbell. Maury would never ask strangers for help and I don't care to find myself face to face with a priest, trying to explain the situation.

Wind buffets my Honda as I park at the bus station where Quinn and I picked up Maury a couple of days ago. I felt safe and inconspicuous then. But now I cross the lot conscious of my bad leg and white skin. Black boys in ball caps bop around in their drooping blue jeans. Unfazed by the freezing night, Asian and Hispanic girls strut and preen, their tummies bare, jewels winking in their navels.

In the waiting room the plastic chairs are full of passengers—or are they homeless bums?—and piled belongings. Maury couldn't bear the noise and the crowd. Still, I clomp up one aisle and down the next, searching.

Outside the men's room I pause, thinking he might be in there. The smells, the fizzing lights, the shouts, the faces, the tattoos and scars—suddenly I feel that I've been through all this before. When it hits me where, I bolt from the bus station, convinced that Maury has hitchhiked to Patuxent to visit his friend.

Plunked in the middle of a treeless field, the prison is lit like an airport. Spotlights crisscross the big flat yard and glint on the barbed wire. In the gatehouse, behind the thick glass door, uniformed guards glide with the slow motion of underwater swimmers. They notice me, but because it's not visiting hours they pay no heed to my knocking. I shout that I have a question, a single question, nothing more. They pretend not to hear me, and when I act out a pantomime of begging, pressing my hands together in prayer, they go on ignoring me.

With its bright lights inside, the gatehouse door looks like it'd be hot. But when I lean my forehead against it, the glass is cold as a glacier. Mom would break it down or bloody her knuckles in the effort. More easily defeated, I trudge back to the car.

It's then I notice my brother at the far edge of the asphalt, hands jammed in his pockets, hair whipping around his face. "Maury," I call. "Come get warm."

I flick on the Honda's heater full blast. He slouches around to the passenger's side with the defeated look of one of those men at an intersection holding a sign saying, "Will work for food." For a minute we sit in near silence. There's only the chattering of our teeth and the whir of the heater.

"Why are you here?" I ask.

"I don't know."

"Is it to visit your friend?"

"My friend's dead."

"How do you know? Did the guards say so?"

"They didn't talk to me. I just know."

"We'll find out this Sunday."

"I won't be here."

"Well, not if you don't want to be," I say. "Look, Mom's locked out of her house. A neighbor drove her to my place."

Maury warms his face at a heat vent, his hair blowing flat on his head.

"She says you two argued."

He leans away from the vent. "I don't want to talk about it."

"Okay. But we better get back."

"Where?"

"To drive Mom home."

"I don't want to see her." For Maury, who rarely speaks with much emotion, this sounds close to anguish. "I'll stay at Quinn's hotel."

"He's not there." I swing around on the parking lot, and when the wind catches us broadside, it rocks the car. "He's with Mom."

"I'll wait for him outside."

"It's too cold."

"I'll wait in a chair in the lobby." Maury clamps his hands between his knees and stares into the high beams of onrushing cars. "I planned to catch a bus home. But I don't have any money on me."

"Home?"

"Slab City. Nicky's."

"You weren't going to say good-bye to us? Look, you don't have to leave. We'll work this out."

"I don't want to see Mom," he says again.

I take him at his word and drive to the Hilton. The swarming headlights that seem to hypnotize Maury unnerve me. When I phone Quinn from the lobby, I'm jangled and my voice sounds wrong. So does his. "Has Mom said anything about Maury and what happened?"

"She's on the couch," Quinn says. "Resting. Sleeping."

"Is she all right?"

"Has she ever been all right?"

"You sound as frazzled as Maury."

"I'll tell the front desk to let you into my room. Stay there with Maury. We'll sort out things tomorrow."

"You're not making sense. What did Mom say?"

"Can't talk now. It'll wake her up." He cuts the line.

I debate whether to call back and warn him. I owe Quinn that much. He deserves to know. But know what? I'm not positive what Mom asked Maury.

I collect a swipe card at the reception desk and reassure Maury that it's all right to use Quinn's room. In the elevator, he rivets his eyes on the rising floor numbers and whispers, "The rope is made of steel."

The spread on one bed has been turned down and a chocolate gleams on the pillow. Maury says it's candy and offers it to me. When I shake my head no, he slips it into his already bulging pocket.

"Are you hungry?" I ask.

"My stomach hurts." He sags onto the couch, zipped up in his Windbreaker.

I bring him a Coke from the minibar. But when I hand it to him, his shoulders start shuddering and his face is wet. "What's wrong?" I sit close, but not touching him.

"Mom," he blubbers.

All our lives that one word has been enough. Neither of us ever needed to say more. Yet Maury goes on, "She called me a retard and a killer."

"Oh, that's terrible. That's cruel." But by Mom's standards not out of the ordinary.

"She wants to die." He clamps his hands between his knees like he did in the car. "She told me to hold a pillow over her face."

I jerk to my feet so quick, Maury jumps too. "She's not in her right mind," I say. "She's sicker than we thought. Stay here. I'll straighten this out. If you get hungry, call room service."

"Do they have pictures?"

"Of what?"

"The food."

"I don't know, Maury. Order a hamburger and fries. You know what they look like."

He rubs the heel of his hand at his tears. "Don't tell Mom what I told you."

# Quinn

The moment Candy drives off to look for Maury, Mom's attitude changes. Her tone, her tune, the set of her sloped shoulders all pick up, as if her daughter's presence had constrained her natural sprightliness. "It's been ages since I've tasted wine." She grins conspiratorily and sips Candy's glass. "How bad can it be for me?"

"Red is good for your heart."

"My heart, like the rest of me, is a mess."

"You're not a mess," I protest, presuming that's what she wants to hear.

"Oh yes, I am. Physically, emotionally, spiritually—any way you look at it, I'm a wreck."

"You look fine."

"Don't BS me, Quinn. You and I have always been honest with each other," she blithely unburdens herself of a whopping lie. I long ago lost track of the numerous untruths that mine the ground between us. "That darkie who drove me here talked to me like I'm senile. But don't you do it."

She downs some pinot noir, then pats at her hair, which the wind has beaten into spiky wires. "I was worried being out in the cold might bring on one of my panic spells."

"Funny. I can't picture you panicked. I don't think I've ever seen you scared."

She chuckles. "That's because you were too scared to notice. As a kid, every time you passed me you ducked."

"Yeah, that's one of my golden childhood memories." Following her lead, I keep it light, playful. "You always kept me guessing when you'd take a swing."

"The truth is—" Her face abruptly darkens, her voice drops an octave. "—I've been terrified my entire life."

"I don't believe you."

"Trust me." She cants her head in a challenging cyclopean fashion, favoring the big brown eye. The wine—or is it the dispute with Maury and her brush with spending the night outdoors?— hasn't just made her feisty. It's put her in a ruminative frame of mind. But unlike those oldsters who dwell on an idealized past, she dredges up a litany of woes, of crippling accidents in her family and premature deaths of friends from diseases now cured with a single shot or pill. "People forget what it was like in those terrible days," she says.

Lament follows lament. Yet I'm strangely lulled by the anecdotes. As usual, as long as she's talking, I feel safe; the flow of words feels almost like love.

"What scared me most as a little girl," Mom scrolls further back in time, "was lugging the garbage pail down to the cellar after dinner. We kept the trash cans between the furnace and the coal bin, and it was dark in that corner. I'd hear rats skittering around.

"When it got to where I couldn't stand it anymore," she says, "I stopped halfway to the trash can and emptied the pail in the coal bin and buried the slop under chunks of coal. It was winter, so the smell didn't reach upstairs to the rest of the house. Long as I was the one to stoke the furnace, nobody noticed a thing."

Pausing, she sips the wine, her timing as impeccable as that of a seasoned actress. "But the first warm spell in spring cooked my goose. You couldn't miss the stink. My mother bustled down to the cellar and straightaway huffed back up the steps. 'Wait till your father gets home,' she said. And I had all day to fret over what he'd do."

In another theatrical gesture, she lifts the glass and sniffs its bouquet. Duly prompted, I ask, "What did he do?"

"He called me into his bedroom, took off his belt, and told me to pull down my drawers. I was eleven, old enough that this was humiliating. I pleaded and cried and explained that I was scared of the dark and the rats. He said, 'I'll teach you to be scared.' Then he beat my butt red.

"I suppose he meant to teach me to be scared of him, not the dark. But I learned a different lesson. I learned if you're scared you better not show it."

While there's much to admire from a professional angle, Mom's Hallmark card performance grates a little. The script's too neat, the message aimed too blatantly at the heartstrings. When I offer neither praise nor encouragement, she says, "I've been doing that ever since. Hiding my feelings. Hiding my fears."

"Don't we all."

"Some of us a hell of a lot more than others. Am I boring you, Quinn?"

"Not a bit. I was trying to picture you as an innocent young girl."

"This wine's gone straight to my head. Why'd you let me drink it?" Bracing her palms on the table, she pushes herself to her feet. "I better lie down."

Cradling the pillow, she wobbles into the living room. I'm free to join her. Or be a bastard and stay here. Reluctantly, I leave the bottle and trail after Mom.

She's lying on the couch with the pillow under her head. She might be a patient composing herself for a session with a shrink. Her arms are rigid at her sides, her legs crossed at the ankle. I deposit myself in a chair beyond her sightline. The resemblance to my appointments with Dr. Rokoko would be complete were it not for her ratty housecoat and the copies of *Modern Maturity* and *Consumer Reports* on the coffee table.

"Move around where I can see you," Mom orders.

I do as she demands, perching uncomfortably on a corner of the coffee table.

"I guess you're wondering why Maury and I argued."

"You made it clear that's between you and him."

"He's probably already blabbed to Candy. You deserve to hear it too."

"We're beyond that, aren't we, Mom? Worrying what we do or don't deserve?"

She stretches out a hand and clamps onto my knee, destroying any illusion of therapeutic boundaries. "He's shook up because I asked him to kill me."

"Jesus, Mom!"

She grips my knee tighter. The veins on her wrist engorge in high relief. "Don't take the Lord's name in vain."

"I hope it's not in vain. I'm praying you didn't do that."

"Well, save your prayers. I did."

"How could you?"

"Who the hell else am I supposed to ask? Candy has her head in the clouds these days. She doesn't care about anything or anybody

except Lawrence. And you're not the type to get his hands dirty."
She speaks as if she were asking for no more than gardening help.
"You're so concerned about Maury's tender feelings, ever stop to
consider mine? You know I'm fed up with life. You know I can't
look after myself. You know I hate the idea of wasting my savings
on assisted living."

"I told you I'd pay for everything."

"I don't want everything. I want one thing. I want to die before
it's too late."

"You're a Catholic. You should believe it's never too late. It's
up to God when you die."

"Don't lecture me about Catholicism." Her eyes blaze behind her
lopsided glasses. "You don't even go to Communion."

"I'm not the one who wants to die."

"You will. Mark my words, one day you will. And I hope to
Christ your kids don't abandon you like mine have."

"Nobody's abandoning you. We're all still waiting on you hand
and foot. What more do you want?"

She yanks the pillow from under her head and pushes it at me.
"Smother me."

I shove it right back at her, and she hugs it to her chest like a baby
and breaks into great gulping sobs. "Wait until you're old," she says.

"I don't have long to wait."

"Wait until you're alone."

"You're not alone. You're cut off. That's your choice, not
mine." My impatience has given way to piercing anger. "You're
the one that abandoned us. God forbid that we might need you.
It's hard enough getting you to answer the phone or the front
door."

She wilts and for once seems to be weighing what I've said.

"You're right. I'm an awful mother. Please put me out of my misery. I'd do it myself, but that'd condemn my soul to hell."

"What about my soul?"

"You can go to confession afterward. You have all the time in the world to repent."

"What about my sanity? Having murder on my conscience?"

"A guilty conscience might bring you back to the sacraments."

"So this is all for my sake?"

"Don't be such a smart aleck. Sooner or later, you have to make peace with the Lord."

"I'd rather make peace with you," I say.

"We're not at war. We've had our differences, our disagreements. Nothing we can't patch up." Her voice turns treacly. "Come here on the couch beside me."

As much as I might complain about her detachment and the distance between us, I'm more fearful of being close to her. I never know what she'll do. I'm never sure what she'll ask of me and what my answer should be. Still, I move over to the sofa.

"Lie down," she says.

"There's no room."

"Sure there is. I'm skinny as a minute and don't take up any space."

I lie back, precariously balanced, half on the couch, half off it. Her body radiates no heat, and the hand she latches onto mine feels dry and fragile.

"Remember how we did this when you couldn't sleep?" she says. "I'd stretch out beside you and we'd talk. Even when you were a little boy we had wonderful conversations. You always understood me."

"Since we're on the same wavelength, Mom, tell me something. What is it about me that makes you believe I'll do what Candy and Maury won't do?"

"You're different."

"You mean I'm the heartless type who'd murder his own mother."

"I mean you're strong, decisive, merciful. Candy's scared of her own shadow. Maury's afraid too. I told him I'm leaving him money in my will. So he's worried the cops'll suspect he had a motive."

"And I don't have a motive?"

"Correct. I'm not leaving you a cent. And if the cops ever questioned you, you'd have them eating out of your hand. Maury, he'd fall to pieces, just like last time."

"Yeah, last time," I say, then go silent. It assumes a shape, a palpable weight, this silence. It slowly presses things to a single sharp point.

Mom stirs beside me. "I suppose you read the papers in the cedar chest. I left them there for you."

"I guessed that. What I haven't figured out is why."

"You get to be my age, close to the end, you like to put your affairs in order. Fill in all the blanks."

"There are still plenty left. I didn't notice your statement. Didn't you give one?"

"The cops asked some questions."

"So what did you tell them? Did it happen the way Maury described?"

She springs to a sitting position, like a puppet from a box. "What's that got to do with what we're discussing? You think I enjoy going over it again and again?"

"You've *never* been over it with me. The one time I asked, you cracked my head against a wall."

"I was a couple of years younger, that's what I'd do now."

"I bet you would. You ask an awful lot for somebody who never gives."

"Never gives? I gave you life. I gave you love. I gave you opportunities. A damn sight more than your brother and sister ever got. Why are you torturing me?"

"I'm not torturing you. I'm saying you're one-sided. You ask for a final favor. And such a small one! But you won't even talk to me about Dad's death."

"Shit on this." She tries to stand up; I pull her back onto the couch. "Get your hands off me!" she screams. "I'm not bargaining with you."

"Of course you are. That's what this is. That's why you left Maury's papers for me to see. It was your opening bid."

"What kind of monster, what kind of doubting Thomas, have you turned into?" She's straining to break free.

"The kind whose mother taught him never to trust anybody."

"I feel like I raised a snake. Why are you doing this to me?" She stops struggling and rolls onto her side, pulling her knees to her chest. The slippers drop from her pitiful, swollen feet.

"I sacrificed everything for you three kids," she wails. "I loved you and didn't want to lose you. Now look how it turns out. You hate me and I've lost everything."

"I don't hate you, and it's up to you how things turn out." Then I wait, and the solid block of silence resettles.

Turtling her neck, Mom slowly raises her head. "If I tell you, will you do what I asked?"

"Let me hear what you have to say. I'm not making any promises."

When she buries her face in the upholstery, I fear I've lost her. But in a muffled voice she says, "Hope you're not squeamish. This is more than any child should know about his parents. Jack and I never had a peaceful marriage, but the sexual part was strong. We went at it most nights. When I was pregnant with you, though, he calculated you couldn't be his. He kept track of his bets on the calendar and he figured he'd been on a bender for days around the time I got knocked up. He wanted me to have an abortion. But I said hell, no."

"I thought that was Tom Trythall."

"They both pressured me." With her face against the upholstery, her words sound slurred, as if coming from an old radio speaker. "That's what Jack and I were fighting about that day—whether you'd be born or not. Candy had gone off to a movie, but Maury was home, listening to the blow-by-blow."

"Dad was hitting you?"

"No. I smacked him. It wasn't a love tap either. He just grinned to make me madder. He had this trashy habit of staggering home half-crocked and washing up in the kitchen sink. So he didn't have a shirt on. I went on yelling at him and he went on sponging himself. Afterward he was as likely to kiss me and carry me off to bed as he was to grab and shake the daylights out of me."

There's a catch in her voice. "The thing of it is," she says, "I was holding the butcher knife. To get his attention. I'd done it before— waved a knife around and threatened to chase him out of the house unless he changed his ways. Normally he'd sweet-talk me. But this time . . . I don't know."

She starts to rock, like Maury. "I don't remember stabbing him. I honestly don't. In my mind's eye, he bellies up to the butcher knife and it just slides into him. Like times when we were drunk and dancing naked in the dark and suddenly he slipped inside me. Simple as that. He groaned and his eyes got real wide. Then they shut. I pulled out the knife and the blood started gushing like water from a fountain. It splashed all over me. I screamed, and Maury ran into the kitchen and started screaming too. He grabbed the butcher knife, and I grabbed it back. He grabbed it a second time, and I went to call the ambulance.

"By the time I came back, Maury was on the floor beside Jack. At first the rescue squad didn't know how many were dead. Maury and Dad looked like two corpses laid out on a slab. But when they felt for a pulse, Maury went nuts at being touched and thrashed and kicked. It took three of them to wrestle away the knife and pin him down.

"Maury yelled at them, 'He was hurting her. He was always hurting her.' The cops handcuffed him, and before I could say a word, they dragged him out of the house and tossed him into a squad car. That's the last I saw of him until that night in jail. Detectives took me upstairs for questioning. Wouldn't even let me change my clothes. I was blood-soaked to the skin. Meantime the ambulance crew was in the kitchen working on Jack. But it was too late. I could have told them that."

"What did you tell them instead?"

"Who?"

"The detectives."

"They asked so many questions, I don't recall all I said. Basically it's what I told you—Jack bellied up to the knife and next thing I knew it was in him."

"I don't suppose you mentioned that the knife was in your hand, not Maury's?"

She rocks harder in a negative shake of her head. "A cop from the squad car rushed upstairs and said Maury already confessed. I saw then how things stood, how they were slipping away from me. The state I was in, the only chance of this situation working out, I thought, was to let things take their course."

"You mean"—I squeeze her hip to stop her from rocking—"let your son take the rap."

With a gust of her old belligerence, she asks, "What was I supposed to do? I thought the best thing was to claim Maury was defending me."

"And what did you expect the police to do? Pat him on the back?"

"I expected them to put him in a mental hospital where he'd get treatment—which he damn well needed. I never in a million years thought they'd indict him for first-degree murder. But the state doctor examined Maury and said he knew right from wrong and could stand trial."

She flips onto her back, and her voice gains firmness as she goes on. "I went to the pastor and confessed the truth, and he swore he wouldn't give me absolution unless I set the police straight. So I admitted to them I was the one with the knife. But they didn't believe me. They accused me of being a good mother, taking the blame for her son."

I switch from the couch to the chair. My every emotion is undermined by skepticism. I should be shocked, horrified. But how much of her story can I believe? I wouldn't put it past her to trick me into euthanizing her. "Why didn't you go public and plead for your son?"

"Jesus, Quinn, that's something you'd do in a movie. This was real life. I wanted to help Maury, not make a spectacle of myself."

"You should have helped him by saying he wasn't a murderer."

"I did. Every Sunday at Patuxent I said, 'I love you. You're not a murderer.'"

"But he still believes he did it."

"You think it wouldn't have made him crazier to know he was behind bars for a crime he didn't commit?"

She doesn't let me answer; she bulldozes on. "Besides, I had Candy to worry about, and a baby—you!—on the way. I had to scrape together the money for Maury's plea bargain and a transfer to Patuxent where he had doctors and a chance for parole. Of course you'd have talked to the newspapers, you'd go on TV. And with your gift of gab, maybe you'd persuade people. But then what? Say the cops did believe I killed Jack, I'd have gone to prison. Then what would have happened to you and Candy? Hell, what would have happened to Maury? You think you'd all have been happier growing up in an orphanage or being split up and adopted by strangers? Well, do you? I can't hear you." She flaps at her ear. "It's easy to claim you shouldn't live a lie, but sometimes lies are all that let us go on living."

I pitch out of the chair and prowl the room, desperate to set distance between my mother and me. I'm choking on our closeness. Even the thousands of miles between Maryland and London may never be enough to let me breathe again, to let me digest what she has said and make sense of what she goes on saying.

"Day and night all I did was lie. One minute I was lying to the police, the next to Maury's lawyer, then his head doctor, then the pastor. And the whole time I had to remember what I told this person and that. It was as bad as being a little girl again, down in the cellar with the garbage bucket, hiding it here, hiding it there, scared I'd get caught and punished. Knowing that's what I deserved. Hating myself for being such a chickenshit. Hating you kids even though I loved you. Terrified by these nightmares where I murdered you and Candy by mistake."

I don't know whether to be appalled or to applaud this bravura performance. Mom's operatic scenery eating is all the more re-markable because she's flat on her back, barely moving, a wizened, white-haired woman croaking a last aria that I haven't a clue how to interpret. She has morphed into a combination of Agamemnon and Clytemnestra—a tragic figure who both sacrificed a child and killed her mate—and yet all the while she remains my mother, a tiny, untidy, loving, hateful, scheming, sad human being.

"Now you're probably thinking," she says, "okay, she didn't confess to Maury, but why didn't she own up to me and Candy? Well, I figured you had enough to cope with. Why heap on more? And if I told you, I was afraid I'd be left with nothing. It was a long shot, the kind Jack used to lose his shirt on. But considering the odds, I believed I did the right thing. You and Candy haven't had it so bad, and Maury isn't doing life in prison. That's about the best we could hope for. I'm the only one that lost out. Candy stayed with me, but hates me. You boys ran as far as you could get and you hate me too."

"I don't hate you."

"I don't buy that. I only hope you hate me enough to keep your end of the bargain." She hands me the pillow.

"I can't."

"Yes, you can."

"Did you make up this story to drive me to murder?"

"I didn't make up a damn thing. You asked for the truth. Now you've got it." Removing her glasses, she folds them on her chest, interlaced with her nicotine-stained fingers like rosary beads on the deceased's hands at a Catholic wake. With her eyes shut and her off-white hair in a halo around her head, she resembles a relic in a medieval church, some obscure saint, preserved, yet disheveled after centuries on display. The sight of her, to all appearances already dead, paralyzes me.

"If you won't do it for me," she breaks the silence, "then do it for Maury and Candy so they'll have a little money. Do it for yourself so you can get on with your life and give us grandkids."

I kneel next to the couch. The wine has churned to vinegar in my stomach. I feel drunk, hung over, and achingly sober at the same time. "Are you sure?" My voice quavers, my hands shake. I don't have any clue how to play this part.

"I'm sure. Give me peace."

I've witnessed this scene before—an actor delivering the coup de grâce, putting an old woman out of her misery. I'm following stage directions, I'm operating under Mom's explicit instructions, just as I've done so often in the past. I kiss her and tell her I love her, then place the pillow over her face.

The instant I exert pressure, she scissors her legs and flails her arms. She's changed her mind! Elated, I lift the pillow, assuming this has been some biblical test of my devotion. But she says, "Don't cover my eyes. I want you to be the last thing I see. Promise me your memoir won't make me look horrible."

I press the pillow to her face again and peer into her eyes. It's not clear what she feels or thinks. It never has been. Do I detect anger in the brown eye and love in the blue one? Or a mixture in both?

That's how I suspect my eyes appear to Mom as I go about the grim business of extinguishing her life. There's anguish in them. But there's love too, and maybe a single poisonous drop of the hatred she has accused me of.

Words, endless words I've said to serve the moment. So many half-remembered scripts and scattered quotes. If only I could bring myself to speak straight from the heart, there's time. There's so much time. It takes far longer than I imagined. Far, far longer. And never once does Mom look away. Still, I don't stop, and when it's over, there's no mistake about it and not the slightest resemblance to a death on stage or screen.

The color drains from her eyes by degrees until they're dull and fixed. The pupils dilate and darken into black holes that admit and emit no light. An opposing force that I wasn't aware of until now eases under my hands. When I raise the pillow, her jaw drops and her mouth gapes at an angle.

I tuck the pillow under her head and close her eyes. Her mouth won't shut. Then I stumble to the kitchen and wish I had something stronger than wine to drink. Something to deaden the trembling that starts deep inside, then spreads to my fingertips.

When Candy calls from the Hilton and says she's there with Maury, I almost blurt out what I've done. I hurry her off the phone, but she's caught the alarm in my voice. Minutes later, it doesn't surprise me—even if it does amp up my inner turmoil—to hear her key in the front door. I rush to her the way Mom described Dad rushing at the knife. "She's gone," I say.

"You let her leave?"

"Mom's dead." I hug her face to my chest so she can't see my eyes.

"You said she was asleep."

"I thought she was. But when I went to check on her, she wasn't breathing. I tried CPR. I tried mouth-to-mouth."

Candy breaks into deep racking sobs that spread from her core to her extremities, like the shaking in me. I dread letting go of her, and she doesn't seem to have any desire to leave my arms. We're more than willing to postpone whatever comes next and stay locked together in grief and relief.

Finally, though, a priest, an undertaker, Maury, and Lawrence have to be notified. I phone Lawrence, while Candy goes into the living room to have a last look at Mom. I call the local funeral parlor, but can't bring myself to dial the Hilton and break the news to Maury.

Candy comes back from the living room dry-eyed and purposeful, behaving with the same ritualistic calm as she does in her role as a Eucharistic minister. Taking the telephone from my hand, she calls the church and almost immediately a young, smooth-skinned Filipino priest arrives and begins administering what used to be referred to as extreme unction or the last rites. He calls it the anointing of the sick. It doesn't matter that Mom isn't sick; she's stone dead. The priest thumbs oil from a gold container and dabs it at her ashen skin. Candy and I station ourselves on either side of him. She responds to his prayers while I, the former altar boy, act as little better than a dumb witness.

Then two sturdy fellows, black-clad and solemn, show up in a hearse and shoo us out of the living room. Over my shoulder, I catch sight of them unfolding a zippered body bag. I can't bear to see more. In the kitchen I shamelessly slug down the last of the wine. It's not enough. Nothing will ever be.

By the time Lawrence arrives, aromatic of aftershave lotion and crisp winter air, I'm quite drunk, not just from pinot noir, not only from all the booze I've swilled today, but from the magnitude of the moment, the enormity of what I've done. At last I break into tears, and find myself crying on Lawrence's shoulder. He comforts me, murmuring, "There's nothing worse than losing your mother."

Meanwhile Candy takes charge. She thanks the priest, discreetly palms an offering into his hand and promises to get back to him about the requiem mass. She escorts the undertakers as they wheel Mom on a gurney out to the waiting Cadillac. Through the venetian blinds, I watch my sister assure the neighbors that nothing is wrong except that a very old woman has passed away.

When she returns, I'm still sobbing and have an excuse not to discuss practical details. As soon as I can decently do so, I say that I have to leave. "I want to tell Maury in person."

Candy doesn't object. She appears as eager as I am to be on her own.


My dazed drive to the Hilton has the quick cuts and illogical leaps of a dream. There's no continuous landscape, just a chaos of flashing lights, billboards, street signs, and franchise names. It's a miracle I keep the car on the road. For an instant I question why I do. But I reach the hotel, climb out of the Chrysler, and slouch against the front fender. For a time—I can't estimate how long—I gaze at the acre of asphalt. When the yellow lines of parking places start strobing in my watery eyes, I go inside.

The swipe card turns the red light green and I step into a room that smells of congealed grease. Maury, in his Windbreaker, waits on the sofa like an expectant schoolboy. On a tray in his lap there's a half-eaten hamburger, an untouched plate of French fries, a Coke, and a lengthy menu of cable channels. He hasn't turned on the TV.

"I have some bad news." Careful not to crowd him, I sit at the far end of the couch. "Mom's dead."

"I didn't do it," he exclaims.

"Of course you didn't."

"I don't know what she told you and Candy. But I never hurt her."

"Calm down, Maury. No one's accusing you. She took a nap and just quit breathing. We should be grateful she died in her sleep."

Maury's agitation grows. He has to set the tray on the floor to prevent his food from spilling. "She asked me to kill her. But I couldn't. I wouldn't!" Desperation pours off him like a desert flash flood races over rock.

"I understand." As much for myself as for him, I wish he'd let me touch him, let me slide an arm around his shoulder.

"She didn't want assistant living," he says.

"No, she didn't. Mom lived a long time and had a rough life. Now she'll rest in peace."

I hear a faint buzz in my ears. Is it the sound of my inner shaking? Or one of the noises Maury makes?

"I need to get down on the floor," he says.

"Go ahead. I don't mind."

"I need to be alone," he says.

I withdraw into the hallway. When he starts moaning, I walk to an alcove where a soft drink machine and an icemaker hum a lonely lullaby to each other. I'd like to lie down on the floor myself. I'd like to sleep, never to wake. Instead, I dip into the ice bin and press a fistful of freezing nuggets to my face.

When my cheeks are numb, I toss the ice into a rattling trash can. Then I return to the room and listen at the door. Out of politeness, I knock before opening it.

Maury's in the bathroom, readying himself for bed. Although

I've eaten nothing since noon and long for another drink, I get ready too and am grateful when we are both in bed and the lights go out. The silence, the separate beds, the sense of words unexpressed— all this recalls the excruciating, drawn-out dissolution of many an old love affair. Now, as then, the distance between person and person, between what I've done and what I've failed to do, feels un-bridgeable. The urge to apologize battles with an instinct that I've talked enough, that I've already done too much damage. Still, I dither. Do I owe it to Maury to reveal what Mom told me? Will it lift a burden? Or drive him to despair?

Had he known the truth, he might have agreed to Mom's request. Nobody could blame him—nobody except the sort of merciless Furies who sentenced him to life in the first place. But rage and re-venge aren't Maury's style. That's me. That's Mom. Maury's no murderer. The fact that he was framed falls into the same category as my finding out that I have a different father. News he can't use.

"Quinn," he speaks up, as if from the end of the world.

"Yes."

"I'm sad."

"I'm sad too."

"I'm sad that the last thing I did in her life was run away from Mom."

"You did the right thing. You're a good person," I say.

"Why did she ask me to kill her?"

"She was so old, she was off her rocker and didn't know what she was doing."

Maury sinks into what I trust is sleep, but I don't dare doze off for fear of nightmares. Mom was no more off her rocker at the end than she was at any point in her life. She had her reasons for choosing to die. Among them, I'd guess, was the habitual desire to absent herself. In this instance she took her toxicity to the grave and left behind something for Candy and Maury. As for what she left me, perhaps she believed that by dying at my hands she bound me to her for eternity.

I'll never know. She was, after all, a liar from a long line of liars. As I reflect on all that I don't know, I add to it all the people I never really knew before—Dad, my biological father, and in some respects Mom, Candy, and Maury. But at least now I know myself. I am a doting son. I'm everything Mom yearned for me to become. A success. A source of pride. An object of envy. The family money-bags. And obedient to the end.

I could argue that she asked for it. I could excuse it as a mercy killing. Or I might maintain that I acted out of the same twisted love as she showered on me. But none of this changes anything. I am a man who murdered his mother. At last the guilt I've felt for so long has found its crime; my dread has discovered its source.

Even if I were inclined to confess, who could I tell? Apart from an anonymous priest, who would it matter to? Not Candy. She doesn't deserve another crippling blow. Not Maury. He probably wouldn't believe me.

No, I'll keep my trap shut and I won't do the *Oresteia*. I've done it. I'm not going to ghostwalk through it a second time for the benefit of the BBC. But I'll finish my memoir. I'll restart it and stick to the facts. I'll keep Tamzin on the payroll and, I hope, in my life, but I won't depend on quotes to tell the story. Whether or not it's what the publisher wants, I'll recount my personal history as it happened, settling the debts that the dead bequeath the living. Primary among them is the truth about Maury, telling on the page what I cannot bear to tell him in person.

"Quinn," Maury speaks up. "You said you have your own way of praying. Can we do that now? Pray for Mom your way?"

It's too late to explain to him that I've lost my way and need to find a different one. So I recite the Hail Mary, and Maury joins in at the end, "Mother of God, pray for us sinners now and at the hour of our death. May the souls of the faithful departed through the mercy of God rest in peace. Amen."

## Candy

Did I cause it? Did I try to control it? Could I have cured it?

Rattling around in my brain, like pebbles in a bucket, these questions echo the key lessons I learned years ago at Ala-Teen. During Dad's drinking days, Mom sent me to meetings where they taught the cardinal rules that you should never assume you caused or can control or cure anybody else's problems. But as I kneel in a church pew examining my conscience, I feel guilty on all three scores; I'm to blame for Mom's death.

Sure, she'd been hinting for years, not so subtly manipulating me. Her worst sin, it crosses my mind, may not have been her foul temper, her vicious mouth, or her relish at smacking around me and the boys. Her worst sin might have been her conviction that she had a right to bully us into doing her bidding right up until the end.

But why run on about her faults? Today isn't about Mom's sins. It's about mine. And the darkest smudge on my soul comes from thinking that somebody owed me a favor. After nursemaiding Mom for years, I counted on Maury or Quinn to step up to the plate. I knew what she wanted. What I, deep down and in secret, wanted. So when Maury told me what Mom asked him to do, I could have warned Quinn by phone from the hotel. Instead, I took my sweet time driving home. If I hadn't, Mom might be alive today.

Then where would we be? A lot worse off—reluctant as I am to say that out loud.

After the sacrament of confession was repackaged as reconciliation, I expected it to become more popular. I mean, no more breast-beating, no more shame-ridden whispering. Just a friendly chat with a priest about toning up your soul. Not that different from talking to a personal trainer about losing weight. But this Saturday after-noon, the traditional time for penance, the church is practically empty, and the parish has cut down on its utility bill by dimming the lights. I almost trip over three nuns in black habits gliding quietly up the center aisle.

When I slink into the confessional, it's not an old-fashioned cu-bicle, dim and hushed, with an unpadded kneeler and a screen be-tween the penitent and priest. It's a bright canary yellow room with two armchairs and a pole lamp in the corner. Any chance I'll feel at ease flies out the window when I find that Father Ramos is on duty. I was hoping for the pastor, not the priest who anointed Mom on her deathbed.

He grins and gestures to the empty chair. I mutter, "Bless me, Father, for I have sinned," and staring at my boots, I let go. What pours out of me seems hideous. "I loved my mother," I say, "but sometimes I hated her, too, and wished she was dead. I've got to admit I wished one of my brothers would kill her. And that's what I'm afraid happened. I'm afraid my younger brother killed her."

"Why do you say that?" Father Ramos cheerfully inquires.

"Just, you know, an intuition."

"Is there any proof?"

"No."

"Have you told anyone else?"

Do I dare be honest? Maybe Father Ramos won't grant me absolution unless I run to the police and rat on Quinn. "I haven't mentioned this to a soul."

"Good." His smile brightens. He's so young and beardless, I have the uncomfortable feeling that I'm confessing to a child.

"For sure, you're sad about your mother," he says. "You were very close to her. But the closeness between a mother and daughter can be hard and confusing. Such talk belongs here, though, under the seal of the sacrament, not outside where it could cause trouble for your brother."

"I blame myself, not him," I say. "I really did wish she'd die so I didn't have to take care of her anymore and I could get married and move to North Carolina."

"You deserve a husband. Your mother wished that for you."

"Still, I'm worried about my brother and what will become of him."

"That's between him and his conscience, between him and his confessor."

"He doesn't have one. He lives in London."

"There are priests in England."

"He doesn't go to Mass."

"Maybe he'll start. Pray for him."

"I will. I do. But I feel guilty."

"That's natural when a parent dies and a child goes on living."

"Father, I'm no child."

"You're still God's child. You're your mother's child," he says in a fake paternal voice that doesn't match his hairless face. "This will all pass with time. Now say a decade of the Rosary for the repose of your mother's soul and make a good act of contrition. Go in peace and God bless."

And that's it. After he absolves me and I say my penance, I'd like to claim I feel cleansed, that, as the talk shows say, I've achieved closure. But it's crazy to think I'll ever recover from Mom's death.

Still, I don't have the luxury of falling apart. Too much remains to be done. She named me executor of her will, and I have to obey her wishes. Like always, she spelled them out in no uncertain terms. She wanted no wake, no open casket. She wanted cremation and a requiem mass. She wanted hymns at the service, and one old-time torch song, "Laura," which, in my opinion, belongs in a cocktail lounge, not a church.

As for her estate, she divided it between Maury and me. The house, Lawrence estimates, will in this inflated market fetch the flabbergasting sum of a quarter of a million dollars. Her insurance policy will pay us fifty thousand apiece, and in the biggest shock, her savings account contains a hundred thousand dollars hoarded up from Quinn's monthly checks. By rights this money should be handed back to him, but Quinn says no, it's my dowry and Maury's trust fund.

The other dreary, teary details I've postponed until after the boys leave. Before I put it in the hands of a real estate agent, the house has to be cleaned and repainted. There's also the rust-bucket Chevy that has to be towed from the driveway and Maury's sawdust boat that needs to be . . . I don't know, shoveled out of the attic. What I dread most is sifting through Mom's personal belongings, giving stuff to Goodwill, getting rid of junk, and deciding who keeps what. It figures to be summer before I'm free of worry.

• • •

As if I didn't have enough on my mind, at the last moment on the drive to church for the memorial service, Quinn volunteers to say a few words. It stands to reason that he's the one to do a eulogy. I couldn't speak without falling to pieces, and Maury talking in public would be a nightmare for everybody, especially him. But while Quinn has the stage presence for the job, I'm frantic that he'll spout stuff totally off the wall or slip into one of his accents or imitations. That's the thing about Quinn—you never know which one of him will show up.

Dressed in solid black, he'd be easy to mistake for a priest. Or since he's not wearing a Roman collar, a Protestant minister. Lawrence looks nice in his blue blazer and gray wool slacks. Sadly, only Maury seems out of it in his Windbreaker and jeans, kneeling at the end of the pew like the church custodian.

During the mass, Mom's ashes rest in a wooden urn on the top step of the altar, next to her favorite photograph—a full-length shot of her in her wedding gown. That's not how I'll remember her. At her best—and she did have good moments—I think of her down on her knees, not in prayer, but planting roses and azaleas in front of the house. She loved flowers, and they knew it and flourished in her care. Tears come to my eyes.

After the last amen, Quinn strides up to the urn and takes the measure of what has to be the smallest audience in his experience. Apart from the priest, an altar boy, an organist, and a couple of choir members, there aren't a dozen of us under the steepled roof of the A-frame. Everybody else Mom knew is dead. Yet Quinn throws himself into this performance like he's speaking for the ages on a worldwide broadcast.

"As the poet Horace wrote," he starts off, and I cringe, afraid he'll quote that rhyme about how our parents fuck us up. "Every one of us walks on a fire hidden by treacherous ashes. We're never sure what lies beneath our feet much less how painful the path is for others. We don't know what's ahead of us and half the time we're blind to what we've left behind. But we all know we're going to die, and so we mourn the death of those we love because we miss them and realize we're bound to end up like them.

"My mother, I feel confident in saying, is in heaven. She was a saint who raised three children as well as she could under very difficult circumstances. But she was also a human being and she had her faults. I don't need to dwell on them now, and it's not my place to judge her. That's God's job, and as the church teaches us, there's nothing that He won't forgive. There's no sin too great, no crime or betrayal or failure beyond absolution.

"Mom knew that, and from the time I was a little boy she swore that if I told the truth, she'd always forgive me. Even if I killed somebody, she said, she'd love me just the same. She said this so often I wondered whether she had someone in mind that she wanted me to kill. But of course she was just impressing on me that she was forgiving and God is forgiving. I hope it won't sound presumptuous then if I say I forgive my mother even as I pray that I am forgiven."

For my money Quinn should've stopped right there. But he's on a roll. Like an Oscar-winning actor who loves the sound of his own voice, he rattles on and on, throwing in a quote from, of all books, the Koran. The Prophet, Quinn says, wrote that God is as close to a man as the vein in his own neck. He swears that Mom, in death, will stay that close to him.

Well, let him speak for himself, not me. I need space. I need to marry Lawrence and wave farewell to Maryland. I don't care to think that Mom is as close as Quinn claims. This is a happy ending. The answer to my prayers. I refuse to let anything ruin it. Quinn will return to London and Maury to California. May God guard them both and grant them good fortune. And please grant me the strength to move on.

# Maury

Mom asked not to be buried in a box. She left word to burn her. But her ashes come back in a box. A little wooden one. So she's going to be buried in a box after all.

Once the funeral mass is finished, the three of us go to Candy's kitchen, and she opens the box lid and spoons some of the gray powder into an envelope. In her will, Mom wrote for her ashes to be sprinkled over the grass at Dad's grave. But the cemetery said no, that's illegal. They don't mind, though, if we spread a handful.

Candy jabs the spoon and hits a hard spot and makes a face. It sounds like a rock or a root. But it's bone. At the bottom of the box, there are solid chunks of Mom, and when I hear the spoon hit them again, I hurry into my room and hold onto the floor.

I bet Candy and Quinn believe I hurt Mom and that's why she died. I half believe it myself. But I know I didn't. Like Quinn said, I'm a good person. People change.

In church the priest told us Mom was dust before she was born and now she's dust again. He doesn't say what she was in between. My mind's on the frogs in the woods that sleep underground in winter, then wake up in spring and squirt black eggs on the creek.

In a couple days the eggs grow fishtails, then legs. Then the tadpoles lose their tails but not their legs and become frogs for a summer before they go back underground. Over and over, year after year. I've changed. I'm different and I'm not dust yet.

On the trip to the graveyard in Candy's car, Quinn tells me I'm not riding the bus back to California. I'm flying. They'll drop me at the airport at domestic before he boards at international. "We're all too old to waste time traveling by road," he says. "You're a rich man now. You can afford it." Then he asks, "Is there somebody you trust?"

"I trust you."

"I mean somebody in the States."

"I trust Candy."

"He means somebody out west," Candy says, "who'll look after your money."

"There's Nicky."

"Maybe we should fix it," Candy says, "so you get paid in installments. That way you'll have what you need each month."

"Whatever you want." Cars tear past us with a tire noise that I'd like to imitate.

"It's not what *we* want," Candy says. "It's your money. It's what *you* want."

"Send me a little every month." The tire noise is like a Band-Aid pulling off a cut.

The cemetery has a big clock at the gate, and everything except the circling red hands is made of flowers. In this freezing weather, they have to be plastic is my first guess. But up close they're cabbages, pink, purple, and yellow cabbages planted in the shape of numbers. The cold wind that bends the tree branches and kills the grass doesn't bother them.

On the roads going past gravestones and statues and stone houses with iron-spear fences I don't notice any street names. But Candy knows the directions. She drives real slow, and even though there aren't any other cars, she switches on the blinker light at each corner. I like it best when she turns right then right then right. When she goes left it feels wrong in my head.

Dad's grave marker lies flat on the ground, like the cover on a well. You can't read the carved writing on the stone unless you stand right over it and stare down where it says Beloved Husband and Father. He was young. Forty-something. And here I am almost an old man. Candy with her gray bangs and Quinn with his bald head look old too, and tired. We're all ready to sleep a long time.

I expect Quinn to start talking, like he did in church. But he keeps his mouth pressed into a tight line. Candy undoes the envelope and before she has a chance to sprinkle the ashes, the wind blows them everyplace. Not much ends up on the grass. It dusts Candy's hair and the front of Quinn's coat, and they both cough. When I breathe in, it shoots up my nose. You'd think ashes would smell like smoke. Instead, they sting like fire and I sneeze. Still, a lot stays inside, in my chest.

Candy cries a little, and Quinn wraps an arm around her. When the wind slaps at my hair, I imagine it on his shaved head. His skin is purple-red with cold. He looks like he'd rather be on the plane, flying home to London. I'm the same myself, ready to be up in the air and going back to Slab City. People complain there's no color, nothing growing in the desert, just sand and sky. But they should see this cemetery in Maryland when the grass is dead and clouds cover every inch of blue sky. Cabbages and nothing else grow in this weather.

Candy shakes the ashes from her hair, and Quinn brushes at his coat. I feel like I should be doing something too. But what? Mom said she had something to tell me and something to give me. Well, she told me to kill her and she gave me money in her will. It wasn't what I wanted but it's too late now.

On the ride to the airport, Candy asks again if I packed all my stuff. Do I know my flight number? Did I phone Nicky to pick me up? Do I understand I have to take off my shoes at the metal detector?

"The security guards may frisk you," Quinn says. "Don't get upset or say anything suspicious."

"Don't scare him," Candy says.

"He's not scared. Are you, Maury?"

"No, I went through plenty of pat-downs at Patuxent."

"Better not mention that," Candy says. "You don't need to check your bag. It's small enough to carry on. Just go to your gate."

"I have to buy something first."

"What?" she wants to know in that voice she has when something's wrong.

"A present for Nicky."

"Don't wander around and miss your flight."

"Like me to keep you company?" Quinn asks. "I could wait with you until they call your flight."

"No, I'm okay."

"Sure, you are." He smiles at me from the front seat.

Near the airport, planes roar over the road so low they look like they're about to crash on our car. I can see the windows, but not the people behind them. The wheels hang down like bumblebee legs

with balls of pollen. The noise zooms into my ears and zigzags off
where Mom's ashes are.

Candy parks at a curb crowded with families and cabs and suit-
cases and black guys carrying people's bags. The two of them climb
out to say good-bye. Quinn shakes my hand and seems about to say
something, but doesn't. Candy puckers up for a kiss and I let her
have one. There's already so much electricity forking through me,
I barely feel it. A traffic cop blows a whistle and hollers for them to
move it.

"Visit me," Quinn calls out in his London voice.

"Phone me soon as you land," Candy says.

They pile back in the car and wave, and I wave too, flinching as
a plane roars past.

In the terminal, a two-seater plane dangles from the ceiling by
cables. It's full-size and has a pilot wearing a helmet and goggles. It
doesn't take a minute to realize that the plane's real, but the pilot's
a dummy.

In the shops there's clothes and shoes and food and beer. Carts
up and down the hallway sell sandwiches and salad in plastic boxes.
I find what I'm looking for at a newspaper stand. A tiny airplane on
a key chain. It's silver. Even the windows are silver, and when I look
in them it's like a mirror, only so small you can't make out more
than a slice of your face. To see inside, I scratch the silver off one of
the windows, and the girl at the cash register says, "You break it,
you own it."

I pay her three bucks and go to my gate and sit on a bench and
snap the key chain off the plane. This cracks a hole in the side.
Careful not to poke the wing in my eye, I hold it up close and have
a look.

"Watching the in-flight movie?" asks a man beside me, much too near.

I slide away from him and take a second look at the inside of the airplane. It's like the bus—a bathroom in back and a seat for the driver in front. Now that I know where he'll be and I'll be, I feel the noise dying down. Mom's still in me, but her ashes aren't stinging and I'm not afraid. I've always wanted to fly. I'm just waiting for my call.

# Author's Note

## *Lying with the Dead* and *Life for Death*

The genesis of most novels is as opaque as the human psyche and as elusive as dream logic. But *Lying with the Dead* had its origin in specific childhood experience that shaped the man I became, and has now been reshaped by the imagination.

In 1961, a friend, Wayne Dresbach, age fifteen, murdered his parents and was sentenced to life in prison. If the event was devastating for the Dresbach family, it was only a little less monumental for me and my family. It changed the already precarious emotional equation of our lives, as Wayne's younger brother, Lee, moved into our home, and as my mother became increasingly obsessed with the case. For more than a decade, while raising four children of her own and running a day nursery for other kids, my mother served as a surrogate parent for both Dresbach boys and worked tirelessly to overturn Wayne's conviction and get him released.

Like Maury in *Lying with the Dead*, Wayne did twelve years at Patuxent Institute for Defective Delinquents, and like Maury's siblings, I passed an adolescence in the shadow of the U.S. penal system. Sunday was visiting day. Christmas brought the annual convict party celebrated in a cell block with pretzels and Kool-Aid. Each New Year commenced with another parole hearing, an emotional mixture of hope and dread.

As Wayne did his time, I went on to college, then graduate school, and became a writer, always intending to do a novel about murder and its ongoing effects on a family, the Greek tragic cycle of hubris, nemesis, and catharsis. But when Wayne was paroled, he moved in for a time with me and my wife and son, and I became persuaded that at least at first, I owed it to him to tell the events from his point of view as nonfiction. I did so in 1980, with the publication of *Life for Death*.

But inevitably the story and its aftermath remained lodged like a stinger in my brain, and so now I have circled back to it, not just revisiting the past but reimagining events, reconstituting a family forever teetering on the brink of discovery and dissolution, and reexamining elements of personal biography and reframing everything as fiction. The result is *Lying with the Dead*, my eleventh novel, a tragicomedy almost fifty years in gestation.